PUBLIC
OPINION

PUBLIC OPINION

NATHAN PETTIJOHN

Cordurouy

Cordurouy

ISBN: 978-1-5445-3223-3 (Paperback)
ISBN: 978-1-5445-3225-7 (Hardcover)
ISBN: 978-1-5445-3224-0 (ebook)

LCCN: 2022911366

This book is a work of fiction. Any references to real people, including quotations, are fictitious. Other names, characters, places, and events are products of the author's imagination, and any resemblance to actual events or places or persons, living or dead, is entirely coincidental.

Front cover art by Diana Kathleen Bradbury.
Book cover design by Anna Dorfman.

Printed by Cordurouy LLC in the United States of America.

First printing edition 2022.

Cordurouy Books
665 Valley Dr
Hermosa Beach, CA 90254
www.cordurouy.com

This book is for Winston McCrary,
who was a great friend.

"With enough cleverness,
anyone can be manipulated."

MARK TWAIN

PART 1

CHAPTER 1

THEY SAY IT'S Christmas.

It's early morning, and it's still dark in Los Angeles. I'm driving through the Hollywood Hills all but lost, and the streets are nearly empty. With the front two windows of my car rolled down, the air is crisp, and the temperature is somewhere in the mid-sixties. Cold for around here.

My body is achy and weary from these long hours. And heavy drinking. I don't sleep much, but I'm wide awake and driving north, drinking a coffee and plotting. Plotting like a kid who secretly stays up late on Christmas Eve to catch Santa Claus.

You can sleep later. You only get one chance a year to catch old Saint Nick. That's how I feel right now: I'm on a futile mission to which I'm somehow obligated. I'm a barking dog chasing a car, not knowing what I'd do if I caught it.

Driving through these dark hills playing Sinatra Christmas tunes through my car's crackling stock speakers and humming along, I'm trying to convince myself I'm cool like Sinatra and sneaky like Santa. The perfect combo. Though I feel more like I'm in the middle of a five-year-long panic attack, and I'm amazed I was sober enough to drive this late. The coffee is working.

There's a spotlight up ahead illuminating a hollow tube of foggy air shooting toward the stars. Everything else up here is dark, so I just keep driving toward the light, moving toward the lighthouse on a hill in this pretentious, mountainous desert. Curving uphill and downhill and uphill again, careening through narrow, moonlit roads.

Every few minutes, another car comes roaring past me headed in the other direction, and I must move to the side of the road so they can squeeze past on the narrow street, but the other drivers never feign any attempt at slowing down. These people up here have the confidence of knowing I'll move over and let them pass. And they're right. Each time, I slow and move to the side.

With clear skies and daylight, you could witness the entirety of Los Angeles from up here, but right now, it is merely humid darkness, a haze of mist and smog, and the lines of the road up to about a school bus's length ahead of me. I slow my car to a crawl and squint to read the house numbers on my right. 2638. 2640. I'm tired, and this starts to feel like a bad dream. I want to say I'm sick and go back home, but I can't. Maybe I should puke in the ditch.

The party is at 2648, so this is close enough. I pull my car over to the curb, roll the windows up, and park. Taking a sequence of deep breaths like I'm about to go free diving, I try to give myself a pep talk. "Just breathe…" "—don't stay too long…" "—in and out."

I step out of my car and look around. There isn't a house on the block worth less than $15 million. I should call Elmer, but my almighty phone has no reception up here, and that makes me feel even more embarrassingly helpless.

Each house has a few lights around its driveway and front gate, but they're otherwise walled off, and it's difficult to tell what's what, as there aren't any streetlamps on this hill. Parked cars line the road, and I can tell where the party is by the spotlight in the backyard and the wafting noises of partygoers hooting and hawing. I follow the sounds.

The cars parked along the street include Porsches, Maseratis, Rolls-Royces, Bugattis, and Aston Martins. I haven't even gone inside yet, but I can smell the phoniness and self-importance of the crowd already. These kinds of guys need to own a Porsche 911 to feel like they belong, and they're compensating in every way you would imagine. It reeks of new money and celebrity privilege, and I'm anticipating the frivolous small talk of their first-world problems. My dark maroon 1994 Jaguar XJR stands apart in this gaudy row of cars, with its bluebook value of around $10K—by far the cheapest car on the street.

I'm still far enough from the house that no one else is around, so I approach the driver's-side door of a brand-new yellow Aston Martin and take a deep breath. I need something to calm my nerves, but I shouldn't have a drink before going in. A random act of vandalism feels like the appropriate move here, so I clench my right hand into a fist and swing it downward like a flesh-and-bone sledgehammer onto the top of the side mirror.

The first swing causes a cracking sound. I immediately tighten my fist and swing down again. The second impact hurts my hand and makes the car alarm howl, but the inertia this time cracks the mirror so it separates from the car and hangs barely attached. I swing one more time and dislodge the mirror entirely. It dangles just above the ground, connected only by a few colorful wires. The alarm is still blaring. I quickly shuffle down the road and toward the address I'd been given, feeling a bit calmer and more distracted than when I parked.

Elmer texted me this address and said I needed to meet someone here with him tonight, on Christmas Eve no less. His text didn't convey anything else. Honestly, the last-minute summons doesn't bother me so much, as I don't have any holiday plans and suspect I might know why Elmer called me out here. Which is why I'm nervous to witness how the night unfolds. I'd say there's a fifty-fifty chance I'll be beaten to a pulp and leave this party on a stretcher. Part of me feels like I've set up an intricate Rube Goldberg chain of events to play with someone's life, but I am not certain what any of the levers or pulleys of my machine actually do. It all just needs to happen to find out what it all does.

Elmer texted, and that set off the evening, and so, of course, I came. I had no choice. Elmer runs a PR firm in Los Angeles. He has an excellent reputation as a decent and trustworthy guy, which isn't easy to maintain over three decades in Hollywood as a publicist. Elmer is old school, and he's met as many slimeballs and scam artists as anyone, so his bullshit radar is on point. He legitimately cares about his clients, and from what I can tell, he only represents people he at least somewhat respects. That's why I like him. Plus, he occasionally sends me business. I'd say he's both a friend and a mentor. Whenever he needs assistance in cleaning up some gross online PR debacle, he calls me in to help with damage control, reputation management, and crisis management.

There must be a guest list for this party. It isn't my crowd as much as it's Elmer's. Celebrity elites have never been my cup of tea, not that they'd have any reason to invite me. Part of my opinion about them is rooted in disgust, and the rest is probably rooted in envy. Who doesn't want to be a rich and famous movie or rock star and party in an incestuous in-circle of the well-to-do while being admired by the befuddled masses? No child dreams of becoming a glorified IT person: the silent helper of celebrities' reputations.

The cyber bodyguard of our betters.

Stepping from the street to the paved path going to the front door, I watch a well-dressed young couple enter the party ahead of me. She's wearing a Santa hat along with a silky dress. The man holding her hand is in a sharply tailored suit, and the top of his head is adorned with a fuzzy headband of faux reindeer antlers.

The outside of the house is dressed with lights and Christmas decorations. It seems quasi-normal and expected from out front, but there's undoubtedly turmoil and unrest pacing around the upstairs of this house. That's why I'm here, after all. Not for the back-patting and elbow-rubbing and hobnobbing.

There are two men in tuxedos near the entrance, and one of them is holding a clipboard with the guest list. They look more like security guards than door attendants. One of them tells the other, "I know it's a Christmas party, but just say happy holidays to the guests." He notices me, points at the clipboard, and makes a motion with his finger that implies he needs me to announce my name or some secret password but doesn't have enough time to explain the process to me out loud or even say as much as, "Good evening."

Their expressions tell me they aren't yet convinced I belong here. Like I'm just wasting their valuable time. I'm not wearing a fancy suit, shoes, or watch. I do look like I might be lost, I must admit. Or like I'm a paparazzo trying to sneak into an exclusive event for a tabloid photo. Both men have menacing builds, and I'm confident either of them could take me down with one arm tied behind his back.

"Merry Christmas. I'm Melvin Ritkin," I tell them. "Elmer and Titus are expecting me. Also, Fred's a good friend of mine." I sigh and nervously look at my phone while I wait for a response from them. Still no reception or internet. It's just a nervous habit of mine to look at the screen for some sense of order.

One of the men takes a few steps away to whisper into his walkie-talkie. He returns and tells me to follow him inside while the other tuxedo stays at the entrance with the clipboard.

We go in, and the party is loaded with enough people to form an army battalion. The men look like young Hollywood and tech big shots, all dressed in fancy tailored suits with manicured haircuts and almost-beards. About half of them are fit and chiseled, while the others look like they grew up on computers. Most of the women look like early-twenties models paid to show up and make the party feel memorable. In LA, it is common practice to have attractive women paid to go to parties and events like this to flirt and socialize so the powerful men in attendance feel validated. The ratio of women to men is around three to one by my count. It may be four to one; I'm not great at math.

It's a safe bet that nobody here has kids since most rational and responsible parents are back at their homes getting ready to open presents in the morning. Only single degenerates that need attention would be here so late.

A MODERN DAY GATSBY

The house is that of a thirty-two-year-old narcissist worth over $400 million. Titus himself. A man born into money and privilege who became a movie star in his own time and made several lucky investments.

Power begets power. Titus's attitude and personality remind me of Charlie Sheen before he got HIV but more handsome and stoic. I haven't met Titus in person before, so I'm basing this on what I've seen in interviews.

The house is ostentatious in the usual ways homes are in the hills: thoroughly modern with plenty of glass, marble, and cement. Tall ceilings. Abstract art. Recessed lighting. High-tech smart-home appliances everywhere. There's enough square footage to warrant having an elevator from the master bedroom to the garage so you aren't summiting three flights of stairs several times a day.

The spotlight is lit up deep in the backyard, and several parties are going on simultaneously. Holly, garland, wreaths, and a giant, decorated Christmas tree fill the living room and downstairs area. The house is meticulously decorated, as if it were a Christmas scene from a Hallmark movie. The backyard has a pool and a giant treehouse, tennis court, and basketball court, and they're all decorated with lights for the holidays. That's at least what I can see from the foyer.

This party will surely be going until the wee hours. There are little platters with piles of cocaine conveniently placed around each room along with utensils for inhaling the powder through one's nostril. When one mound of nose whiskey is depleted, the staff promptly replaces it with another entire pile. Enough for everybody who wants some.

I tread into the backyard, and it's even more bizarre and raucous than the sounds I had noticed when parking my car had seemed. There's a band playing and people laughing and singing along to "Grandma Got Run Over by a Reindeer," and it seems slightly unbelievable to me that so many people know all the words to the song.

To confuse things even more, Miley Cyrus is standing on a chair leading the chorus, and the surrounding crowd is singing along with her, smiling, and dancing to the music being played by a live band behind the pool and in front of the tennis court.

It is an evening of excess and self-absorption for the luckiest of the luckiest generation. They are spoiled, coddled, and selfish, and they're confident they deserve it all and more. This is a party to celebrate themselves as much as it is to celebrate Christmas, Hanukkah, Jesus, or whatever. Miley is excellent, though, so I exclude her from my generalization.

Next to me are two thin nerdy guys talking to each other. One says to the other, "Sure, if you eke by in obscurity and never make a dime off your art, only then are you an artist, according to the miserable and tired at least."

"Yeah," the other guy responds, "well, M. Night Shyamalan wrote *Stuart Little*. Sometimes you just have to pay the bills."

"Hey, that's his best movie," his friend responds, and they both chuckle. "Movies used to be more subtle because people used to be more subtle."

"A talking mouse," the other responds. "Can't get much more subtle than that."

Right as I think I recognize Cuba Gooding Jr. dancing and singing along madly to Miley's rendition, the security guard in the tuxedo who escorted me into the house reintroduces himself by grabbing my right arm and forcing me back inside and toward the stairs. He issues a stern summons to follow him up there.

The partiers downstairs are oblivious to us as we climb the staircase.

We go to a door in a hallway. The tuxedo opens it, shoves me in, and presumably hurries back to his post out front.

This room smells like the expensive colognes of five different men about town mixing in the air and fighting with each other. My first instinct is to ask if we can open a window or turn on a fan, but strangely, this is a room without windows or fans, so I settle for not saying anything yet.

Looking around, I recognize a few faces, but Elmer's is the only one I know personally. He has grown out a beard, which matches his graying hair, and he has on a brown suit that doesn't feel festive or chic. He is standing between me and the door. He nods. "Good to see you, Melvin. Thanks for coming."

Titus is sitting in a large leather swiveling chair behind his desk, scratching his famous chin. I recognize him right away, seeing as this is his house and he's a successful movie star. Movie stars are rarely as impressive in person as you'd imagine, but Titus does have a certain air of sophistication and confidence I can't help but admire. And I'm at his party, in his office, surrounded by his confidants.

Many movie stars can pretend to be a badass on camera, but few are in real life. Daniel Day-Lewis and Samuel L. Jackson come to mind as two who I'd believe are badasses in both environments, but they're the rare ones who were born with charming intimidation and skill. Titus, however, strikes me as the type of person who has learned to act this way through years of practice. He has been groomed to fit the part, which he now does as convincingly as anyone.

Put on an act long enough, and it can become a reality.

A STUFFY OFFICE

I'm guessing this room is an office by the look of it. A room with no windows and three doors feels ominous to me, but I'm no expert on home design. The decorating of this room is not like the modern, stale, Apple Store aesthetic I saw downstairs but more like a study from an old British detective novel. Big mahogany desk; dark wood walls; two ornate globes; an oversized hourglass; a chess table with the pieces handmade from gold and bronze. No computer or electronics other than an antique phonograph and some dim lighting fixtures. It's unexpected, but also it's appropriate somehow, like he's practicing to play Sherlock Holmes in a movie.

Titus is sizing me up as he lights a cigar. On his left are two of his management people, but I can't remember their names. On his right, standing and bouncing the heel of his foot up and down nervously, I recognize an up-and-coming actor named Oscar. He's in his early thirties and has a boyish face that I know is hiding dark secrets, though he hides them well. Seeing Oscar here makes me feel like shitting my pants. I was worried he may have been why Elmer called me here. Oscar and his fucking computer.

Put on an act, and it can become a reality, so I display my most convincing expression of confidence and clench my cheeks.

Oscar is gripping his laptop like it's an ancient relic. He walks over and hands it to me. "You the computer guy? Here, take this."

Nodding, I accept the laptop with both hands out, palms up like a samurai being given a new katana. I look to Elmer just in case he feels like making a proper introduction.

Elmer sees the look on my face and chimes in. "Yes, of course, sorry. This is Melvin, who I told you about. He helped us out in the Puerto Rico situation. I think you should be open. You can trust him."

"I'm Oscar. Look, some rat shithead hacked my computer and has all my files and says I have to pay a ransom or he'll leak all of it.

Some of that stuff can't be seen by anyone. Emails. Photos. Personal shit. It'll ruin me. And it'll ruin Titus, too." I exhale my despair as Oscar admits his debacle, and now I am confident. "So what, are you an engineer or a developer or a hacker or something?"

"No, but I stayed at a Holiday Inn Express last night." I look around, and nobody thinks I'm clever except for Elmer, who barely breaks a smirk at my reference to an old commercial.

I set the laptop down on the desk, and Titus looks up at me for the first time since lighting his cigar. His eyes connect with mine so intensely I can't look away. He stands and walks toward me, making eye contact the whole way. Titus comes right up close to my face like he's trying to look into my soul. His face is as close to mine as it can be without my having to bring up the awkwardness. He sticks out his hand, and I instinctively shake it. "Melvin, Merry Christmas, and thanks for coming so late. This sounds pretty straightforward. Elmer tells us to trust you. He says that you're some sort of digital alchemist. If you can help us out here, we won't forget it. So can we?" Titus speaks as though we're the only two people in the room, and it's both comforting and terrifying at once.

"Can you what?" I'm not sure what he wants, but maybe I wasn't listening closely enough.

"Can we trust you?" Titus is speaking in his deepest voice. It sounds like he's performing lines from a movie and needs to come off as intimidating. If so, it's working.

Everyone in the room is staring at me, waiting for my response. My hands begin to sweat, so I put them behind my back. "Well, I've never known a truly honest man," I say, desperately wanting to cut some of the tension in the room after my Holiday Inn line bombed.

"That's not a very satisfying answer. Look, this isn't The Comedy Store. We're concerned about this. That's why the party is downstairs, and we're up here."

"You can trust me as much as you can trust anyone, is my point." I try to smile to let him know I'm on their team, and somehow, they seem content enough with this answer. "So how did they get access? And how long ago?" I ask.

Titus returns to his big desk and motions for Oscar to go on with the details with a simple wave of his hand as he plops into his leather chair.

Oscar speaks with some degree of composed confidence now, as if he'd been reciting this part before I showed up so as not to give up too much information. "It was stupid. A catfish or something. This girl I matched with on a dating app, it's called Raya—have you heard of it?"

I nod. Raya is an exclusive dating app for celebrities and verified social profiles of which I am aware. I would venture to guess I know more about it than anyone in this room.

"Well, we were texting for a few days, and she sent me this link. I get my texts on my laptop too, so for some reason, I opened the link there, and that's what caused it. I thought it was a video of her, but instead, my screen locked up and was covered in symbols, and then it restarted to a page that just says their demands. I don't know. It was around noon today, I guess, and I've been freaking out ever since. It says we can just pay them, but we wanted to make sure we involved an expert just in case there's anything we should do, or if there's a way to catch these rat bastards. Like, how do we know once we pay them that they won't release the files anyway?"

I open Oscar's laptop, and the screen refreshes to a black background and an all-caps, red-font list of demands, with the familiarly whimsical hacker speak of, "OOPS, YOUR FILES ARE ENCRYPTED," at the top in a bigger font and a list of instructions below it for sending $100,000 in Monero to a specific account number within twenty-four hours, or else.

Oscar looks at me expectantly, appearing as innocent and vulnerable as he can manage. He's the real victim here, according to him. "So can you help?"

Five faces in the room, and they're pointed at me again, waiting for my answer. They want a solution to poor Oscar's stupidity. Digital neophytes, hoping to be told that everything will be okay and I'll handle it so they can go back to their partying and their privilege. No problem, your reliable nerdy tech geek will fix your mistakes, sweet child. Don't worry. "They're asking for a hundred grand?" I start with the rhetorical. "If you're worried about what's on this device, then you should just pay them. I'm not sure why you'd need me for the transfer unless it's to help with the Monero part? It's basically like most other cryptocurrencies but is impossible to trace."

Titus gulps the rest of his glass of whiskey and stands again to address me eye to eye, puffing hard on his cigar now. "I'll pay the money. That's not a problem. But we're worried that after we pay, he can still post this stuff. Stuff that will hurt me inextricably. Oscar can show you the names on the accounts for the catfish that tricked him. We're hoping you can help make the transfer for us and see if you can find out who was behind this. We know it's a long shot, but we can say we tried. According to Elmer and Fred, you're the guy for this kind of thing."

This is what Christmas must feel like for the unimaginably spoiled children of billionaires. I'm getting everything I hoped for and more, but I try to portray a demure expression like I'm still on the fence about whether to help them. I make this uncomfortable silence last a few extra moments, savoring my Christmas present. I answer coolly, "Sure. If you tack on 20 percent and send me $120,000 by wire tonight, I'll handle the payoff and investigate the usernames and stuff to see if I can find the culprit. You should know, ransomware like this is nearly impossible to trace if they're half competent. It's doubtful that I'll come up with anything. Maybe an IP address on the Raya account if we're lucky, or a billing address on the cell phone account Oscar was texting. Hard to say. Also, if they have control of this device, they can probably hear everything we're saying right now."

Everyone else looks at Oscar's laptop in surprised disdain.

"Fair enough," Titus responds. "Like I said, as long as we can say we tried to investigate this. Well, there it is. Justin, handle the wire for Mister Melvin and get him whatever else he needs." And with that, Titus leaves the room like he has a few more equally important meetings to tend to, and now I know one of these guys is named Justin.

Oscar starts to leave but first puts his hand on top of his laptop. He gives me his business card with his other hand. "Take the laptop with you, and let me know whenever I should meet you to pick it back up. Here's my number. Text me, and I'll send you the screen-shots for the catfish bastard if you want them. And thank you in advance for your discretion. We won't forget this."

"Should just be a couple of hours to get the laptop unlocked if everything goes well," I say. "I'll text you."

"I'll be up, waiting." Oscar nods at me gratefully and follows Titus out of the room. Of course he'll be up with all that coke down-stairs. The remaining men in the room are Elmer, Justin the business manager, and Titus's talent manager, whose name escapes me, but he gives off vibes of a budding Harvey Weinstein. I give Justin my account number and watch him make a real-time wire for $120,000 to me.

Once I see the confirmation, I take the laptop and head back downstairs with Elmer. He's smiling like a proud father as we descend the steps. "Well done, kid. They're coked out of their minds, and I think the paranoia was pushing them over the edge. Good that you came and played the consummate pro. Not a bad Sat-urday night. Twenty grand?"

"I appreciate the work, as always, sir. I'll send you your piece in the morning."

"Attaboy. Now go get to work." Elmer gives me a wink and a quick rub of my shoulders. He then disappears into the backyard in the direction of what looks like a pool full of skinny-dippers. The party has fewer people now but is only getting wilder, with an even greater female-to-male ratio.

I'm in the living room taking it all in, and I deserve a drink before I go to celebrate a grand scheme well-schemed.

CHAPTER 2

THERE ARE THREE open bars at this Christmas party: two outside and one in the dining room, each with hired bartenders handling the pouring. I go to the one by the dining room and join the queue. There are a few people in front of me, but the bartenders are fast. There are two women talking by the piano, and I recognize them both, but I'm not sure from where. The one with red hair is shorter than the other and wearing a white dress and big, floppy hat. The other is a taller brunette wearing a red dress. Both are beautiful and laugh along with each other like old friends. Two other women behind me in line are talking loudly about a new movie that just came out, and I can't help but overhear pieces of their conversation. "You know, I'm just shocked that it got such good reviews. I didn't get it at all."

The other woman responds, "No, me neither. It was so weird. I bet they paid for good reviews."

Then a familiar man's voice speaks into my left ear, right up close and personal. "Herb, it's so serendipitous to see you here."

There's a tap on my shoulder to accompany the awkward greeting, and I turn to find Fred, a man I've worked with on more than a few occasions. Fred owns a security firm and handles private security for movie stars, athletes, and rock stars. The kind of job that if done well, you never even notice him. It's only after someone gets attacked that you ask where security was. Fred and Elmer are probably the only people at this party who know my real name is Herbert, or Herb for short. My namesake, Herbert Hoover, was one of the worst presidents in US history, and so my parents named me Herbert for some reason I'll never understand. I clear my throat and shake Fred's hand.

He turns to see who I'd been staring at.

"Which one are you interested in? I'll introduce you. I think they're both single. The movie star or the porn star?"

"Huh? Do you really know them? Which one is which?"

"The redhead is a porn star. Ruby something. The other one is Sequoia something, a huge fucking movie star. A-list. Do you not own a television or a phone?"

I hold up the laptop. "I have a laptop. Can you really introduce me to Ruby? That'd be great."

"I was just fucking with you. Don't be a creep. I haven't met either of them yet. They're probably busy talking about astrology and crystals and shit anyway. Plus, they are way out of our league."

"Speak for yourself. You got my hopes up. Thanks a lot. I haven't heard from you in a while. I was beginning to think maybe I did something to offend you." I give a pouty frown as if to tell him I'm kidding but not really.

"It takes two to stay in touch, kid. It's good to see you. Merry Christmas. Listen, Elmer told me you'd be stopping by. I just love how Hollywood people always call everything serendipitous, so I thought you'd think my reference was funny. Do you notice that? 'This chance encounter is so serendipitous. Everything is so fucking serendipitous in our corner of this magical, floating, spinning planet.'" Fred flails his arms.

"Yeah, I get that at least once a week." It's our turn to order at the bar. I get tequila. Fred gets gin. We take a few steps away from the bar to continue. "So porn, huh? That's where I've seen her? Are you on the clock all night?" I ask.

"No, I've been off since midnight. My guys are working security for Titus, though, so a few of them are here to make sure nothing gets out of hand. Herb, listen, I need your help, and I've meant to reach out to you. I have a decent budget for it. Should be worth your time, and I want to get it going right away."

"Sounds good so far. Cheers." We clink our glasses together. I'm still on a high from fleecing the host and his flunkies upstairs.

Fred keeps on with his pitch as we both sip our beverages. "Do you remember that guy Dan that I've told you about? He screwed me over in Athens?"

Everyone who knows Fred well enough knows all about Dan. The gist of it that I can recall is Dan hired Fred to handle security at some rock concert in Greece that Dan produced. Then Dan stiffed Fred out of sixty grand for his work. This was three or four years ago, and I vaguely knew details of legal battles since then.

I provide a miniature eye roll and nod in confirmation. "Of course I remember who Dan is. And please, call me Melvin when we're around other people." I give Fred a wink and look over at the piano to find Ruby looking at me. My first thought is that she just saw me wink at Fred like I was hitting on him.

Fred chuckles and puts his face close to mine, and I figure my already slim chances with Ruby are quickly deteriorating.

"Sure, Melvin. I need your help taking Dan down. With the stuff you do online, you know? I want to put you on retainer to just go wild on his reputation."

"Take him down? What do you mean, exactly?"

"The worse, the better. A year from now, I want him to be terrified of opening his phone or going online. I want everyone to know what a lying piece of shit this guy really is. I finally got the settlement money over this, and I just want to pour it all back into getting back at him."

"Well, it'd be easy to put out a bot that trolls him online. Could do some AI shit and have it constantly fuck with him for the rest of his life." I'm getting more excited about the notion of putting my sinister know-how to good use. "I've got something built that could literally do just that."

"No, I mean, I want this to be ten times worse than that. Nothing passive. Total cyber warfare against this guy's reputation—anything you can imagine. Go wild. We should meet up to talk about this tomorrow, if you're free. But I'm serious. What I want is if you search for Dan on Google, I want the first page of results to just be about how he's a scam artist and a fraud. I want anyone who ever looks him up in the future to know what a scumbag he is before they get into business with him. That sound like something you can help me with?"

"If the court got you the settlement, why don't you just let it go? Agonizing over this shit will give you ulcers or something. Why not just take the money and relax?" I'm talking myself out of a gig, but I believe in the advice. The truth is, I would love to destroy some stranger's life, but I'm not sure Fred will like where that path leads.

"I've more than slept on it. I want to do this, and I think it could be a lot of fun for you." Fred is frazzled by the fact that I didn't immediately agree to his absurd request to destroy someone's life.

The tequila is hitting me in the right places, and I'm still on the high from earlier. I look down and remember I'm still holding Oscar's laptop and should leave after this drink. "Reputation management is right up my alley, though it's usually the other way around. Look, I'm free anytime, just let me know, and we can meet up. It does sound fun if you're determined to do it. I've got to go take care of this." I show Fred the laptop, and he nods knowingly.

"Well, you know we're doing all the security for Titus. Elmer and I were the ones who told him to have you handle the catfish mess. Oscar is such a dumb fuck. You go handle his laptop thing tonight and call me tomorrow. We can meet and talk more, if you don't have Christmas plans."

I shrug—no holiday plans.

"Good. Let's connect in the morning and grab lunch somewhere. Can't spend Christmas alone all day, buddy. My treat."

Right as Fred says this, a stout man in a colorful flowery shirt with a deliberately manicured Captain Hook mustache approaches, daintily holding a glass of champagne like he's toasting us. A friend of Fred's, I presume.

"Merry Christmas, gentlemen. Oh, Fred, it's good to see you." He has a slightly drunk stammer and a sarcastic feminine voice that makes me assume this guy is fun to be around, just not right now. Fred's friend with the mustache hugs both of us like we've all known each other for years.

Fred keeps talking to make it seem like we weren't just conspiring to destroy someone's reputation. "Well, basically, I just don't know much about crypto, is all."

"Oh, it's easy. You just buy high and sell low." I try to make myself sound drunk, and the mustachioed man laughs.

"That's what I hear. Listen, you need to handle that thing on the laptop. Get out of here. Let's chat tomorrow." Fred shoos me out, and I hurry back through the front door and past the doormen.

While walking back to my car, I see two men examining the broken side mirror on the yellow Aston Martin. "Motherfucker," one of the men says to the other as I stride to my cheap vehicle, toss Oscar's laptop into the passenger seat, start the engine, and drive myself home.

As soon as I'm on the road again, I reflect on how the night played out. I can hardly believe my luck. Oscar literally handed me his laptop, which I already know has sickening material on it ripe for blackmail. Trust is a hell of a thing, and it is easier to trust someone when you desperately need someone to trust. Someone once told me Hollywood is all about who you know and when you know them.

◊   ◊   ◊   ◊

People get catfished every day. Even rich and famous people. Even if you don't hear about it. If you're a victim of ransomware and you pay, there's an 80 percent chance you'll be a victim of it again. Oscar and Titus already know it's a long shot that I'll find any answers for them, but twenty grand is the appropriate amount to charge them to appear to be making an effort.

What will actually happen is, I'll keep the full one hundred and twenty grand, unlock Oscar's computer myself, and return it to him repaired a few hours later, as if the evil hackers had unlocked it once they received payment.

Good as new.

I wouldn't need to pay any ransom in this case. After all, I was the one who had catfished Oscar and locked up his computer earlier that day. Yes, I had engineered the whole ordeal and hacked his computer myself since I had a hunch he wouldn't want anyone else to see what's on his hard drive. After baiting Oscar, I got him to install the ransomware on his own device by pretending to be a cute young woman on a dating app, and his big-shot friend's publicist called me in to help him. I had no way of knowing I would be brought into the fold, but sometimes, you catch lightning in a bottle and you just have to roll with it.

One of the best tactics a hacker can count on is human error. As careful as you think you are in setting up your security protocols, you can always get bamboozled by a brief lapse of stupidity. I didn't have to break into Oscar's computer—I just fooled him into clicking a link, and he gave me access on a silver platter. A true thing of beauty, and all in a dishonest day's work. If you can get paid on both sides of a deal, you know it's a good deal. Or as my grandma used to say, "You're either the one doing the fucking or you're the one getting fucked."

Once I'm home with Oscar's laptop, I have a brief passing notion I should make a show of trying to find the culprits who hacked the device. Earn my $20,000, as it were. I took over Oscar's computer by lunch, and I've already seen everything. His cloud account hasn't changed in ten years, and I found a trove of damning photos and videos. His emails and texts have some incriminating exchanges that could damage a lot of notable people. His internet history and some of the content on his hard drive would be of interest to the proper authorities, but sadly, there's nothing in those files I haven't seen before on similar hard drives of similar creeps I've hacked.

I save another backup copy of his hard drive, shuffle a few Monero payments around, and unlock the ransomware. I free his laptop by entering a password on my device. None of this takes longer than it takes for me to heat and devour a Pop-Tart. I text Oscar my address and say he can come retrieve his computer.

Oscar texts back almost immediately that he'll be here within the hour.

DIGITAL ESPIONAGE FOR DUMMIES

The naive never know they're being naive. That's why we call them naive, but it is essential to remember that anyone can be manipulated—even you.

To be completely honest, all I ever wanted was to get to live like a Russian oligarch a few weeks a year. Just a little taste of that kind of opulence and decadence to blow off steam and decompress like the worst of them. Is that too much to ask? To drift on a yacht off the coast of Majorca or Florianopolis or someplace the general public hasn't ever heard of, crewed up with a private chef and a captain, and skinny-dip in crystal-clear ocean water every day with a dozen fashion models. Call me old-fashioned. Call me a shallow, misogynist pig. Call me a sociopath with borderline personality disorder.

It doesn't matter what you call me. At least I know what I want, and it's simple.

In digital strategy and crisis management, most people would categorize my techniques as gray or black hat, meaning I'm ethically agnostic. *Whatever needs to happen to get the job done* type of consultant—a fixer. I'll accept that title with a badge of honor.

I'm no hero, and I'll admit that early and often.

What I am is a dirty, slimy opportunist: a grifter and a liar, a catfish and a cyberbully. I enable deep fakes, spread vicious rumors, and sling bullshit far and wide on the almighty internet for whoever pays me the most. I perpetuate my own cycle of spambots, infomorphs, and sockpuppets to no good end. My ex-wife would add to my multi-hyphenate that I'm an arrogant asshole to boot. We didn't have any kids, and I think she's somewhere in Arizona now, though I haven't checked in a while. She took her last name back and left, and I never heard from her again. A few months ago, I did look her up and saw some photos online of her with a new husband and a happy, quiet life in the desert, and it made me jealous and resentful to the extent I never wanted to look her up again.

Technology perpetually dissolves one reality and replaces it with another, causing paradigm shifts of perception for each new generation. When I started working in digital, it was still novel and just for geeks or hustlers. Over the years, though, some of us have acquired enough knowledge about how it works to pervert the web and disseminate fake news and misinformation in worrying ways. How to influence an election should be taught in universities alongside how to market a new film or product nowadays. It's all the same thing.

Those who know me well would probably categorize what I do as social engineering, growth hacking, or reputation management, though these douchey titles come and go like passing fads. According to my LinkedIn profile, I'm a consultant. Harmless. I work mainly with publicists. But my profile there also claims my name is

Melvin, not Herbert. Only a few people in LA know my real name, and I can't think of any reason to change that. Not just because I hate the name Herbert, which I do, decidedly, but because I prefer some version of anonymity by way of pseudonyms.

People only hire me when they're stuck between a rock and a hard place in some life-changing crisis. Someone cancels them on social media. A hit piece comes out in a magazine. Someone hacks their computer or installs ransomware. They'll usually throw any amount of money at the problem to get rid of it at that point—meaning if I get a few decent jobs a year, I can still chase after that oligarch yacht fantasy. So anyway, it is mainly out of an abundance of caution and a deep sense of paranoia that I conduct business under the alias Melvin Ritkin. I funnel my revenues through offshore accounts, cryptocurrencies, and shell companies before I ever touch it with anything connected to my real name. It's impossible to see around every corner, but I always try to assume and plan for the worst possible scenarios.

Things can always get worse, and you should plan accordingly.

To put it simply, people with too much money call me when they need to suppress one narrative online and spread their own instead. There is a shadowy art and science to digital public relations, and it becomes imperative to err on the side of paranoia once you know enough about the field.

CASE STUDY: JEFFREY EPSTEIN

In 2008, Jeffrey Epstein pleaded guilty to a 2005 crime involving his actions with a then-fourteen-year-old girl. He served thirteen months with work release—meaning he got to leave prison for twelve hours a day, six days a week while serving his time. It wasn't until 2019, when he was arrested again for the same sorts of crimes, that there was widespread public outrage in the media. Of course, he famously died in his jail cell under mysterious circumstances while awaiting trial at the Metropolitan Correctional Center in New York City in August of that same year.

This is all to say that for over ten years, Epstein rubbed elbows with dignitaries, celebrities, and executives on a casual basis like any other disgustingly rich elitist even though he had been convicted of and served time for sexual crimes against a minor. Public opinion during this time was that he had paid his debt to society, or at least paid off whoever he needed to so as not to be ostracized from the well-to-do any further. Some, of course, did not embrace him back into their inner circles, but many did, or at least they tolerated him because of his wealth and perceived status.

Epstein's conviction didn't matter to many people during those ten years because he'd ensured the public forgot about his unlawful perversions. Once he was released from prison, he slunk away like a harmless pearlfish to commit more crimes under his shadowy umbrella of misinformation. A lot of this was accomplished by Epstein's proactive and extensive public relations strategies. After his conviction in 2008, Epstein's PR team began systematically flooding the web with positive press releases and fake news stories about him to spam the internet with enough content and links to help push down his negative search results. Until 2019, much of these efforts were successful, and I assure you countless people with enough money are doing the same types of things right now, whether to cover up their old crimes or help lay the groundwork to hide any unwanted future revelations.

People like me help curate what shows up when people search any specific phrase or person online. This can take months or even years to have an effect depending on the project, but it makes a lasting impact once enough groundwork is laid. For Epstein-level reputation management, someone could pay a PR firm around $20,000 a month for twelve months, which is $240,000 for one year of crisis management PR, if you're interested. The people out west who made money during the gold rush were the ones selling shovels and picks. The same is true here, so take note.

Perception is reality. Seeing is believing. If you search online for "How to cyberbully" or anything similar to that, you will only find guidance to the contrary. You'll be provided with content explaining how to respond or what to do if you are being cyberbullied. Search engines like Google simply won't promote instructions for cyber-bullying or character assassination because that's the way things are, so I'll provide what I can on the topic as I'm able to here.

This is my equivalent of Gorgias telling Socrates it's not his fault if the students he teaches sophistry to wind up using it for evil instead of good. He said if a boxer teaches someone to box, it's not the teacher's fault if the student uses those skills to pummel the inno-cent instead of other fighters in a ring, as boxing, sophistry, social media, and the internet are, in many ways, all morally neutral.

REAL ACCOUNTS VERSUS FAKE ACCOUNTS

Anytime you create a fake account and have it spread information, that account is called a sockpuppet because you control it, and it isn't an actual, separate, individual person. If you pay someone else to manage a fake account on your behalf, that shill is called a meat-puppet because there is another person beyond you behind it, but it's still not a "real" person.

I've made more sockpuppets over the years than I can count. Many of my most successful ones would regurgitate ideas from other people or paraphrase them. I had a client once who encour-aged me to build up a small army of accounts in the blockchain ver-tical just in case it could ever be valuable to have some influential personas in the space. This was when the idea of blockchain was still relatively new. I created about fifty personas tangentially related to blockchain and built their influence over the next six months or so.

For these accounts, I needed affable causes, news, and stories for them to promote and feed their content machines. One peculiar middle-aged man I stumbled upon was a self-proclaimed scholar on blockchain and cryptocurrency, and so I told him about my plan for the fake accounts and shills. I asked if I could mine his papers and speeches and repurpose his ideas for my fake accounts to use. His reply was immediate: "Of course, but there are no fake accounts. Only real accounts."

I sipped my coffee and tried not to look too dumb while raising one of my eyebrows, waiting for more.

"You see, if one of your so-called shills is regurgitating my opinions, that is helping them spread further into society. As long as I care about my ideas being spread far and wide, why should I care who gets credit for spreading them? Or what account shares them? These accounts spread real ideas originated by real people. Therefore, they are real accounts. All of your accounts are real accounts."

CHAPTER 3

WHEN ACQUIRING A burner phone, it must be purchased with cash. And you need to get a stranger to buy it for you. Someone who doesn't know you and can't identify you. The location where the phone was purchased can be traced, and the worst-case scenario is that someone could review the security camera footage and see who physically purchased the phone, or you could be stupid enough to use your credit card. If you can convince a total stranger to buy it for you with cash, you'll be much better off.

You need to meet them off-site, somewhere without cameras, to make the exchange. If you don't take this step seriously, there is no need to read further. While you're at it, have them buy several pre-paid minutes cards for your new phone. One hundred dollars should set you up for at least three months. You just need an old flip phone, the kind where you can remove the battery when you want to know the phone is off. Be mindful of where you use the cell phone since the cell towers will ultimately let authorities know where you were using it. Setting up fresh social accounts can require a cell phone text verification, so the flip phone can handle at least that.

Similar precautions should be taken when acquiring other hardware, such as your laptop. You can have a third party buy one on your behalf with cash via Craigslist, a pawn shop, or a similar location. Or you can buy one online with cryptocurrency if you know how to hide your tracks and have it shipped to a PO box that you set up with a phony ID. You must also use an encrypted email address, probably one based in Switzerland, where privacy rights are more protected, and only use encrypted text and email to speak to anyone digitally. You must use the Tor web browser, or a browser that has Tor built into it, and a good VPN. This simple combination of Tor plus VPN gives you the ability to crawl the dark web anonymously from any coffee shop in the world.

The other requirement for this line of work is Tails, which is a portable Linux distro. You can install Tails on a thumb drive that can be plugged into any computer to boot your own operating system without leaving a trace. This will route all your traffic through Tor by default. If you need to be anonymous, Tails is necessary. It's used by anyone serious about their privacy, like whistleblowers, activists, military agents, and journalists and their sources.

CYBER WARFARE

Before you make up your mind about just how despicable I am, please remind yourself that at least I'm not some state-sponsored hacker or cyberterrorist wiping entire countries' computers clean and crashing planes and power grids to sow chaos and death. That's how our civilization is destined to end: more sinister and tech-savvy individuals than myself looking to dismantle a culture and ethos on behalf of their own. America, in particular, is vulnerable to these sorts of attacks since our general public has hastily and readily embraced the concept of the internet of things enough to connect our systems to a single grid with little concern for encryption or security. We are light-years behind China in this regard.

However harmful you may find my actions, bear in mind that there are such things as post-roll video ads on sites like YouTube. These are the inexplicable advertisements that run after your video has finished playing and serve no purpose other than to line Google's pockets after you've finished watching your video, even if it is not auto-playing into another video. The idea for such an ad should cause outrage. People should be out marching in the streets right now and stomping on Android phones over this, but instead, we celebrate the ingenuity in finding more of our eyeball moments to monetize and chalk it up to another success of capitalism while we applaud Google's stock going up another few points. In any case, keep a healthy dose of objectivity when judging what you think is evil online and what is just opportunism.

Technology evolves quickly, and there is no time like the present to take advantage of errors in the system, especially when it is increasingly likely our civilization has already peaked and our distracted minds will not notice that our inevitable decline has already begun. The great empires of the Romans, Greeks, and Mayans most likely did not have leaders sitting around saying, "It is a pity that none of this will last." Our species' eternal belief in constant progress is an egotistical blindfold shielding us from history repeating itself. We call it optimism, but it is just selfish wishful thinking.

Whatever society follows in our footsteps hundreds of years from now, they may find our media, literature, and philosophy to be a form of archaic and self-obsessed religion. For the first time in history, a human society's values will be enshrined everlasting in digital form for our distant descendants. They could potentially discover our reality shows, documentaries, and representations of ourselves and our past, echoing the mindsets of mankind's manifest destiny. They will understand our missteps with the kind of clarity that only generations of hindsight can provide, and they will know that our obsession with pleasure and laziness assuredly led to inadequacy, unsustainability, and irrelevance on this planet.

BACK TO THE POINT

You don't have to steal a Social Security number or anything that complex to assume an alternate identity, though on the dark web, it is possible to obtain such things. If you want your alias to hold up in a police station, you'll need a complete persona. Otherwise, everything is a veneer and nothing is tangible anymore. If you can spice up the appearance around the edges of a new identity enough, no one will ask you any questions, especially online. Regurgitate other people's ideas and say whatever you think the fans will retweet. Come up with an easily forgettable name, like Sarah Thompson or John Riley, as your pseudonym. These accounts become your sockpuppets. I have hundreds of them at this point and can control thousands through my relationships with other nefarious entrepreneurs and their meatpuppets and click farms.

Melvin Ritkin started this way: a useful idiot who became an alter ego. Back home in Indiana, I was Herbert, but once I moved to LA and started creating these accounts, I found I could speak more freely through microphones held by shills than I was able to when I spoke as myself from my own personal microphone. Melvin became whoever Herbert couldn't be, and over time, Herbert stopped existing, at least as far as the public was concerned.

We all have weird knacks, fears, and worries. One of mine is that I'll slip and fall on the wet bathroom floor tiles while I'm cleaning my ear with a Q-tip, despite the warnings on the label not to insert them into your ear canal, hit my head square on the floor at just the proper angle to plunge the Q-tip into my brain, and have that painful experience be the last thought running through my mind when everything goes dark. Another misplaced fear of mine since moving to Los Angeles has been that a large earthquake will strike just as I am naked and soaped up in the shower, vulnerable and likely to slip as well. Actually, the shower may be a safe spot to be in during an earthquake. I do not know about such things, but the anticipated shock runs through my mind each time I step into the tub. What should worry us is too ephemeral and intangible to notice: that nothing ever goes away on the internet, that anyone can be manipulated, and that everyone has a price.

Anytime you fire off a text message or email that you immediately regret sending, or whenever you search online for something scandalous that you know will live in your search history long after you "clear" it, the prospect may pop into your mind that the desperate act of hitting that return button may come back to haunt you someday. In your imagination, there may be the expectation of some climate-controlled deep-state data server somewhere far underground in the desert with an ever-expanding file with your name on it that machines have automatically populated with key-logging software and AI. This file, you imagine, would also have sensor data, location data, purchase history, and financial information and would be the equivalent of having dirt on every person in the world. When needed, someone with the proper clearance could download that file and your entire online history, and they could potentially blackmail you with it, or worse.

I doubt it's all as organized as that, but your data is out there and ready to be exploited by at least one group, if not many. One merely needs to take the time to collate the materials.

❖   ❖   ❖   ❖

My phone buzzes. It's a text from Oscar saying he's parked out front of my place.

I go outside and give him his laptop, along with the good news that he now has his data back and can access his computer.

He gives me a big sincere hug before driving away, and it feels strangely personal, like we are friends now, but I chalk it up to it being Christmas and him being on a heavy dose of drugs and alcohol. I feel a sense of bittersweet satisfaction. It's like the feeling of finishing a video game or a long novel. I hoped it would last longer, and now, I'll have to find my next victim online and start the process all over.

First, I need to look online for Ruby, the adult-entertainment celebrity from the party. For research purposes, of course. During the span of my evening viewing, I recognize a few of her videos as ones I've watched many times. It seems odd that I hadn't ever paid attention to the performers' names in these clips, but I was already a fan of Ruby before realizing it consciously. Many of my favorite scenes in adult videos include her in a critical role, and now, I wish I had been the one performing those acts with her.

Never before had I watched X-rated videos with the intention of asking one of the performers on a date. Still, during my research, I start to fall madly in love with the idea of her. There are, of course, scenes I stumble upon that are taboo and kinky to the legal limits, which tear my emotions between feeling nervous and insecure about the prospect of ever actually approaching her, as much as I might wish I would.

CHAPTER 4

A TYPICAL CATFISHING SCAM might go a handful of ways if you're doing it to make money. Some people just enjoy catfishing and have no deeper motive other than to mess with someone and stomp on their dreams. In general, I try to catfish rich, entitled, arrogant men, with blackmail or money as the endgame. I start by creating a few accounts on dating apps posing as beautiful, young women. This is easiest if I already have fake social accounts to connect with the dating apps to make the facade more believable and three-dimensional.

Once you connect with a mark, you want to lure them over to another platform where you can talk outside of the dating app. This might have to be text, WhatsApp, or something else, but the point is the same. One method is to ask the match to do a video chat. When that happens, the woman he sees is actually a pre-recorded video. You can control her actions by clicking to have her wave or say one of a few phrases, and you have numerous reasons to end the call within a minute or two. That video is automatically recorded and almost always includes incriminating evidence that you can use to blackmail or embarrass them if they're a public figure or married or otherwise compromised. With AI advancements and deep fakes, the capabilities to have more than a few phrases or a short conversation will soon expand to much more disturbingly realistic digital interactions.

Another method is to build trust and come up with reasons for them to send you money with Venmo, PayPal, CashApp, or something similar before ever meeting in person. As you can imagine, there are all sorts of sob stories and explanations for why you need the money, and enough people will fall for it to make the scam worthwhile to some. You can make a few hundred bucks on a mark, but not anything substantial, unless you're doing tons of these every day. Sure, you could automate some processes if you have a cell phone farm with the right protocols in place, but it still takes a fair amount of physical labor. For that reason, these types of scams are usually scaled offshore in places like the Philippines, and people like me don't typically spend their time nickel-and-diming random guys like this on dating apps. I would've found it entertaining in my teens, but nowadays, I'm focused on what I call elephant hunting.

It takes nearly the same amount of energy to fleece an average Joe as it does to catch someone like Oscar.

The offshore cell phone farms repurpose existing photos of attractive women to imitate actual, live human beings. They create an imposter profile with the real person's photos and link them to fake socials, email, and phone number. Within a few messages, they come up with a reason for you to send them $50. If I ran this scam and spread it across several target cities, I figure I could likely set up bot funnels to convince twenty guys a day like this, automatically, and that's per account. With ten accounts, that's theoretically $300,000 per month just running a simple $50 scam with template responses and minimal human effort. In the same way *The Wolf of Wall Street* could write a script for any penny-stock trader to use and close a shady deal, you could attempt to take lonely men's money while keeping them lonely.

Honestly, it can be amusing to create fake dating profiles, and I encourage everyone to try catfishing at least once in their life. You don't have to do it with the malicious intent of bullying or thievery. You can log in and give a few compliments and digitally stroke a few egos. I have a fake young female account I made named Darlene. Her bio says, "I'm like all five Spice Girls put together," and I have another one named Jessica whose bio says, "bicoastal and bicurious." Being quirky always helps put people at ease, like creating a profile of a young Asian woman with a bio saying something like, "best parallel parker." The bios generally end with a suggestion to add me on Snapchat, which about 60 percent of matches do, and less than 5 percent of those are worth scamming, so the fictitious ladies just tell them something nice and give a reason they're unfortunately too busy to meet up or ghost them.

These scams aren't my main focus, and I don't spend much time on them anymore, but I enjoy putting someone in their place when I see the right match. Especially people who are used to putting others in their place, like Oscar or Titus.

Catching an elephant requires more work than the bush-league catfish assignments scaled overseas. Celebrities and other people with verified social profiles have their own dating apps to which we simpletons aren't invited. That's where my verified profiles come in, and once I use one of them, it generally gets burnt, and I have to start over. So I can't monkey around with them too much or for too long. It is a fast process—maybe a week or two of use on the dating app before the shill is garbage. For that week of activity, I might spend a month preparing the profile and potential targets. It's a lot of work if you want to do it right—the way I do these things.

I met a guy once at a bar who told me he had used fake accounts to hurt people. Some guy, we'll call him Steve, slighted the man at the bar once, and so he decided to make Steve pay for it. He took his time and was methodical. Evil, even. He would set up a Grindr account with Steve's photos and within the same general area that

Steve lived. He'd proceed to message guys nearby from this account, giving them Steve's home and work addresses. Steve was heterosexual, which is a key part of the sinisterness. To top things off, he'd say in the messages he had a rape fantasy and wanted for someone just to break in and force themselves on him. After a few encounters, Steve got wind of this and tried to complain to Grindr and report the account. Sometimes Grindr would deactivate a particular profile. Still, they couldn't do much to prevent future accounts with his name and photos from popping up on the site or even attempt to catch the person responsible. Thanks to the Communications Decency Act, Section 230, tech companies aren't legally liable for what you do on their platforms. They are just the platforms in the same way the postal service could not be sued over the actions of people like the Unabomber.

This guy kept making new Grindr accounts with Steve's info, and when one would get deleted, he'd make another. Over six months, according to what he told me, he sent over one thousand men to Steve's home and workplace, until finally, Steve and his family moved to another state. He'd gotten whatever sick revenge he needed on Steve and seemed cool as a cucumber while explaining his tactics to me a few years later at a bar, about half an hour after I'd met him.

He said this to me casually over drinks, just like a neighbor telling you about repainting their house. He was proud of his efforts, and I was obviously impressed.

RED FLAGS

If you notice any of the following red flags, you may be getting catfished:

(a) The person has a sparse online presence. It shouldn't be difficult to do some quick digital stalking to find them and message each other on social media channels to verify the photos match what you saw on the dating app. If you can't find them online, that should be an obvious red flag. The account might make some claim of recently deleting their socials because they were sick of them or something, but it's a lie. Real people leave breadcrumbs that you can find, and it is unlikely a dating app is their only online profile.

(b) They make quick moves and share overly personal details to escalate the impression you have of where the relationship is heading. This one is harder to realize as a red flag because they may share something sincerely severe and personal that makes you more empathetic and want to believe them or help them out of some situation. As a general rule, empathy should be withheld until you meet someone face-to-face.

(c) If they seem too good to be true, they probably are. If you matched with someone who could be an underwear model, and you don't usually match with those types of people, and this one needs money—you can bet it's a catfish.

(d) If they ask for money before meeting you, they're the definition of what I consider to be a catfish. Even if it's a specific amount for an Uber trip to meet up with you, and they say they just need you to send them $31.48. They might say they don't get paid until next week. Their credit card hasn't been paid yet. A crisis came up in their family. Whatever their excuse, they're a scam artist. I promise. Trust me.

Even when you meet with an escort and have them come to your house or hotel room, there is still a certain likelihood of getting scammed after they arrive in person. There are different schools of thought about whether you should pay before or after the service. One man I know is adamant you should never pay until the following morning when they're leaving because they should be obligated to stay the night as well. He says if they ask for money right when they show up, he has a stash of counterfeit bills he'll give them instead of real money, as often when they ask for money up front, they find a reason to step outside and are into a friend's car and off to the next house.

When I catfished Oscar yesterday, I had the figure online of a tall, skinny, French, brunette, twenty-three-year-old model named Josephine who loves yoga, travel, and modern dance. She told Oscar she recognized him and loved all the shows and movies he was in, and he was hooked. Beauty and flattery will fool most men online, just as it has in the real world for millennia.

Whether the catfish scenario plays out as a home run or not, after every exchange, I take screenshots and save those in a file named after the person with whom I'm interacting. If they're married, the screenshot's existence is already damning. Sometimes I'll say it's two girls messaging them. Sometimes I'll say I'm a minor in case I can make them propose something illegal. Most of the dating app accounts I have are female, but a few are male, and they're constantly collecting messages and photos from temporary accounts that pop up and get deleted a few hours later. I keep the screenshots. Nothing vanishes on *my* internet.

One ruse I like using on dating apps whenever I'm pretending to be an attractive woman is after we match and he says something to open the conversation, I'll say, "Do you not remember me?"—and wherever that ends up going, it's always a good diversion. Usually, they'll vaguely claim to remember meeting me, especially if I pepper in a few details about where we supposedly met. This takes a lot of homework, but you get their guard down. In Oscar's case, it was child's play. We had maybe ten exchanges of texts between us before I sent him a phishing link. He clicked it. I took over his laptop, and it was over.

At least $150 million gets swindled away from people in the United States in online dating scams every year. The number is likely much higher since many victims are too embarrassed to report such a loss. Among corporations, over $400 million a year gets taken in ransomware attacks, which is also increasing. Someone was sending those emails about a down-on-his-luck Nigerian prince back in the nineties, and hundreds of new scams hit the web every day. This is innovation, and it's something to be studied and admired, not swept under a rug and ignored because we disagree with their ethics. Too often, we think about these perpetrators as ratchet sleazeballs who will surely get their comeuppance someday, and we quickly turn our minds to other more-pressing matters.

The black market has a range of people employed in the supply chain of illegal goods and services. There are certainly some lousy cartel guys at the top running the illicit drug business, but many of the people involved below them are just good people getting by and working a decent-paying day job. I look at internet scammers the same way. If someone is going to take the time to come up with a novel method to steal my information or extort me without my seeing it coming, they deserve the win. We're supposed to be more cautious, paranoid, and protective of our information, and if we're not proactive, they will help teach us why we should be. These hackers are hardly the image you have in your head from nineties movies anymore, where the characters are furiously typing lines of code "inside the system"; instead, modern hacking is more like launching and installing scripts that are prewritten, easily procured, and ready to go. Nowadays, there is ransomware on the dark web that can be purchased and initiated by software virgins.

In a world constantly more connected and with less privacy each day, more people should learn how to go anonymous. Be a contrarian. Say what shouldn't be said. Publicly shame total strangers. Cause a riot. Because someone has to.

A little bit of anarchy can be healthy sometimes.

Bing. My computer chimes that I have a new email. It's from Fred, and he's encrypted it. It has links about Dan and his arrest history and asks if we can meet for lunch today at 1:00 p.m. to discuss moving forward. He doesn't say anything about ruining Dan's life. He keeps it vague. Fred is a true pro. I respond that lunch works for me. I suggest a diner a few minutes from my house and say I'll be there at 1:00 p.m.

FRED'S MASTER PLAN

I'm seated at a booth waiting for Fred to arrive. I am just waiting and looking at my magical phone to pass the time.

It's Christmas, and I only got about four hours of sleep. Not many places are open, so I chose this old twenty-four-hour spot I can walk to from my house. The establishment is nearly empty aside from a few other lonely stragglers and scant restaurant staff. There are two women having lunch at the table next to my booth. A waitress brings me a glass of water and a coffee and tells me to holler when I'm ready to order. She has a warm motherly vibe, and I wonder why she isn't with her family for the holiday as she turns to check on her other tables. Perhaps she doesn't have any family here in LA, or maybe she was one of the ones who moved here in search of fame but settled for a regular paycheck and mediocre tips. I pull out a flask and add some whiskey to my coffee.

Fred is fifteen minutes late. Since he had requested this meeting at the last minute, I consider being peachy with him about it, but Fred scampers in and waves at me like he's already apologizing, and it's Christmas after all, so I brush it off. I didn't have anything else to do today, so to Fred, this whole meal is probably a gesture of holiday friendship. Fred looks clean cut, well rested, freshly showered, and shaved. He's draped in khakis, a polo shirt, and aviators as he takes a seat across from me in the booth and removes the sunglasses. "So sorry I'm late. Have you ordered yet?"

"No, I was waiting. No worries. Merry Christmas."

"I hear the chicken parm here is excellent, and the fish and chips. Yeah, Merry Christmas to you too, buddy. Lunch is on me."

The waitress looms back over the table. "Merry Christmas. How are you all doing today?"

She seems happy enough about working during the holiday, and her smile and energy are almost contagious. Fred and I wish her season's greetings and both order beers and fried fish before she disappears again.

Fred speaks to me while peering out the window and taking off his jacket. "Okay, I'll keep this quick. I've got to be back on the other side of town in an hour. You get the links I emailed you? Oh, by the way, you should've seen this broad I brought home from that party last night. A bit older, maybe thirty-five, but great big, huge tits." He uses his hands to show me the size.

He's talking loudly, and the two women sitting nearby can hear every word. They look over on the word "tits," but Fred continues like he doesn't give a damn.

"Here, I've got some pictures. Will you look at this?"

He hands me his phone, and there's a photo presented with tits as described. He reclaims his phone and looks out the window again, like he's either tailing someone or thinks he's being tailed.

"Yeah, so about the email. I read through it." I look over at the window to determine what he's looking at, but it just looks like a regular parking lot. "This Dan guy is a scumbag all right."

Fred looks back at me and forgets about the window.

"A scumbag, yes. A fucking shitfuck. Now, here's what I'm thinking. There's a clear record of this guy breaking the law, embezzling, lying, scamming people. Some big people. Some have even taken him to court and won like I finally did. The thing is, other people keep hiring him to produce concerts. He's doing a concert for KISS next month in Rome. I want to make it where if people search for Dan online, the first things they see are about his frauds and scams and lawsuits. That's the short of it. There should be an article going out right now saying, 'Why Is Gene Simmons Working with This Known Scam Artist,' or something to that effect."

"Fred, this sounds wonderful and all, and I've been thinking about it, but this is going to be more involved than just updating his Wikipedia page or putting out a press release. Placing stories, making a few dedicated websites and socials about the allegations, tons of content—this is a big ask if you want to give him a nervous breakdown. It's just like building a brand from scratch but an anti-brand."

"I know. I've thought about this for a while, trust me. I'll spend a hundred grand over the next twelve months on this if you can make it really work. That's how much the settlement was for, even though he only owed me $60,000 before the trial."

"You know, when Eminem dissed Michael Jackson in 2005, Jackson just bought Eminem's entire catalog and made money off his music every time he performed. That's how you get back at someone."

"If I had the money Michael Jackson did, I would buy Dan's company and burn it to the ground. This is my next best option. We just burn it to the ground."

"Fair enough," I say and scratch my chin. "It's definitely up my alley, Fred. Though it's usually the other way around. Would you be willing to be the face of any of this? Maybe do a byline somewhere, or we could produce a short docuseries about his crimes that you could be a talking head in?"

The waitress approaches and sets down our beers, already poured into glasses, and heads back toward the kitchen.

Fred and I clink our glasses together and each take a sip. He sets down his drink, cracks his knuckles, and interweaves his fingers into a prayer pose on the table in front of himself. "Yeah, I can be the face of this, and I think I know a few people that would be willing to be interviewed on camera. That's a good idea. I don't mind being blamed for ruining him. I just want him ruined."

Another gulp of beer. "All right, I'll start working up a plan. I just worry about this somehow coming back to bite me, is all. But if you want to take the heat..."

"Take the weekend and think about it some more and where the budget would go. Then you should come join us for New Year's Eve, and we can get the ball rolling. Do you have any New Year's plans?"

No Christmas plans, no New Year's plans. I shrug pathetically and shake my head.

"How much do you know about ghost towns?"

"I don't know." I shrug again as Fred's tone and question both seem a bit menacing and suggestive. "The usual amount, I guess. You mean like an old mining town where everyone left once the gold or silver or copper was gone?"

Fred leans back like he's getting comfortable before telling a decent story. "That's pretty much it. There are a lot of those towns. Over a hundred just in Nevada, but they're in Alaska, Montana, those kinds of places too. Most of them were disestablished by the 1920s. Thousands of people lived in these towns at one point or another, but now, they're empty and dilapidated, and in some cases, you can buy the whole town. So Titus bought one a few years ago for four hundred grand, and he's been renovating it. First, he rebuilt the saloon and hotel, and now, he's fixing up some old homes and hooking them up with solar power, water, sewage, and whatnot."

"Sounds like quite a project."

"Well, Titus's cousin Larry has been living there the past two years overseeing the renovations, and the New Year's party this weekend is the first time it's being used for an event. Larry's the mayor, technically, so it should get wild."

"Mayor of a city with a population of one. Must be some ego boost. Funny, I didn't realize you could buy those towns. Why would you want to? Or why would a movie star want to?"

"For four hundred grand, why wouldn't you want to? At least if you've got the bankroll. Titus has to fix it up properly still. In Nevada, there are counties where gambling and prostitution are legal, so he bought a town called Cortez, where both are already legal. I think his pipe dream is to turn it into a skanky little party spot eventually, with a brothel and casinos and hotels—all keeping with the old-mining-town vibe. I don't know if it'd be open year-round, but I think it'd only cater to other celebrities and Hollywood people. It's actually a hell of an idea."

I try not to smile too obviously, but I too appreciate that Titus has been secretly building his own makeshift *Westworld*, presumably with less crime, so I fight it off and end up with some sort of unexpected grimace. "Sounds classy," I say.

The waitress walks back up with our orders and sets down our plates. "All right, can I get you all anything else?"

"No, thank you, everything's perfect," Fred says with his mouth already full of fish, and the waitress backs away somewhere between disgusted and amused. "Yeah, about as classy as a waterbed motel. But it'll be a fun party, I promise."

"I don't know. It doesn't sound like my crowd. How about I call you next week, and we meet up to go through the plan to take Dan's life down? I've got a lot on my plate right now."

Fred tosses three fries in his mouth and looks at me while chewing them down with a stupid smirk like he knows I don't have anything on my plate. We're having lunch at a diner on Christmas Day, so there's no way I have much going on in my life. "Ruby is coming. That redheaded porn star from the party last night. She's helping one of the actresses in Titus's new movie, so they're bringing her along." He washes the fish down with the rest of his beer.

"Really? What movie? How is she helping?"

"Well, now I've got your attention. Titus is directing some big movie this spring in New Orleans, his directorial debut. I guess one of the characters gets into sex work or something, so the actress has been shadowing Ruby for a few weeks to get her vibe or style or whatever. They're friends, grew up together, so I think they just wanted to hang out and add her to the payroll."

"I actually researched some of her work last night before bed," I say.

"I bet you did. So I'll see you there? I have to jet." Fred tosses some money on the table and takes the last bite of his fish.

"Okay," I tell him. "Yeah, I'll see you there. Sounds fun."

CHAPTER 5

BURBANK AIRPORT IS deserted around noon on New Year's Eve, at least in the section where we enter through the private-plane area. This section is equipped with a metal detector and two men with plastic placards hanging around their necks as the entire security apparatus. You could walk through here with whatever you want and fly it somewhere else privately, but that's probably just one of the many advantages of having your own plane, and I feel like an idiot for just now realizing that in my late thirties. There's kinetic party-type energy on the flight the whole way there. One of the ladies in front of me has on headphones, and her arms are in the air dancing most of the journey, as if she took some molly just before takeoff.

I don't recognize anyone else on this jet, but we're heading toward the same place: some seedy, western, ghost-town, party-retreat brainchild of an eccentric movie star: Cortez, Nevada, USA. A modern-day rustic pleasure palace.

When we arrive, there is no airport, just a single landing strip with two airplane hangars and a handful of valets in vests waiting for us with golf carts. As passengers and their belongings are loaded into the transport, there is a man next to me loudly talking business into his phone. Something important that apparently needed to be handled immediately after disembarking. "Well, I find 65 percent leverage to be quite interesting, obviously." I shoot him a sideways glance that implies he should find a spot with fewer people to continue his deals in private, yet he continues in place like everyone needs to hear what a big shot he is.

The golf carts take us in small groups to the main street of Cortez and drop us in front of the central hotel and saloon. It has the same western decor and style as the older buildings but has been rebuilt from the ground up. There are a few other newer buildings in the town square as well, possibly lodging for the staff or private residences. More people wearing vests appear and bring our bags in for us and offer us cowboy hats and drinks in the same way you may have been given a lei when arriving in Hawaii in the seventies.

Walking through the café doors, I find old-timey piano music playing in the saloon. The pinewood floors, ceilings, shutters, and beams throughout make you feel like you've stepped into a classic Clint Eastwood western. I am certain they've done a great job at the restoration, as everything in here is new and old at once. The wood has been freshly sanded and stained, the appliances and electrical are state of the art, but the foundation and layout feel like they've been rebuilt as they were initially.

Titus, Oscar, and a few other people are at the bar handing out champagne to everyone who enters. There is a festive flurry of partyers in the lobby and plenty of people in vests around the building working as staff for the weekend. Caterers, bartenders, valets, servers. Judging by their vans and cars in the parking lot, they all came in from Las Vegas. The town's mayor is some flunky cousin, and there is no local police or authority, so it's assumed anything goes here.

When I enter, Titus is in the middle of a strange conversation with another man who looks like a soccer dad in an expensive suit, which means he's probably from the studio. The man in the suit is aggressively lecturing Titus. "There's no way you can include the scene of her getting gang-raped by priests. It just can't happen, and this is the third time I've said it. You'll realize it today or next month, but there's no way."

Titus is calm in receiving the lecture and in his response. "But we have to. That's the beauty of it. Oh, give me a minute. Melvin Ritkin, so glad you made it." Titus brushes past the man he was talking to and approaches me. I feel oddly honored that the conversation needed to pause for him to acknowledge little old me.

Oscar and Titus both shake my hand, and Oscar grabs my shoulder like an old friend while the studio executive walks off, frustrated, in another direction. Two young men are hovering around Oscar and Titus, who I quickly determine are their assistants. Titus is a bona fide movie star, so it makes sense his assistant would be with him here. Oscar, however, is the type of phony LA guy who has an assistant even though he isn't busy or famous enough to warrant having an assistant. Oscar is just a short, average, clean-cut, Midwestern guy who has successful friends and been able to ride their coattails to his own limited status.

Oscar speaks close to my ear to keep others from hearing. "It's nice to see you, Melvin. I owe you big time for helping me out with my computer. Damned hacker assholes. Any idea who was behind it yet?" He hands me a glass of champagne and raises his glass, so I return the gesture.

"My pleasure. Thanks for inviting me. No, I doubt we're going to find out who did it, but I'll keep looking."

Titus raises his glass to me now too. "Starting the year with a computer wizard by our side. We're glad you're here."

We cheers again, and I take another gulp of champagne. I excuse myself to find something better to drink while Titus and Oscar continue their train of hugs and handshakes of the latest arrivals. A subtle man in a vest with a stocky build and Latin accent is waiting for me behind the bar. "Hello, sir. What will you have?"

"Tequila and lemon on the rocks, please."

Flying always makes me anxious, and I'm relieved to be at the destination, if only for the night. With my drink order placed, I look around the bar. There are poker tables, slot machines, blackjack, craps, and roulette on the main floor. The other end of the building holds the reception for the hotel. A sturdy woman is behind the reception desk, passing out room keys and information to the other guests from my flight. Obviously, no one is being charged anything for the travel or accommodations.

Fred descends the stairs and catches my attention at the bar. With his index finger, he commands me to follow him outside, which I do unquestioningly with my fresh drink in hand. He's seated in a rocking chair on the front porch, and I take a seat next to him, sipping my beverage.

"You made it."

"Yeah, here I am. And I've got a plan for the campaign against Dan all ready for you. I'm getting more excited the more I think about it."

"All right! Let's hear it." Fred leans back and folds his hands over his lap.

"I found a production team that can make a three-part web series detailing all of Dan's crimes. It'll eat about half the budget at $40K, but it's a solid crew and worth it. The editor is legit. It'll be like a Ken Burns documentary with a catalog and timeline of criminality. We'll need to line up interviews with other people that despise Dan and schedule about a week of shooting. We'll have a lawyer look at everything to make sure we can't get sued for libel. It'll be super high quality. On top of the three episodes, we'll probably have a bunch of shorter clips that we can put out on socials."

"Fuck yeah, Herbert."

"Melvin," I scold him with a glance of concern, but no one can hear us above the jubilations inside the saloon.

"Shit, right, Melvin. Sorry, I got excited. Go on. I like everything so far."

"I've lined up someone to ghostwrite some bylines for you that we can push out, and she'll just need to do a few recorded phone calls with you to put the story straight. We'll also get a few designers working up Dan memes, like a 'Bad Luck Brian,' but more like a 'Bad Guy Dan' sort of vibe, so we can get those images to show up higher in searches for his name. I think we've got a few avenues we can take with getting articles placed in music and trade pubs and sites, and I want to book you on podcasts to get the story out there too. Once the episodes are ready to launch, we can use that as a PR moment to pitch you for interviews. We'll want to do other stuff like updating his Wikipedia and putting out a bunch of press releases about him and the web series. And we'll have hundreds of bot accounts share every article and tag him to make sure he's being reminded of it daily. Whatever is left in the budget, I'll put toward paid media to drive video views of the series and traffic. I won't really make anything off this, I just like the idea of helping you fuck this guy."

"Sounds fucking fantastic. Traffic to what, though?"

"Oh, I already started buying domains that will be relevant later on. I bought some like DanielCastilloIsAFraud.com and DanCastilloIsAScamArtist.com and a few other domains like that."

"Brilliant. Send me a monthly invoice, and let me know when the interviews are. I like the plan. I can't wait. Good work." Fred giggles like a young boy.

"Yeah, so it'll probably be three months or so before we have the episodes and content ready to launch, and six to eight months before the top search results for his name start to be impacted. We'll want to be methodical about timing the release of this stuff so that we don't tip him off. I'd prefer he doesn't realize what's happening until it's too late."

"Agreed. In the next three months, you put together the pieces underground, and then we'll strike like cobras. I'll await your green light to say anything to anyone else. Otherwise, I'll start reaching out to a few people we can interview." Fred hands me a cigar and lights his own. Once his is burning, he hands me a lighter. "You remember in the movie *Trading Places* when they give Eddie Murphy a job and a house while they take everything away from Dan Akroyd? They destroy his engagement to his fiancée by making her think he's cheating. They take his home, fire him, and have him framed and arrested on drug charges. All in the name of a scientific experiment and a wager over one dollar. Well, we are doing a scientific experiment of our own, but at the end of it, I want Daniel Castillo to be completely ruined."

I smile at the comparison. "So you don't want this to end like the movie ended?"

"No, not at all, but I think the first seventy minutes or so of the movie is a good touchstone for us." Fred and I both take long puffs from our cigars. "So are you planning on making a move on your porn star this weekend?"

"Yeah, if it happens naturally, I guess. I didn't see her on my flight."

"Her and the actresses came in late last night. She's here. Staying at this same hotel."

"Any chance you can get her seated next to me at dinner tonight?"

"I run security, not seating arrangements."

I finish my drink and go inside to find my room and shower.

DINNER IN CORTEZ

We're all seated at a long wooden table on wooden chairs outside the front of the hotel and saloon. Servers scurry around, bringing us our drinks and appetizers. All fifty or so guests in town are here at one long table, and Ruby happens to be across from me and just to my left. Not close enough for casual or intimate conversation, but I look over at her nervously until she looks back, then I dart my eyes away in shy embarrassment like we're in middle school. I look at her and attempt a flirtatious smile, but I'm sure it just comes across as awkward.

I have to check on a few of my shills, so I pull out three identical phones and place them on the table in front of me nonchalantly and check different social accounts. A few clicks later, I slide the three phones into three separate pockets in my blazer.

I'm wearing my typical black pants and black V-neck shirt with a black blazer. Ruby has on a letter jacket that says Pornhub on it. She looks like a younger, hotter version of Jessica Chastain, but one who I've seen get nailed a hundred times.

The man on my left tells a story to the surrounding crowd about a producer with whom he had worked. "And he says, 'I don't care what your damned protocols are. I want what I want, when I want it, the way I want it, where I want it, and however I goddamn decide that I want it!'"

His delivery sounds accurate for a diva film producer, and a handful of those nearby are laughing and smiling along. There's another funnyman on my right making the crowd laugh, and I feel more than out of place. I sneak a smile at Ruby and see her dart back a half smile of her own in between cringing over how out of touch those around us are. One couple near Ruby recounts the troubles they had with their adopted preteen daughter before deciding to return her to an orphanage.

The man on my right has slicked-back hair and is taking his turn sharing stories. "I helped a blind man once. It's true. I try to help out whenever I can, you know. So I saw this one blind man crossing the street on his own one day, and he had a cane, but as soon as he got to the other curb on my side of the street, the door to a Jamba Juice opened, and he almost walked right in, so I tapped one of his shoulders and said, 'Excuse me, sir, but you were about to walk into a Jamba Juice.' Like I had just saved him a huge mistake. And he was like, 'Yeah, that's where I'm going.'" The whole end of the table laughs.

Someone starts clinking a wineglass to get our attention, and it's Titus at the head of the table standing, preparing to give a toast. Our conversations muffle, and everything goes quiet.

"Everyone," Titus is smiling and looks to be in his element. It's a long table, so he speaks loudly. In this light, he reminds me of what it might be like if James Dean were our contemporary, but if he also had a trust fund and hated Porsches. "Thank you so much for joining us for the first of many Cortez getaways. The town is still coming together, but how about the Sinner's Saloon and Old Towne Hotel that my cousin Larry has delightfully reincarnated?"

Titus motions toward a man to his left, cousin Larry, who stands and smiles as we all clap. Larry waves a thank-you and returns to his seat.

"There are a lot more improvements we're going to be making to this little town over the next few years, so if you have any ideas for cool things we should have here, let me know. One more thing, and I promised I would keep this short. Aside from bringing in the New Year together, I am also excited to be celebrating that our film, *Justine*, is officially in preproduction and that we'll all be in New Orleans this spring to shoot what I know will be a memorable film. Everyone told Kevin Costner that no one cared about westerns anymore, and still, he financed and directed *Dances with Wolves* because he believed in the story. It ended up winning Best Picture at the Oscars." There are a few mild laughs and stuttered applause. His delivery is that of a seasoned actor, even if his speech isn't that of a seasoned writer. "A lot of people told me that no one would want to see a period piece in New Orleans adapted from the Marquis de Sade. But here you are, the people who have believed in this project since day one."

The table mumbles in agreement and awe, along with a few claps and here-heres.

"So, I'd like to raise a toast and quote the marquis himself," says Titus. "Oh thou, my friends! The prosperity of crime is like unto the lightning, whose traitorous brilliancies embellish the atmosphere but for an instant, in order to hurl into death's very depths the luckless one they have dazzled."

Titus raises his glass and winks at us like an asshole. Who knows what the hell that quote is supposed to mean in this context, but still, someone whistles. Everyone else responds with cheers and applause, and they all merrily continue drinking.

As the table of sycophants raise their glasses in gushes of mutual gratitude, I catch Ruby rolling her eyes while downing her drink, which makes me smile, which she sees, and she smiles back at me. I raise my glass to her, and we have our own private cheers, although her glass is now empty.

FIREWORKS

After dinner, Ruby starts walking in the opposite direction of the saloon, which is where everyone else is headed. I grab a freshly opened bottle of wine from the table and follow her. Almost on the edge of this small ghost town, she climbs up into the back of an old wagon cart and lies down.

My eyes dart to the saloon and back to the wagon, wondering if I'll be too aggressive by coming up to her out here alone in the dark. Before deciding what to do next, Ruby's voice, her beautiful, soft voice, says to me, "You look like trouble."

I freeze and look up at her, unsure how to respond.

Ruby breaks the silence by following with, "Are you gonna join me, or are you just gonna creep on me all night from over there? It's kind of making me nervous."

I crawl up next to her in the wagon, trying not to seem too nervous. "Sorry. Hey, I'm Melvin." I put out my hand, and she shakes it gently.

"I'm Ruby."

"Yeah, I know who you are. Or I guess I didn't know if that was your real name."

"Yes, my real name is Ruby, but my stage name is just a different last name."

She glances at me with a raised eyebrow before returning her gaze to the stars. I lie down next to her and join her in looking up at the night sky. There's little pollution and few lights out here, so thousands of stars are visible up above. I'd prefer to look at her, but I keep my eyes up and try my best to seem gentlemanly.

"I thought you looked interesting at dinner," she says. "With your three phones. Must be a very busy man."

"I'm a garbage man for movie stars. I stay pretty busy. So what do you think of this town?"

"I hate the desert. I like the beach, but at least you can see the stars out here."

I look up again at all the stars you can't view from smoggy Los Angeles.

"Well, what do you think of Titus? Of this movie he's directing?"

"Oh, I don't know much about the movie. I tried reading the script, but the characters all talk so weird. What do you think about it?"

"I didn't know what it was about until that toast at dinner, but he said it's an adaptation of *Justine* by the Marquis de Sade, so that does seem like strange source material. How do you wind up with the job of being shadowed for a movie part?"

"Sequoia is a friend of a friend. We're all three from Texas, and my friend from high school knew her in college. She introduced me to Isabella last year, and we all hang out sometimes."

"What about Titus? Do you know him well?"

"Not really. You sure have a lot of questions. I think part of him scares me, same with that Oscar guy. When they've been around me and Isabella and Sequoia, I can tell those guys make them uncomfortable too. I don't think guys notice that as much."

"A lot of directors like to make actors feel out of their element to make them seem more vulnerable on camera."

"I don't think it's that. I don't know much about mainstream stuff, but I saw the way he was treating Isabella before dinner, and it was pretty cringey."

"What happened before dinner? Who's Isabella?" I ask, oblivious.

"Her and Sequoia are the actresses starring in Titus's movie." She says this like it's something I should have known. "I don't know, I saw him touch her leg, and she tried moving away, and then he put his arm around her. It just felt gross. You can sometimes tell when a girl is too scared to say anything."

We share a silence and lie on our backs, next to each other.

"Are you religious?"

She looks at me, surprised by the question, and laughs in a sort of snorting way that is both embarrassing and adorable. "No, I do porn. I'm not religious."

"I mean, are you, like, spiritual? Do you think certain things happen for a reason?" She locks eyes with me for the first time, and it's more intense than I expected. She doesn't respond, just looks into my eyes for a minute, like she's calculating something immeasurable. "Yeah, I guess so. Kind of."

"I think it's almost midnight. Do you want to go back with your friends?"

Ruby glances at her watch, and it's the first time I've noticed she's wearing one. It's a Chanel watch that must have cost over $25,000.

"Yeah, it's almost midnight. I can't stand to be around that crowd any longer. Did you hear that couple complaining about the girl they adopted and then returned to the orphanage? Let's stay here. In the back of this wagon, in some sleazy millionaire's private resort cowboy town." Her lips curve upward, and I'm more nervous that it seems like she likes me.

"That's a really nice watch." It's a dumb comment, but I'm plain out of smart ones.

"Thanks. Yeah, when I was twenty-one, I won the AVN Award for Best New Starlet, and I got a lot of work and made a lot of money all at once, so I bought this. I have a few other nice things, but I've decided to save my money now. I can't do porn forever, after all. This watch is a reminder of what I have to be grateful for and what I have to work toward. I don't wear it very often, but tonight seemed fancy enough."

"Sounds like a load of bullshit," I say, and this gets her attention. I want to make it known up front to her that I'm callous but not a star fucker. She hasn't responded, so I try with a question. "So do you have a boyfriend?" What a stupid thing to ask.

Ruby scoffs, snorts, and smiles. "No, I don't. Do you have a girlfriend?"

"No, I'm single. Why don't you have a boyfriend, though?"

"Well, it's hard in my industry. All the boys I date end up being assholes. Most men are just assholes, I'm pretty sure. And I'm kind of shy. That's why I came over here by myself."

"I'm not an asshole." She looks at me skeptically. Right on cue, a barrage of booms set off, and the star-filled sky explodes with colorful fireworks. Our eyes are drawn back upward. "Would you prefer if I leave you alone?"

It could be the sounds of fireworks exploding, but Ruby doesn't acknowledge hearing me. "I don't think I've ever even been in love," she says. I'm expecting her to say more, but she leaves it there. We bask in the booms of the pyrotechnics and the awes from the rest of our crowd down the road, and she puts her hand on top of mine. "I mean, I've said 'I love you' to people before, but I don't think I've ever actually been *in love*."

"Maybe you're overthinking it. I think it's funny when people say they're working on their relationship, or that marriage is hard, takes work, or something. I've been married, and it was hard, so we got divorced, but that probably means we just weren't the right fit. Someone once told me that love can be easy, that it doesn't have to be hard. I want to believe that."

I'm saying too much, but her eyes are glossier, and it could be the wine, but she's smiling, and her hand is still on top of mine.

"It sounds nice. Being in love."

"I've got to believe there's a way that love can fit just right that it doesn't feel like work. It should feel fun and exciting, I think. Hey, happy New Year."

We both smile. I lean in and kiss her, and she kisses me back. Fantasizing about someone before falling for them, secluded in a wagon with explosions above—it is a magical start to a new year.

As the fireworks continue, we disrobe and proceed to have the best sex of my life on top of a rickety old wagon. At first, I am as nervous as you would be if you were about to sleep with your favorite porn star. She lies on her back with me on top of her. Her body is luscious and perfect, and mine merely average and about a decade older than hers. She looks amazing, and she moans and reacts in the ways I imagined she would.

I've been told I look like a disheveled Keanu Reeves—but not like a ripped *Matrix* or *John Wick* Keanu, just a sitting-on-a-bench-and-eating-a-sandwich-by-himself type of Keanu. There's no way I deserve to have such a wonderful experience with her, and there's no way I could have dreamed she would enjoy it as much as I would. It's our first time together, and I finish more quickly than expected, though she seems to enjoy that she turned me on so much.

We return to my hotel room and have sex all night. By the next morning, even my legs are sore.

CHAPTER 6

I F YOU EVER doubt something you say will be taken seriously, just boil your point down to a single phrase and attribute that phrase to Mark Twain. This almost always works. You could make the most absurd claim with confidence, such as, "Dogs never bark when it's raining." But if you say you're quoting Mark Twain, everyone will nod in confusion and assume there is some deeper truth to the statement. Even if it's raining and a dog is barking.

Ruby and I have spent the last couple of weeks together since New Year's Eve. She hasn't even stayed the night at her apartment once since we returned to LA. You could say we hit it off. Sparks flew. Love at first sight. All that cliché nonsense. It's happening faster than usual, but there are no rules about what pace you can fall in love with someone. We're already saying, "I love you," to each other, and it feels good.

The night we met in Cortez, Ruby's friend Miles was taking care of her dog, an ancient, fluffy thing who must be a hundred years old, at least in dog years. As soon as Ruby moved into my place, her dog moved in too. Ruby had rescued the animal, a small, white maltipoo the size of a watermelon, from a shelter when she first moved to LA.

Based on its teeth alone, a veterinarian at the time had guessed that it must have been eight years old when she adopted it. That was five years ago. She named the mongrel Frankie, and he is a cantankerous old man of a dog with a peculiar personality. Already, he has specific spots on my couch and bed that belong to him. His eyes droop, and the area under his eyelids build up with an obscene amount of dark crust. He's nearly deaf and blind, and his back-right leg limps when he walks. If Frankie somehow hears a noise outside, he will yelp out his fiercest high-pitch bark, which would never scare anything.

Ruby has gone to her apartment a few times to pick up more clothes and belongings, but she's slept at my place every night, and I've cooked us dinner almost every night. I wake up to her and go to sleep next to her, and it's just about everything I thought it could be, living with my dream girl. Around the house, Ruby wears fluffy, pink slippers. She listens to Miley Cyrus and Rihanna and other popular female singers. At her apartment, she has three framed Miley posters in her living room. She watches trashy reality shows like *90 Day Fiancé*, and we both enjoy watching home-remodeling shows, commenting on different styles and design choices we'd like in our theoretical future home together. She uses an electric toothbrush, she's a vegetarian, and she's liberal, but she doesn't vote. Ruby hates driving, so she doesn't have a car, preferring to take Ubers everywhere around town or ride with me. She keeps in touch with most of her family and talks on the phone with her mom a couple of times a week. She only doesn't talk to her oldest sister, who turned her back on Ruby when she got into the adult industry.

Ruby has a queer temper sometimes about the smallest of things that will set her off, but so far, we've been finding a flow together while playing house and enjoying it. When she gets upset and starts yelling at me about something, my strategy is to give her space so she can let it out, and I'll come back to her about half an hour later to give her a hug and a kiss and usually more.

PLAYING HOUSE

Ruby and I fall into a smooth routine. We usually go for a morning walk together with Frankie before having breakfast. After eating, we both spend a few hours getting our respective work done. I will sit at my computer and type away on projects I've been assigned, and she will either respond to messages on her phone or get dolled up and go into the bedroom to shoot solo content or customs or occasionally do a live stream for two or three hours. She has a ring light set up on her side of the bed and several sex toys in the room, along with a tiny, spinning wheel like the one from *Wheel of Fortune* with different things written on each section in marker that she will do on camera for a live stream when tips come in, like "suck dildo" or "play with feet."

Largely, the day-to-day life of being a digital garbageman like me is dependent on either having contacts at social media companies or the patience to deal with the tediousness of their customer support processes and submission forms. It isn't sexy work. One crisis I'm helping with this week is a local businessman who got a drunk-driving arrest that was covered in the *LA Times* due to his high public profile. That story is now appearing on the first page of results when people search his name, which he fears will hurt his business. There is little I can do to push the result down, but I can improve results for other news about him and create new social channels, content, and press releases that I will steadily push to the top. Creating his new pages, scheduling content, updating his Wikipedia page, and issuing press releases take me about six hours, and I charge him $15K up front, although it could take a few months for the search results to improve.

The other project I am absorbed in and need to complete is for a team in the National Women's Soccer League. The short of the situation is that the team is in the midst of being sold to a new majority owner, but the conflict is centered on who will be allowed to buy the team. There is a woman who already owns 48 percent of the team, and the coach and players all like her and support her being the new owner. The current majority owner, however, says he will sell the team to anyone except her. The deal could be finalized within a matter of a week or two, so I am tasked with hiring influencers to voice their opinion that a women's team should have a female owner, especially if the team and coach both support her. I am also buying thousands of likes, shares, and retweets of these opinions to pressure the ownership into making the right decision.

Ruby, despite her occasional meltdown, is usually a sweet and cuddly princess. On one of our first nights together, I got sick with food poisoning and was dehydrated, and I began having cramps and fever chills. Ruby instinctively took care of me for two long days and nights, bringing me soup, water, and medicine, taking my temperature, and putting cold rags on my forehead. Those memories with her are far less dramatic than our fights but showed me the heart of who she is and made me love her even more.

Granted, I have known her only a short time, but I already love Ruby because she is honest and doesn't pretend to be anything she's not. She can be fiery and explosive in stressful and dangerous ways but equally expressive in loving and nurturing ways, wanting to please those she loves. When she is sweet, she is the sweetest person in the whole world and will snuggle up in such a way that it feels like her body was molded to fit atop mine in bed, with her leg wrapped around my leg and her head nestled on my chest. Plus, since I'm dedicating my prime working years to protecting certain slimeballs online while destroying others, something deep inside me can sense that Ruby's emotionally erratic behavior could someday destroy my life. There is, perhaps, some twisted sense of inevitable karma that subconsciously turns me on.

We are both introverts, so we avoid going to the beach on weekends when it is crowded. Instead, we go during the week when we have more privacy. We never go out to bars or clubs, preferring to stay in together. Yesterday, we got day-drunk and took some mushrooms together and went to the beach and played paddleball for hours. Ruby is unbelievably talented at Ping-Pong and tennis and apparently also paddleball. The mushrooms kicked in about an hour into playing, and it felt like we were so in tune we could spread out and deliver the ball directly to each other from thirty yards away. It was hypnotic.

We ate some food, walked Frankie, and went back to the beach at sunset. I suggested we take a night swim in the ocean, half-expecting her to shut down the idea. She is usually wary of being in the ocean, saying that's where all the fish pee. Last night, though, her inhibitions were gone, and once the beach was empty and dark enough, we stripped down and went skinny-dipping under the moon. Swimming in the ocean at night is terrifying and exhilarating—not knowing if a shark may be out hunting in the murky depths.

We played in the water and made out for a while before drying off, getting dressed, and heading home. Nobody's perfect. But she's close enough. Sometimes you can meet someone at the right time, when it feels like you are both looking for love and hoping to find it in each other. At least in the honeymoon phase, it can feel like you've found it, and everything makes perfect sense.

After about a month together, I booked us a vacation for ten nights in Tulum, Mexico, sparing no expense on the most luxurious rental homes and hotels I could find. As my grandpa used to say, "I spent all my money on fast cars and women. The rest, I wasted."

She was scheduled to do a porn shoot the day before our flight. I knew this all week leading up to it, but I didn't ask for any details. I knew what she did for a living when I met her; I just hadn't grappled with the idea of her continuing that work after we became serious. I couldn't just step on her independence by suggesting she quit now that I'm suddenly around. So I simply tried not to think about it. She went to her place, got ready, put on her makeup, and packed her shoot bag. She called a ride to the set—some rental house in the valley that is used for shoots all the time. Ruby texted me she had gotten in the wrong Uber, and the driver had been a jerk and let her off next to a highway. She got stressed and canceled her shoot and went back to her place.

When she came over to my place later, I asked her about the premise of the shoot. She proceeded to tell me it was supposed to be her and another girl and a guy in a threesome video. The production company in question is known for step-sibling content, and that's what she was supposed to shoot the day before we went on vacation together. Until then, I'd successfully managed to compartmentalize my feelings of resentment and jealousy from seeing the taboo fantasies she played out on camera with other men, but she hadn't had one of these shoots since we met.

I told Ruby I was glad she missed her shoot because I would've felt sad during our vacation, and she said she was glad she took the wrong car too and didn't feel right about shooting that scene now that we were together; it had just been booked well before we ever met. Later that day, she called her agent and changed her performing availability to girl-girl and solo work only, so no more shoots with other guys would be offered or considered.

Ruby says she'd prefer to shoot POV scenes with me where my face isn't shown, and it all feels like her way of saying I am her man. This fortunate series of events boosts my ego and makes me feel much happier than I would have if she'd taken the right Uber, like inadvertently dodging an emotional bullet. Her friend Miles happily agrees to watch Frankie while we are in Mexico.

We both dress comfy for the flight. Me in black sweatpants and a black hoodie, and Ruby in matching pink sweatpants and hoodie with the Playboy logo on them along with a white hat with the Vixen logo. From what I've seen of her public outfits so far, this feels tame. Often when we go out, she will have on a Pornhub hoodie or a T-shirt that says something like, "Spank Me, Daddy." Despite her shyness, she likes the attention and can always be taking and posting photos that cross-promote her platforms.

We get off the plane in Cancún and go through immigration. I've had a few too many drinks on the flight, and Ruby and I start arguing about who spilled a drink on whom. She's winning the fight somehow, even though I know I'm right. She's talking much louder than I am, and it sounds like she's talking down to me, with lots of people around, and I feel emasculated. "Babe, I can hear you. You don't have to talk so loud."

"What the fuck? Are you trying to water down my personality? What is your problem?" She speaks louder with each word.

"I could throw my shit at the walls and call that having a personality." I regret saying it as soon as it leaves my mouth. Some guy on my right smiles, and I stop regretting it as much.

"You're an abusive asshole." She's just getting louder, and people are watching us now, which I'd hoped to avoid. She starts walking faster. She's up ahead of me, and I'm giving her more space by shuffling my feet a little slower.

Ruby gets to the front of the line and is called to a counter to present her documents. Her passport is quickly stamped, and she moves through the checkpoint. The woman operating the immigration counter to the left of Ruby's line waves that she's ready for me, so I walk over and present my passport.

The woman at the counter doesn't look up or acknowledge me, so I stupidly speak up as the arrogant and impatient American because I am drunk and my mind is on fire from arguing with Ruby about absolute nonsense. "Excuse me, how long is this going to take?"

She doesn't take kindly to my question or my tone as she lifts a walkie-talkie and says something into it in Spanish that I don't understand. She looks back down at her desk for a moment until a security guard comes over and puts his hand on my shoulder. "This way, please." The woman behind the counter looks up to hand my passport and paperwork to the security guard while giving me an evil grin like she'd gotten some twisted revenge.

The guard leads me to a room with a bench, scattered luggage, and a counter with two airport employees talking: a man and a woman in matching black pants and white button-up dress shirts. The woman is seemingly enthralled by whatever story the man is telling her. I sit and wait. Minutes go by, and I am still waiting. There's a mundane circular white clock on the wall behind the two of them, and after ten minutes have passed, I raise my hand as politely as possible. "Excuse me, but how long is this going to take? I have to go to the bathroom."

Ruby enters the room and plops down next to me. She sets our checked bags down and whispers to me, "What's going on?" Her attitude is cool now, and she's over whatever drama we'd been fabricating.

"I was rude to the lady at the passport counter, so they're punishing me by making me sit here in time-out."

Ruby smirks like she knows I deserved it.

The man behind the counter waves me up to stamp my passport, possibly because of my desperate bathroom plea but more likely because they saw they were punishing my girlfriend by making her wait too.

Stamps are now dutifully applied to both our passports. We enter another area, where Ruby is again waved quickly through while my bags are thoroughly searched. After an hour of professional delaying techniques by the Mexican immigration officials, we're finally on our way to a resort in Tulum.

A week in Mexico with a porn star. Not just any porn star, my favorite one. Which, in some ways, must make her my dream girl. Not to mention, she is the first girl in LA I've met who listens to country music, and I like that even though I don't necessarily love country music. I do like all kinds of music but don't like the LA types who on dating apps say they specifically love EDM and hate country as though that disdain qualifies as a personality trait.

Ruby was born in Texas, and I appreciate how being a little more country makes her seem more approachable, sincere, and capable than many women I've met on the West Coast. Despite what Katy Perry may tell you, California girls are not undeniable.

The first few nights in Mexico, we stay at a posh five-star resort in the presidential suite complete with a private chef for dinners each night. We lounge by the beach or pool most of the time, drink, and go snorkeling. Our room has a balcony, so at night we have sex outside with the lights on, and I hold my phone to record the encounters for her to sell on OnlyFans.

For breakfast on our third day at the resort, we go to one of the hotel's restaurants and each order different styles of eggs.

I had watched the film *A Star Is Born* on the plane, and I'm telling Ruby how it is still stuck in my head when I feel a tap on my back. I turn in my chair to find a man in his late fifties dressed nicely in khaki pants and a button-up shirt. He's finishing his breakfast across from his wife and looking at me. They seem like they're from the South, and he speaks with a polite southern drawl.

"I couldn't help but hear you mention *A Star Is Born*. I just watched that on the plane here yesterday."

"Oh, so did I. I was just telling her about it."

I look at Ruby but can tell she can't hear us very well by the way she's cocking her head at me.

"There was a line in that movie," the man continues, "that really stuck with me. When Bobby tells Ally, 'It's not your fault.'"

I nod my head in agreement, but the man speaks softly and carefully, so I wait for more. His eyes start to water, and I forget about breakfast.

The man turns entirely around to face me, and now I notice his wife is stoically looking down at her plate, frozen in time. He speaks even softer now, as though telling me a dark secret. "This weekend is the first anniversary of our daughter committing suicide. I wanted to take my wife out of town to forget about it. Our daughter, Sage, lived in Los Angeles and was around your age. She studied film and was trying to work in entertainment. And we had no idea. We had no idea that she was so depressed. But that line stuck with me. When he tells her it's not her fault."

"Jesus," is all I can manage to say.

The man sees that I have nothing else to add and turns back to his wife and holds her hands as they wait for their bill to pay for breakfast. I turn back to Ruby, who has a quizzical look and mouths the words, "What was that?"

"I'll tell you later, babe," I respond quietly.

We try to go back to eating, but my appetite is gone as I watch the older couple leave the dining area, and all I can think about is how I wish I had been able to say something meaningful.

PUBLIC SHAMING

On the fourth day of our vacation, we check out of our luxurious room at the hotel and prepare to find our rental home in Tulum. We're excited to have a bit more privacy to shoot some scenes in the backyard pool and Jacuzzi. At one of the shops in town, we buy a lucha libre mask that Mexican wrestlers wear so we can shoot some kinky scenes together while still covering my face.

In the days we had spent together at my house in LA before this trip, Ruby would often spend most of her day either making solo content in bed in front of her ring light or on the couch busily typing into her phone responding to fans. Ruby explained to me that some of her fans would request particular JOI videos, which stood for "jerk-off instruction" videos. She would make a custom sensual video that included her addressing that specific fan by name, sometimes ending with a countdown telling them exactly when they were supposed to finish.

Many of her fans are obsessed with her feet, and she will bend her legs any which way to include the bottoms of her feet in photos and videos.

Other fans were submissive and wanted her to tell them what to do. She could message them and say, "Send me $200 for my lunch today," and it would happen. They would regularly buy items from her online wish list, which meant a steady stream of packages in her name showing up at the doorstep. Her screen time report would say she spent around sixteen hours a day on her phone, every day. The work seemed to pay off, though, and possibly helped explain how she got to the top of her field. With the videos she would sell that I filmed in POV, she could earn several thousand dollars within a few hours of uploading. She knew what it took to be a professional, and she put in the hours to ensure her independent success. That said, in the days leading up to our vacation, Ruby had doubled her efforts and scheduled enough content to go out so she would not need to look at her phone as much while in Mexico. At most, she would spend around thirty minutes a day responding to fans, and otherwise, she was the most unplugged I had ever seen her.

I get a bit nervous but have fun every time we shoot content together, and Ruby always handles putting the camera where it should go and directing me on where to position myself. You may argue that a job is a job, and many of these guys may face rough pressure having to last all day only to ejaculate on cue, but from my own limited experience, it seems like the girls have the only difficult job on set. It is their face, body, and reactions that most of the audience wants to see.

When we finish one of our sessions making POV content together, I just feel like we had a kinky, fun afternoon, not like I had to go to work.

Whenever Ruby shoots solo or girl-girl content, and even for some of our POV scenes, she always does her hair and makeup to an exacting standard. Her hair straightened, blush heavily applied, eyelashes fake and long, and lipstick bright red to match her hair. And the outfits, of course. When I first went to Ruby's apartment, I was impressed and surprised by how she had turned one of her extra rooms into a huge walk-in closet with rows of clothes and shoes and a limitless supply of sexy outfits.

The makeup needs to be heavier to make the performers look like dolls on camera, and she always looks great. I am not a big fan of heavy makeup on women, but being involved in a fantasy scenario was alluring for me each time, knowing it was all for the art and commerce of the video. A video where other men would wish they were me and fantasize about what it would be like to be in my position.

Our taxi driver gets lost on the way to our rental home, and the GPS on our phones isn't helping either, as the address just doesn't seem right. We get the house's host on the phone, and she explains in Spanish to our driver how to get there. Another five minutes on a busted, one-way road, and we finally arrive.

The house is gated, and the majority of the neighborhood is lined with dilapidated houses with makeshift storefronts built into them. We go in, meet the host, and thank her for helping our taxi find the place. The weather is much warmer here than it is in LA this time of year, and I'm ready for drinks by the beach with Ruby.

We unpack our bags, shower, change, and explore the town to find food and shopping. The downtown area has bars, restaurants, and shops with an open-air design and hut-like straw roofs. We locate a restaurant with swings around the bar to sit on, hung from way above on the high ceilings with a thick rope.

Ruby looks at her phone excitedly. "Hey, a couple I know from porn are here in town on vacation. I told them they should come meet us for a drink."

We have another margarita, and her friends arrive: an attractive couple with warm energy. We all meet, hug, and take our seats in the swings by the bar. The couple takes a tequila shot with us, but otherwise, they aren't drinking much. They do offer us some cocaine, but we politely decline. Ruby and I have both separately had our days with cocaine and put them behind us. There was a period when coke would make things seem more fun, but after a while, it would stress me out and cause my hands to sweat, screw with my digestion, and make me grind my teeth to the point where my gums would bleed every time I brushed my teeth.

Ruby has a small circle of friends she is close with, but otherwise, she's frighteningly shy, so watching her smile and laugh and socialize here is fun. She says her friend is from North Carolina and notes that most of the porn girls she knows in LA are either from Texas or North Carolina, for some reason.

The girls catch up while the guy and I get to know each other. Apparently, the other couple met while he was working in Miami as a Michael Jackson impersonator, and she was living there and doing online cam shows from her apartment. A lot of people make salacious sex videos, but few ever reach Ruby's level of fame or success. This couple did not.

He proceeds to show me how their OnlyFans account is set up and how he handles the responses while pretending to be his girlfriend. They have a whole system. Ruby is in the top 0.5 percent of accounts on the app, so she doesn't need the lesson, but I find it fascinating. In return, I show him a few videos on my phone that I've shot in POV style with Ruby over the past week while on vacation, and he compliments me on the production, along with some more specific compliments that another man has never given me, and I nearly blush.

The girls are both locked in together in conversation, and they have no idea what we're discussing, just as we have no idea what they're talking about.

"So you guys only shoot content together?" I ask him. I'm desperate for more details about dating someone in this field. The act of shooting porn is always phrased more kindly as *shooting content,* which makes filming sex for money sound less seedy and more professional.

"Always together, we only shoot stuff together, but sometimes we'll shoot threesomes. We also do live shows at swingers events where we have sex in front of everyone to get the party going."

"Do you ever get nervous? I mean, how do you get hard? How do you last?"

"Yeah, of course. It's nerve-racking. You never really get used to it. I take the pills and have a liquid I put in the tip to make it stay hard, and there's a cream that numbs it so you can last longer. I'll text you the names of them."

"That's awesome. It seems like quite a lifestyle." I cheers with him, kill my drink, and point at my empty glass to instruct the waiter to create another one. "You know, just from the few scenes I've shot with Ruby so far, I find it exciting and fun. Just holding the camera and being a human dildo isn't that bad."

"Totally. When I'm looking at my phone recording what we're doing, it kind of helps distance me from the craziness on camera somehow, and that helps make me last longer."

"I know what you mean," I say with a smile.

"Yeah, man, we're spending four weeks in Mexico right now, and her online subscriptions are funding it all. We haven't even shot any new content in six months. We can just cycle through and keep repurposing old stuff for new followers. Plus, when I'm in my seventies and look back on the things I did in my life, I can point to a lot of crazy times on video, smile, and say, 'What did you do with your life?'"

The four of us take a few more shots together, and the guy tells me that we should all have sex in the same bed together sometime and suggests it'd be hot. The girls don't hear this, and I'm a bit nervous and new to this openness. I tell him that being in the same room or bed could be interesting sometime, but not tonight and not a full swap. I say to him that seeing someone else fuck her in front of me may make me even more insecure and jealous, and I'm not quite there yet. He nods, understanding. Then I remember Ruby telling me she has shot with both of them before, so I'm actually becoming friends with a guy she has had sex with on camera, and I probably unknowingly watched the whole encounter at least once online.

Now that we are all properly sauced, we decide to call it a night. They walk back toward their rental, and we walk back toward ours in the opposite direction. Holding hands, we're both drunk and giggly and happy from running into some friends here. Ruby is stumbling a bit, but I'm able to keep her stable by holding her hand firmly enough.

The topic of comedians and jokes comes up, and I try to regale her with some old Norm Macdonald jokes I remember. Ruby laughs at my retelling and says she hadn't heard of Norm before but that she likes most comedians, just not Sarah Silverman or Whitney Cummings. Ruby claims that Whitney has said rude things about porn girls and Sarah made fun of Paris Hilton and Britney Spears. I try to imply that comedians should be able to say anything, but Ruby is fixed in her stance against them both, so I drop it.

Still walking back to our rental home and holding hands, I try to paraphrase a Bill Burr joke about how men can't really be feminists, and she lets go of my hand.

"Babe, I support women's rights. I was just trying to paraphrase a joke, maybe I said it wrong. I can pull it up for you online when we get home."

"I don't want to see that shit. How the hell are you telling me now that you're not a feminist?" Ruby is walking faster now, and I'm just trying to keep up.

"Baby girl, we're on vacation. Just chill out. We can still have a good night."

"No, I can't. How are you not a feminist? Tell me."

"It's just semantics. Come on, you say you're a feminist and want equality, but when we're in bed, you want to be choked and have your hair pulled and be degraded. How does that work?"

My argument works like gas on a fire, and I know right away I should have just apologized and said I was, in fact, very much a feminist.

Ruby turns her anger up another notch with each step, and it's not something I know how to defuse quickly without just backing off and letting her get it out of her system.

We are both drunk, and Ruby is on fire with emotion. "God, I fucking hate you. I don't know why I came on this trip. You should pay me ten grand for all the work I've missed out on since I met you. You're just a fucking pig, like every other boy I've ever dated."

A woman passes us going the opposite direction, and I instinctively glance over at her, which sets off yet another level of fury and jealous rage from Ruby.

I'm drunk and don't feel like I have done anything wrong, but I know there's a chance I turned my head a little too obviously. "We were walking and laughing and holding hands a few minutes ago. Let's just be on the same team like we were then."

"You're just like every other man." She says this like it's an indictment, but it's likely true. She starts power walking faster in front of me, so I drunkenly follow her from a distance to make sure we both make it home safely. We've both shared our phone's locations with each other, so I know I'll be able to track her if she ducks out of view for too long. Letting her get lost in Mexico while mad, drunk, and alone is not a good idea.

She tells me I'm gaslighting her. I hate that shit. I doubt a year ago she had even heard that term before, but now, she throws it around like everything is my fault. The strange thing is, I think I probably am gaslighting her. I just don't want her to feel validated that she's right, and I would rather keep her thinking she's the crazy one. It's more convenient that way.

We turn left off the main road onto our street, just a short distance from home. First, she makes the left, and I follow a minute later. I'm walking on a sidewalk, and Ruby is up ahead, walking in the middle of the road. This seems unsafe, and so I yell to her, "Hey, babe! Get out of the road!"

"Fuck you, you asshole!" she yells back, turning around quickly to flip me off and then turning back again to march toward our place. A dark green, older-model car drives past me and toward her and slows down next to her. I presume they're asking if she's okay. She leans in on the driver's side window and keeps talking, and for a moment, I feel a familiar unease settle in. After a moment passes, the car drives away, and she walks up to the front gate of our rental house, which I'm still a minute away from, and I have the house key, so she'll be waiting.

As I walk up solemnly, the dark green car from before drives up to me, and I realize this guy just made a U-turn so he could follow us. The driver rolls his window down as he comes to a stop beside me. In my mind, the worst of scenarios is playing out. He leans over and speaks to me in a reassuring tone, like he's on my side. "Hey, man, how are y'all doing?" His use of "y'all" surprises me here in Mexico. He looks like an expat.

"I think you saw how we're doing." I gesture toward Ruby, and the man nods. Another car goes around us since he's idling in the middle of the road.

"I've been there, man. If it's that toxic, get out while you still can. Before you wind up with kids or something." He looks at me for acknowledgment that I hear him. I nod even before I notice his young daughter sitting patiently in the back seat. Now I understand what he's saying.

"Thank you, I appreciate that. It's been a rough night." I wave, he drives away, and I catch up to Ruby and unlock the gate to let us in.

AND WE KEEP FIGHTING

We enter the rental home, and Ruby darts upstairs, still furious at me and blackout drunk. Not wanting any of that, I open the sliding doors from the kitchen, go to the backyard by the pool, open a bottle of tequila, and pull off my shirt.

Ruby is upstairs in the bedroom screaming at me, obviously mad I went to the backyard and didn't follow her upstairs to either be berated more or apologize to her. In the few fights we've had, she'll quickly and easily scream and howl like a dying puma out of anger and frustration. I guess it's worked for her in the past, but my strategy for dealing with it so far has been to give her space and let her wear herself out. I'm pretty sure if I went upstairs and just gave her a hug, an apology, and sex, it would calm her down, but I'm too drunk and angry at her childish behavior for apologizing, so I plop down on a pool float shaped like a flamingo, take a swig from the bottle, and light a cigar.

It's relaxing just long enough for me to wonder why the screaming has stopped. The upstairs balcony door opens, and Ruby begins screaming again at the top of her lungs like she's being attacked. "Why the fuck won't you apologize to me?"

"Because you're acting crazy."

"Don't you call me crazy. You're making me act crazy. You're crazy!"

"Gaslighting."

"Fuck you!" Her drunken anger kicks up a gear, and I can feel it from down here.

Ruby throws my flip-flops at me from the balcony. One splashes next to me in the water, and the other lands off in the grass. I know she could have grabbed my laptop or something more valuable to throw, so I figure she isn't that upset if it's just my flip-flops raining down on me.

"You know, I should take my phone out and film this and show you tomorrow what a crazy bitch you are when you're drunk."

"How about I show you a video of how a real man fucks?" she hisses from the balcony, and I can feel a brutal sting in my side as she disappears for a moment.

I go back to my cigar in search of tranquility, then there is a sudden, horrible scream. Ruby is back on the balcony above me, yelling at the top of her lungs.

This causes me to fall off the flamingo with a splash. I get out of the pool and dry myself quickly. One of the neighbors has turned down their music, and a woman's voice from over the fence shouts out, "Hey, are you okay?"

At once, Ruby is the deadly combination of brutal, frustrating, and exhilarating.

Ruby goes back inside and slams the sliding glass door to the balcony as hard as she can. Time to go upstairs and hug her and just apologize. I know that's all she wants, and at this point, I will do anything to calm her down.

My hand hits the door handle, and she's locked it. I look around, and the only other option seems to be jumping the fence to get to the front door, so I sit on the patio chair to finish my cigar.

Then I check my phone and log into social media, and I see nasty comments on each of my recent photos flood in from Ruby's account in real time. One comment was posted two minutes ago. The rest are seconds old. I quickly delete the comments and block her account before she can leave any more. I also block her finsta since I know her handle. She has over three million followers on social media and three hundred thousand subscribers on Pornhub. I have no idea how many subscribers she has on OnlyFans, but I can assume there are a lot as each month since we met has been her most lucrative month to date. If she wanted to call me out or ruin me online, she'd have all the ammunition necessary at her fingertips. Luckily, she was just drunk.

A few minutes later, there's a click on the door lock, and Ruby slowly comes out. She frowns and gives a sad puppy face, and I can't help but love it. She's wearing a tiny, pink, silk robe I bought her, and she speaks softly now, like she's putting a child to bed. "You blocked me."

My lip raises and smiles automatically. I put my arms up, welcoming her in by reflex. "Come here. You're being mean."

She falls into my lap and kisses me on the cheek. "You are. But I guess it's fine. All men are assholes, after all."

"How would you feel if I said that about all women?"

"Well, men are assholes, and women aren't. Women aren't starting wars or causing mass shootings or raping anyone. Will you please unblock me?"

"I guess you have a point. Maybe I am an asshole. Let's go to bed—if you'll let me come inside."

We head upstairs to bed, and I'm killing light switches all the way up. "You know when you start screaming like that, I don't know what to do. It's pretty scary. I don't know how I'm supposed to handle that."

Ruby sits on the edge of the bed and hangs her head down. "I'm sorry. I don't know why I get like that. Only with people I really care about, though."

"Well, what am I supposed to do, then? It's happened more than once now. I feel like I should get a bottle of chloroform and just knock you out whenever you get worked up at me."

We both smile and lay down on the bed, wrapped up together.

"That may be a good idea," she says. "Speaking of which, what should be our safe word?"

I think for a moment and have it. "Pineapple."

"Pineapple?" She snorts out a laugh. "Okay."

I had a friend in college who thought Mike Ditka was the most remarkable man who'd ever lived. While some people might ask, "What would Jesus do?" If he were in a bind, he'd always ask, "What would Ditka do?"

So I ask myself, "What would Ditka do?"

Then I proceed to mount Ruby, and as we get going, she pulls my hand over to her throat to choke her. She says, "Yeah, use me like I'm your fuck toy, Daddy."

We make up and decide not to fight again for the rest of the trip.

Our first couple of weeks together had all gone back and forth like this: from puppy love, to passionate lustfulness, to incendiary screaming matches.

She seems to purposely push me away, possibly so she can avoid getting hurt in the end. If you let everything become either a fantasy or a nightmare, with no in between, nothing will ever satisfy you. Boring and content can't exist, only the extreme highs and lows of joy and despair.

BACK HOME

Ruby and I have a fun trip the rest of our time in Mexico. We go hiking around some Mayan temple ruins. We rent a Jet Ski one day and go zip-lining another.

On the last day of the trip, before we head to the airport, I lose my timidness entirely and ask if she'd ever want to have a threesome with me—the kind with two females and one male. The male being me, specifically.

"It would be fun. I like doing that, and you've done them in a bunch of your videos. Literally, when I search for threesome videos online, a few of yours always pop up in the thumbnails."

"I don't know. I've only ever done that in porn. I've never done it in a relationship," she says, clearly not wanting me to push further.

"You've done, like, dozens of them. With millions of views. It makes me feel like a cuck."

"I don't know," she says slowly. "When I shoot something for work, it's just work. It's not like I like those guys at all. Porn isn't real life, you know? It's just a fantasy."

"Yeah, but you're making those guys feel good, regardless. You treat them like a king, but it's wrong for me to ask for it? It's my fantasy. They make those videos for a reason."

"It's not wrong for you to ask. I just don't have that fantasy. I don't want to share you. I just want you to want me."

"I do. I'm just saying it would be fun and would keep me from being jealous." This isn't going the way I'd imagined.

"There's just a difference between real life and porn. I've never done that with a boyfriend, and porn is just fantasy. It's not real. It doesn't mean anything. I don't care about those guys the way I do for you."

"How about we just do it for content, too, then? I can hold the camera POV just like half of your scenes. I just want to feel like the guys in your videos, being treated like a king like that by you and another girl. If it's just for content, it shouldn't mean anything, right? And you can make money off it."

"I don't want to mix my work with personal. Plus, the girls in the industry that try setting up threesomes with their boyfriends on camera get called out for being predators. It gets out that they used other performers just to give their boyfriends a threesome, and they get called out for it and stop getting work. I don't want that. I don't want you to fuck the girls I work with. I'd rather you just cheat on me, and I never find out."

We stop talking, but the tension stays within reach as we head to the airport. Ruby tells me she'd rather I had a foot fetish like her last boyfriend, but I feel how I feel.

Sometimes Ruby is the sweetest thing on earth, while other times, she will act like we are enemy combatants. For all the fights and headaches, I am still happier than I've been in years. Only 5 percent of the time feels toxic, which is what I keep reminding myself. The rest is incredible. She makes me believe love is infinite. Being around her always makes me feel useful and macho, like when a girl asks you to open a can of pickles because it's too hard for her to twist open and you easily pop the lid for her, and she kisses your cheek and thanks you for being manly and strong.

Now we've landed back in LA and are at each other's throats by the time we get our luggage, and I can't even remember how this argument started.

We walk out into the arrivals section outside the airport where people are filing into buses and taxis, and I suggest she should go back to her apartment, which she hasn't stayed the night at in a month. "We need a few days apart. I can't deal with this fighting right now."

Her eyes go from searing mad to kind in an instant. The sweetness and vulnerability that makes me crazy for her blinds my sense of rationality. "You don't want me to come over?"

"I think a night or two apart would be good. I'm sure you have mail and packages at your place you should get, and you can do your laundry and stuff."

"But I want to stay with you. I'm sorry for how I acted."

"Babe." She looks so beautiful and harmless now, and it is hard to turn her away. "We need a break. Even just for a few nights."

Ruby finally gives in and gets a ride to her house, and I get a car back to mine. For once, she doesn't send me a single text. I drop my bags on my living room floor, take a shower, and lie on my couch to watch television and decompress. Back to a cloudy and dreary spring in Los Angeles, but I am tranquil for a few moments. When Ruby and I fight, it's generally through text messages, as if she can verbalize her emotions better by typing them. Some of the texts go off the rails, with name-calling and heated hatred, and by the next morning, we've usually both deleted the text thread from our phones out of shame, pretending to slide our past fights into the ether and hit reset on our emotions by way of a simple apology.

I am amazed she still hasn't said anything at all. Not continuing to fight, not a makeup text. Nothing.

Then my phone dings.

Slowly, my hand reaches for the phone and swipes to unlock it. It's a text from Ruby along with a photo. The text reads, "Herb, I'm pregnant. And I'm keeping it." Attached to the text is a picture of a positive pregnancy test. For some reason, the first thought I have is how she called me Herb instead of Melvin, and I remember I told her my real name while we were in Mexico. The first woman I've told my real name to in years. I think about the guy in Mexico in the dark green car and what he'd said about getting out before you have kids.

I drop my phone back on the couch and go to the kitchen to make a cocktail: tequila, ice, and a slice of lime. I finish it in one gulp, pour another, and go back to the couch, bringing the bottle with me. I pick up my phone and stare at the image for a hard moment.

I send a text back: "Do you want to come over?"

CHAPTER 7

RUBY HAS RETURNED to my place, and we're continuing our streak of spending every night together since we met. Even more of her things are at my home. Frankie is back also, blindly prancing around my place.

After she texted me about the pregnancy, I invited her over to talk about it, but instead, we lay together in bed with our arms wrapped around each other and fell asleep, exhausted from the day of traveling. We slept without a mention of babies or anything else. All that was needed was an unspoken closeness.

It's morning, and she's still asleep. I have my arms around her as her big spoon, with my right arm tucked under her neck falling asleep with a bit of shaky, pins-and-needles-type pain around my elbow. Frankie is nestled between Ruby's feet.

My free hand slowly caresses her stomach, and I think about all the potential ups and downs of a future together as a family. We have been together a little over a month, but somehow, I can begin to imagine us becoming parents. So my mind sticks to the ups and forgets about the downs. I imagine teaching our kids how to ride a bike, throw a ball, or skip a rock over a lake. Going on family vacations and pouring ourselves into another being rather than focusing on our vapid dreams. None of it sounds as bad as it used to, though it undoubtedly interferes with my oligarch yacht delusions.

Ruby looks unbelievably angelic and peaceful while she's sleeping, so I gently kiss her on the cheek, slide carefully out of the covers so as not to wake her, and go into the kitchen to make us coffee and breakfast. I stop by the bathroom to pee, and there are three more positive pregnancy tests on the counter. I guess she wanted to be sure last night. By the time I finish making eggs and avocado toast, Ruby is up and has already taken a bath. I had always thought of baths as more of an evening ritual, for whatever reason, but Ruby took hers every morning.

She enters the kitchen wearing her tiny silk robe, pink fluffy slippers, and a towel wrapped around her hair, and I hand her a coffee. She sets her coffee down, grabs an ice roller from the freezer, and proceeds to roll it on her forehead and cheeks as part of her daily beauty regimen before eating. If she gets even the slightest cut in her skin, she methodically lathers it in Neosporin. She takes her appearance as seriously as any mainstream actress might. Even if she had just a small cut or bruise, she would tell the producers before a shoot in case it was an issue.

Ruby meticulously manicures every inch of her body, but as far as her pubic hair goes, she lets it grow. I asked her once, weeks ago, about her growing bush out of curiosity, and her tone in responding was immediately hostile, almost defensive.

"This is what a woman's body looks like."

"I've seen videos of you online where you were shaved."

"Yeah, when I was like twenty and was new to porn."

"I think it's fine either way. I'm not against shaved," I said, dumbfounded by how to get out of the conversation.

"What are you, a pedophile that's attracted to prepubescent girls? That seems a little—" she looked at me slowly "—creepy."

All I could do was clench my teeth and nod my head with my

eyes closed, as everyone just loves to be called a pedophile. There could be some deep-rooted feminist agenda that Ruby and some of her female coworkers are striving toward by making a point to grow out their pubic hair, who knows. I decided that day to never bring up pubic hair again.

We sit at our breakfast nook in silence, eating and pretending we'd never even fought on the plane home and that everything is back to normal, yet there is a strangeness that reminds me nothing is normal. You don't date a porn star because you want normal. Frankie chews on his canned food, forcing it down with his nubbed-down fangs.

Ruby sets her fork on her plate and breaks the silence with a soft and loving tone. "Herb, I'm sorry about how this all happened and how I was acting, but I've already had four abortions, and they took a lot out of me emotionally. I can't go through that again. I just can't." Her eyes are slightly red and watery, and I can tell she means every word. "You don't have to be involved with the baby, but I am going to keep it. I can go back home to Texas, and my family will help me raise her." She sounds like she was rehearsing what to say while in the bath, she laid it all out so matter-of-factly. She grabs her fork to finish off her eggs.

I nervously take a sip of my coffee and nearly choke. "Did you say her?"

"I think it will be a girl. I have a feeling. Are you okay?"

My throat clears after another few coughs, and I set my coffee back down. "Yes, sorry, it went down the wrong tube. So you're serious about wanting to keep it?"

She sets her fork back down, her plate clean of eggs now. "Don't say it. Say her. And yeah, I've made up my mind. I'm sure. My mental health just can't handle another abortion. And I think I could be a good mom. Better than mine, at least."

I sigh and put my hands out to hold hers. "Okay, then I'll help raise her. You trapped me." I wink, and she laughs. Her eyes start to water.

"All according to my plan." She lets go of my hands, and her half smile turns into a more demure expression. "Are you sure about this? You can take some time to think about it if you want. I meant what I said. You don't have to do anything if you don't want to."

"No, I want this. I was thinking about it all night and all morning. Let's start our own family, babe." I kiss her, take our dishes back to the sink, and wash them. Ruby follows me into the kitchen and pours us both more coffee.

"I have a shoot on Wednesday. A girl-girl scene. I have to go get tested for STDs today, and then I'll go by my place and pick up more clothes and stuff to bring over here. I guess I'll call my agent later too and let him know I won't be shooting any more content after next month."

"What do you mean? Like done forever?"

"At least until after the baby is born. I know girls who do porn, and they've had kids and then gotten back in shape and did content after. But I might be done forever, yeah. I don't know." She looks a little lost as she says this, like she's just now realizing this chapter of her life is over. I can't tell if she's happy about it or demoralized.

"You don't want to do pregnant porn?" I say it with a smirk so she knows I'm joking.

She scoffs. "I wouldn't do that to my kids."

"Oh, like they'd find out about it when they grow up and see a video where they are in it as an embryo?" As I say this, I realize why she finds it so repugnant for those kids.

"Yeah, exactly," she says solemnly. "How will those kids feel growing up? That's why I didn't ever want any children. I never even considered it before I met you. I never thought that I'd want to have kids. When they start getting to high school and if their friends found out what their mom did for work, I'm sure they'd get bullied and feel embarrassed and hate me, and it just makes me really sad to think about."

There's a silence, and we just look at each other. It's clear she's looking for some comforting words of security. I search for something to say that will ease her mind of the fact that our child will most likely be embarrassed by how she earned a living.

"I'm sorry, babe." I can't think of anything more supportive to say.

"I'm just a normal girl. I just happened to start doing porn when I was twenty, and some people let that define me, including some of my family. I hate that."

"Yeah, that isn't fair, babe. Maybe we can move to another country and raise our kids there, in another culture. Maybe they won't have to find out."

Ruby smiles. I finally said the right thing.

She kisses me.

After the Mexico trip, I decided to look into ways to attain chloroform, as that was my best bet for peacefully solving disputes with Ruby: simply knocking her unconscious. It turns out you can make your own chloroform using basic household ingredients. You need about 3.6 liters of bleach and 100 milliliters of acetone.

Chill the bleach bottle to −2° Celsius, pour out about 150 milliliters from the bottle, add the 100 milliliters of acetone to the bleach, cap the bottle, and shake it. Open the cap, and leave the bottle out overnight to let the chloroform separate entirely to the bottom. Pour the liquid out into beakers, decant off the aqueous layer, and add the rest to a separatory funnel, which will give you the chloroform in the lower layer of the funnel. The chloroform should be washed once with sodium chloride and added to a distillation flask containing calcium chloride. You can go through a simple distillation using a hot-water bath, at which point the distillate should come out as a clear liquid. This should give you around 50 milliliters of chloroform, which you need to pour into a container that shields the liquid from sunlight, and you're good to go.

It took me about a week to figure out the mechanics of this lab experiment, but after a few false starts, I finally had my own batch and used it on Ruby once just to make sure it was effective. While she was lying in bed, I walked up, put the cloth to her face, and asked, "Hey, does this smell like chloroform?"

She was asleep before she could laugh or answer, but at least I knew the stuff worked. As she slept, I realized the drug may not be so healthy for the baby, so I made a commitment to use the stuff only when necessary.

BACK TO WORK

Ruby is on the couch watching TV with Frankie on her lap, so I grab my laptop and sit next to her while I handle some business, most of which just entails sending and receiving emails and occasionally making a PowerPoint presentation. She's watching a reality show, laughing, and providing commentary about the different relationships being followed on-screen. I lock in on my laptop and melt away, and the concept of time dissipates as I work through the emails, screenshots, and presentations.

After I complete each task, I take a sip of tequila. It's Saint Patrick's Day, but we aren't out partying at the bars. Ruby can't drink because of the pregnancy, and I have to check in on Fred's project to ruin Dan's life. The plan is to make the videos, articles, websites, and press releases public starting in July, so I have three months to get my content and tactics ready.

I take my time to draft each email. The first goes to a web developer and details how I want DanielCastilloIsAFraud.com and a few other sites to be designed and what content to include. The next email goes to a journalist who does freelance writing for me sometimes, and I introduce her to Fred so they can set up a call for her to hear his story and start drafting articles and press releases to come out in July. The third email is to the director of the web series we're making about Dan. He's shooting the final interview with Fred tomorrow, so I check to make sure they have everything they need and let them know I'll stop by around lunchtime to see them.

Putting an idea out in the world is a hell of a thing. No matter how absurd the idea, if it's repeated enough, it will take on authority of its own. It occurs to me we could fabricate and disseminate articles and blogs that accuse Dan of pedophilia or cannibalism or coprophilia or necrophilia or any other philia or ism. Even if he denies it, the stink of the accusation will likely sit on the search results for his name for a while, especially if he fights or denies it. This is similar to the Streisand effect, a phenomenon named after Barbra Streisand based on when she tried having an aerial photo of her Malibu home removed from the internet in 2003. In her attempt to suppress that information, she inadvertently drew massive attention to it.

I had spent two months already ruminating about ways to destroy Dan's reputation. I didn't talk to anyone other than Ruby most days. I went for walks, wrote down notes, and thought only about how to ruin this guy's name, piece by piece.

Fred had approved the blueprint, timeline, and budgets and said he could be the face of the campaign, but somewhere in my gut, I know there are some other more serious accusations I may want to toss onto Dan's plate. Though I've never met Dan Castillo, and he's never harmed me, I've convinced myself it will be a fun little project to ruin his life.

"Can you believe he talks to her that way?" Ruby is disappointed in another couple on the reality show she's watching. I put my laptop away and toss my arm around her to hold her and watch trashy television together.

"Oh, I'd never talk to you like that."

CASE STUDY: ANTHONY PELLICANO

Anthony Pellicano was an old-school private investigator in Hollywood back in the day. One news headline called him the "Machiavelli of Muck." Born in 1944, he became a private detective at twenty-five and did all manner of shady things for his clients through the years. His private eye run ended in 2002, when he was arrested.

Pellicano is far from the only example of this sort of character. Still, he's interesting to consider in relation to today's information age, where you can quickly obtain and install spyware on someone's device if you just commit to doing it. You can have access to all their data: texts, phone calls, emails, location, photos, everything. Anyone with enough determination can bug you and catch you on tape. Back in the day, however, you had to do a lot more grunt work to find dirt on someone.

The way Pellicano would operate often included wiretapping home phone lines illegally to record conversations on tape. He'd intimidate the people suing his clients by threatening them. He'd disable your car's brakes and run you off the road—that kind of guy. He'd blackmail you. He'd dig through your trash. That's why they call them Hollywood garbagemen, and Pellicano was one of a kind.

Whenever a famous client hired him to spy on their loved one or enemy or whoever, Pellicano would also wiretap the client. You can read all about him elsewhere and his alleged involvement in getting charges dropped against Michael Jackson for molesting a twelve-year-old boy, or how he helped to acquit the woman who gave John Belushi his fatal dose of heroin, or the work he did for Tom Cruise, Sylvester Stallone, Kevin Costner, and you can just imagine how many others.

He ended up putting a dead fish and a rose on a reporter's car hood to scare her off along with a note that said, "Stop." That journalist called the cops, and that's what got his office searched. First, they found his grenades, then they found his computers. And on the computers, he had thousands of hours of recordings obtained through illegal wiretaps. This was in 2002.

His tapes were encrypted, so the NSA had to help break into them and went through over ten thousand recordings. He'd been illegally wiretapping people of interest for years, as well as his own clients without their knowledge. That's where his genius should be noted: in the way he'd play two people against each other, like agent Michael Ovitz against billionaire Ron Burkle. By investigating his clients as well as whoever the clients wanted to be investigated, he was able to hold all the cards and have dirt on everyone.

You just make one stupid mistake, and it's all over. You put a dead fish and a rose on the hood of a car like Pellicano, or you sign up for a mushroom blog with a personal email account like Ross Ulbricht. Pellicano spent sixteen years in prison and was released in March 2019. The intimidation tactics and grenades aside, what fueled his power for years was information. These days, you should keep in mind how much easier it is to steal someone's data and what kind of opportunities that presents. It's all easier than it's ever been.

FRESH ALLEGATIONS

I arrive at Fred's office to find him and a small video crew milling around, drinking coffee, and eating bagels. It's the team I hired to produce the short series about Dan's criminal allegations, and they do incredible work, but the principal director here is a goofball and has a lot of nervous energy that makes me also nervous for some reason. He's the kind of person that probably claps when their plane lands, but he's a good director.

Fred waves me into his office. "Guys, it'll just be a minute. Finish off the bagels, and we can keep going in ten." The crew nod, and two of them go out front for a smoke.

Fred's office has the chairs all moved around, and there is a camera on a tripod facing his chair behind the desk. There are two lights with flags in front of them, but the lights and camera are all turned off now.

"How's the shoot going?"

"Took me a while to get rolling, but I brought a hell of a lot of notes." Fred holds up a stack of yellow notebook pads to show me how much effort he's putting into this. "Should take another two or three hours, I suspect, but these guys are professional. I like them. Good choice."

"I'm glad to hear it. They have you mic'd up? Can you make sure the lav is turned off?"

"I turn it off as soon as we cut the camera. This isn't my first rodeo, kid. What have you got for me? I'm kind of busy here." He has a straight face that makes it tough to tell if he's kidding, but I don't think he is.

"Here's the new timeline I have in mind." I went to Kinko's and had two copies of my nefarious plans and timelines printed out and bound to look more impressive. The cover page is a photoshopped photo of Dan that gives him devil horns and a Hitler mustache.

Fred flips through his copy, his index finger running along the words as he reads them, nodding now and then. He flips through each page again and tosses the bound agenda back at me. "Looks great. I'm impressed. This is going to be a hell of a thing. I can't wait."

"Yeah. I've been thinking about it. Thinking maybe this should be the whole plan as far as anything being traced back to us is concerned. But separately, I could put another plan in motion that could implicate and accuse him of all sorts of nasty shit, like planting child porn on his computer or something. We could have fake quotes and plant stories in some small blogs that don't fact-check, and that could upstream to the bigger publications. We could smear enough shit on him that it'll take the rest of his life to clear up any of it."

Fred is tapping his finger on his desk and biting his lip. The tapping is annoying, but I think he must be doing it subconsciously, deep in thought over my proposition.

"It's an interesting idea. Let me sleep on it, and we'll talk." Fred says this in a way that seems like he's concluding our meeting.

My phone buzzes, and I remove it from my pocket and glance at the screen, which says that Elmer is calling. "It's Elmer, sorry. I can call him back later."

"No, take it, I know what this is about. You should take it."

"Okay." I stand and answer the call. Elmer is on the other end, speaking calmly but emphatically.

"Herb, I'm going to need your help, big guy. Can you catch a 6:00 p.m. flight from LAX to New Orleans?"

"What? Why?"

"I'm already at the airport. It's about Titus again. Good money. It's a three-and-a-half-hour flight. I already booked you on it and got you a hotel room. Can you make it?"

"All right, I'll be there." I hang up the phone, and Fred stands and walks toward the door but waits to open it.

"Titus is a real son of a bitch, but at least we're all making money. Am I right?" Fred frowns and pats me on the shoulder.

"Can you give me any color on what I'm walking into?"

Fred's head drops for a moment, looking disappointed. Not disappointed in me but in Titus, or in humanity in general. It's unclear. "Just more bullshit. I'm sure you can sweep it up fine. Someday, eventually, the other shoe is going to drop on that asshole. Used to be we'd hire fixers that could solve problems in the real world and erase the situation. Now it's on guys like you that can choreograph search results and press mentions. Just be careful."

Fred opens the door to his office and welcomes the crew back in to finish interviewing him about his legal issues with Dan. We shake hands, and I shuffle outside, feeling unsettled about what he'd just said.

By the time I get back to my car, I've reassured myself I have no ethical dilemma in working for Titus at the moment. With a copy of Oscar's hard drive and entire cloud, I have plenty of information to destroy both their lives later on if I need to.

My car's clock says it's 11:30 a.m., and I have a flight at 6:00 p.m. I go home to pack and ask if Ruby wants to come along and see her actress friends on Titus's film set in New Orleans.

We pack our bags and drop Frankie off with Miles.

PART 2

CHAPTER 8

JULIETTE, A STRIKING, frail, young woman, slams the front door behind her as she races inside this simple but tidy Creole cottage home. Juliette falls to a couch in the living room, covering her eyes and sobbing as her temporary foster mother, Anna, enters the room.

Anna sits on the couch and wipes away tears from Juliette's face. "My dear, what is the matter?"

Juliette's sobbing lightens as she sits up, apparently in need of the motherly nurturing. "I went to see master Antoine today, as you instructed. He had just returned from a duel, which he'd won and was getting drunk in celebration."

"As men do. I told Antoine you would fit his needs, and now, here you sit, crying. Whatever happened today? Have you done something foolish, young girl?"

"Oh, ma'am, master Antoine is a brutal, evil man. I do not wish to see him again."

"Whatever happened, my dear? Spare no detail. Tell me everything."

Juliette, still hoping for consolation, wipes her face and composes herself. "I entered his study, and he was wearing nothing but a robe, which I was not expecting. He asked about my upbringing and had me stand and twirl for him as he sat in his big chair, just drinking and inspecting me. Then he made his intentions clear, as he demanded I undress and submit myself to him."

"And how did you respond?"

"I told him I am merely an unfortunate orphan in need of work and a place to stay. I told him that I am not a tart nor a prostitute. He asked why I should expect the wealthy to relieve me when I am no use to them. He said for me to consent or to relieve him of my presence. When I began crying, my tears infuriated rather than melted him. Then, as I attempted to leave, he grabbed me by my shoulders and said, 'How can a girl such as yourself show gratitude for those who take care of her other than by total and complete surrender of her body?' And he began to remove my dress, forcefully, but I managed to open the door and ran out and ran all the way back here, ma'am."

Juliette moves her hand toward Anna's, and in response, Anna stands and turns away from her, thinking for a moment before facing Juliette again. "Oh, you idiotic twat. Do you imagine men enjoy doling out their hard-earned money to little girls like you without requiring anything in return? If I'd been in his place, I would not have allowed you to leave without having satisfaction from you first."

Juliette's face turns red with embarrassment and worry. "But, ma'am, I am a virgin."

"That is why I told him you would fit his needs, but since you do not want my help, make your own arrangements. You owe me rent money. Pay me by tomorrow, and be out of my home for good."

"Where am I to go? I have nothing."

"I attempted to help you. Instead, you can see how easy life is on the street."

"Ma'am, no, I can't. I will obey. Please give me another chance. Whatever is required of me, I will give."

Anna studies Juliette's face and snorts. "I will go to Antoine now and attempt to mediate the situation, and if I am successful, I will tell him to expect you tomorrow morning, when you will give yourself fully to him."

Juliette sinks back into the couch, resigned. "Yes, ma'am. Thank you."

Titus's voice rings out, as recognizable as any. "Cut! Very good. We're moving on."

Watching their performances, I'd almost forgotten I was watching two actresses in the process of shooting a film. The fifty or so people on set who were quiet and still the past few moments are now moving around performing various specific duties. The camera operator is checking the gate, whatever that means. Grips and electricians turn off lights and turn on other lights, wind up cables, and plug in different wires. Sequoia, who had been playing the role of Juliette, sees Ruby standing beside me and comes over to give us both hugs.

"So magnificent. You are such a skinny legend," Ruby says as she kisses Sequoia on the cheek, followed by a hug and a quick slap on the ass. "This movie is pretty fucked up, huh?"

"You can say that again. What are you guys doing after this? Should we get dinner?" Sequoia suggests.

I try to look disappointed in turning her down. "I have to meet with Titus tonight. Maybe you ladies can do something, and babe, I'll meet you back at the hotel later?"

"Perfect. Isabella can join us at the hotel, and we'll go out for dinner."

"Girls' night." Ruby hugs Sequoia again, and I assume they'd wanted the time to themselves anyway.

ON SET

Over the years, I have been on several film sets. Some are stressful, others are joyous. The crew here look grim and miserable overall, and it feels far from a three-month summer camp together in New Orleans. My initial impression is that Titus is regarded as an egomaniac not only by me.

You can tell a lot about a film director by how their set operates. This one is quiet but also tense and unhappy. None of the crew seem upbeat. They are just here to do their jobs, receive their paychecks, and go off to the next shoot. Undoubtedly, the nature of what they are shooting here is macabre. The menacing and condescending air of Titus is also well apparent. It doesn't appear anyone enjoys working with him beyond the money his presence brings.

Ruby waits with me as Sequoia goes to her trailer to change. Titus goes over to Sequoia and puts his hand on her side. She pushes him away and enters her trailer. Titus looks to his left and casually follows her into the trailer.

Ruby shoots me a glance as if I am supposed to step in and defend Sequoia's dignity, but Titus is out of her trailer and walking back toward us within a minute.

"Melvin, good to see you. How does dinner and poker sound?" Titus seems like he's always acting or putting on a show, as he smiles and talks to me like he's trying to convince me to come work for him when I'm already here.

"I could go for dinner and poker. I think they have a girls' night anyway." I wink at Ruby and kiss her. "You'll be okay leaving with Sequoia?"

"Yeah, I'll just go check on her now. Love you." Ruby walks off to the same trailer without giving Titus any sort of acknowledgment.

Titus waves over some kid working as an assistant and gives him his order like a waiter. "I need a cup with four shots of espresso. Decaf." Titus points at me. "You need a coffee or anything?"

I shake my head no, and the kid runs off. Within a minute, the kid is back and hands Titus the nonsensical beverage.

Titus nods his head toward the exit, and I follow him outside, where a sizable, dark SUV is idling and ready for us. I get into the

SUV with Titus, Elmer, and two other men who are already inside. The men readily, and as if on cue, both hand me their business cards out of their jacket pockets and shake my hand.

One is Lance, some producer I've never heard of who is apparently a studio executive. He looks rich, but he doesn't strike me as what I generally expect film producers to look like. Lance has a sinewy build, with a classically handsome face, chiseled chin, spooky intense eyes, and a shade of gray to his hair that gives him an aura of authority and wisdom. He's good-looking and rugged, but there's a sinister, dark element about him that leads me to believe he's the kind of guy that probably poaches rhinos in his spare time. Lance doesn't say a word to me. He just hands me his business card, shakes my hand firmly, and nods politely. Lance proceeds to stare out the car window, presumably in a trance watching the city of New Orleans pass by. I've known him for two minutes, but he is already who I want to be when I grow up.

The other mystery man is Tony, Titus's talent manager and producing partner, and they seem as close as two straight men can be. I had been too flustered to identify him at the Christmas party when Oscar gave me his laptop, but I remember now that he was there in the office with us that night. Tony is wearing a bespoke suit that probably cost more than the average American's annual salary, along with Prada eyeglasses with a tortoiseshell frame and a maroon cashmere tie. He's balding but still has some thicker hair on the sides of his head, and just the front-top section has drifted away over time. He has a trimmed beard, and he must weigh three times what would be a healthy weight for a man. Tony talks to me, to Titus, to the driver. Always needing sounds of voices speaking to be comfortable, preferably his own voice telling stories about the famous people he knows.

Together, Lance and Tony represent opposites in the extremes of wealth and power. Tony is the glutton: a talkative, overweight chain smoker who is known around Hollywood for being abusive and controlling with young women, especially those hoping to become famous actresses. He always settles before anything goes to trial, but I've heard enough to connect the dots. On the other hand, Lance is fit and pulls off the vibe of a Sunday school teacher. Yet until today, I had never heard of him. Elmer sits in the front seat next to the driver, and I have no idea where we're headed.

"You like massages?" Titus asks me.

"Yeah," I respond. "I could go for a massage."

HAPPY ENDINGS

The SUV parks and unloads us onto a sidewalk. I don't know New Orleans well, but I can tell by the buildings and crowd we're in some central district. Once we are out of the car, the driver takes off in the SUV. I assume he knows where he's going and when to come back for us. Usually, one of Fred's guys would be here as security for Titus, which is a peculiar absence in the group.

We all move from the vehicle to the street and into a building like we've been told the FBI is watching us, in one quick, fluid, tactical motion. Inside, the building has tall ceilings, brick walls, and dim lighting. There is a winding, cast-iron staircase to the right of the reception area, and to the left are several couches and a station for flavored water with sliced cucumber and lemon. The furniture and reception desk are black, and everything else is either painted black or stone tile. Spa music of string instruments quietly plays in the background, along with the sounds of a running water fountain. The woman standing behind the reception counter is a curvy young brunette with glasses and a name tag that asserts she is Marie, and Marie is wearing a short, tight, black dress that hugs her muscular thighs and robust chest.

"Good evening, gentlemen," Marie says to us. "Do you have an appointment?" She smiles. Her lipstick is the brightest red I've ever seen, and she has a small mole near her left cheek.

"It's under Titus. There are five of us here for massages."

Marie hits a few buttons on her keyboard and nods to confirm we are indeed expected and welcome here. "Five massages for Titus at 6:00 p.m. I have it right here. Would you like to choose your therapists?"

"Yes, please." Titus seems at home here, and I imagine it isn't his first visit to this establishment.

Marie turns and leaves the room for a moment. When she reemerges, there is a procession of a dozen young, attractive women, all wearing high heels and the same sort of short, tight, black dress as Marie. They do a short catwalk in front of us and pose in a semicircle as if this is a normal daily occurrence.

"I'll take this one and that one," Titus says quickly, pointing to two young women who both smile at him.

Elmer points at one and says, "She looks strong. I have a bad back."

Lance picks the most petite one in the lineup.

Tony chooses his.

I worry about hurting one of their feelings by not picking them, as if we're captains choosing kickball teams, but on second inspection, they don't look the least bit disappointed.

I point to one and say, "I'll have her."

Marie jots down our choices and shoos the ladies out of the room.

"Good choices," Titus says. "Shall we?"

"You know where the lockers are, sir?" Marie asks.

"Yes, we'll go change and relax in the steam room until you're ready."

Titus leads us back, to the right, and into a men's locker room. We each pick out lockers and exchange our clothes for robes and towels before proceeding downstairs to a dimly lit, subterranean room of Jacuzzi baths and steam rooms. It seems to be an establishment only for men, as we're encouraged to be naked by the posted signs. The area of this room in the basement is vast, the ceilings are high once again, and it looks like all the hanging lights are candles or faux candles. There are so many of them I can't imagine they're real candles.

The five of us move through the room like a herd of deer, not one of us wandering off on our own. We are all independently successful in our respective businesses, but somehow, Titus has the air of an alpha leader in this scenario, and I have no urge to leave the pack. We all hang our towels and robes on hooks and slide into one of the many Jacuzzis.

Tony waddles when he walks. It takes him a minute to get into the whirlpool, and I can't help but notice his member is tiny, crooked, and strange-looking as his belly sinks into the water. Titus's body is on the other end of the spectrum, with a shaved chest, a six-pack, and packing something twice the size of the rest of us and four times the size of Tony's. Good for him. I find a spot in the tub where a jet can hit my shoulder blades, and I shimmy back and forth to loosen up my upper back.

Five fits just right in the Jacuzzi, but six would have been cramped.

We are the only people here, aside from a few staff members. In a place like this, I find that hardly a coincidence and decide to chalk it up to Titus having rented out the entire site, which seems more than likely.

In the Jacuzzi, somehow nobody talks until Titus does. "You know, I read an article one time about how...No, wait, scratch that. I mean, I skimmed a headline one time that said that for every fifty pounds a man gains, his dick gets like a quarter inch shorter, or something like that. Again, I didn't read the article, just putting it out there."

"Who are you putting that out there to?" Tony says defensively but seems capable of taking the rubbing.

"Maybe you could try a few more salads, buddy. I want you to live a long, happy life," Titus says with a smile. Titus is charming and entitled, and I wouldn't be surprised if he stares at himself in the mirror while he fucks like Patrick Bateman in *American Psycho*.

We all relax and enjoy the jets shooting across our backs and legs. Once we're properly tenderized, Lance gets out and walks over to a water station, where he stands naked, takes a paper cup, and fills it with cucumber and lemon water. I follow Lance's lead and have a paper cup of water, and another, and another. I hadn't realized how thirsty I was. Lance grabs a towel and enters a steam room, so I do the same and follow him.

I can barely see in the steam room and hold my hand up above my eyes like I'm saluting the condensation.

"Come on in," Lance says, and I gather that he's on my left. I walk straight and take a seat. Elmer, Titus, and Tony all come in at once, towels in hand, and proceed to take seats around the room. They each have little paper cups of water.

Tony asks, "Hey, Lance, when do you go back to Mexico? Thought maybe I could tag along."

There's a heavy mist of hot moisture in the room, but I can see Lance, and his reaction to this is to be left alone in silence. Lance recognizes he has to answer in order to maintain etiquette and quash the awkward silence. "I go tomorrow, and I'll be back in Aspen by Wednesday."

"What are you doing in Mexico?" I blurt out. Again, Lance seems annoyed, which I can read on his face even through the steam. He's sweating a lot less than the rest of us.

"It's no big deal. Just a personal thing." Lance tries divulging nothing.

"Oh, come on," Titus says. "Tell him. You're a vampire." Titus, Tony, and Elmer all chuckle, and Lance just takes a sip of his water. I have no idea how he's making that tiny paper cup of water last him so long when I finished mine in a single gulp.

Tony says, "You wouldn't know it from looking at him, but Lance here is sixty-two years old. He looks more like forty-five, doesn't he? Every six weeks, he gets a stem-cell injection from some laboratory. And every other week, he goes to Mexico and gets plasma transfusions from eighteen-year-olds. Now tell me that shit doesn't work, or that rich people don't know what's up."

I look at Lance for a reaction, but he just stares off into the steam the same way he'd looked longingly out the SUV window earlier. "This is slander," Lance says.

Titus laughs and sits down on his towel so it will shield his legs from the warmth of his bench, at the same time revealing himself to us again like he wants to brag.

"So, Titus," Tony says, "I'll go ahead and ask what we're all thinking. Especially after getting to choose the girls. Does this place give happy endings or what?"

"You used to seeing legit massage therapists wearing high heels?" Titus answers the question with a question.

"You know, I've found," Elmer juts in for the first time in an hour, "that you can either get a good massage or a happy ending, but seldom both."

Titus smiles. "You just have to know where to look. Every major city has at least one shining light where gentlemen are still treated like gentlemen. I'll be your guide."

"I'm confused," Tony blurts out like a big sneeze. "Do they give hand jobs here or not?"

"Yeah, I'm trying to show you guys a nice time tonight. We're going to get massages and hand jobs, then go back to my place for dinner and poker."

"I figured you'd be the kind of guy to have his own masseuse travel with him for shoots," I say.

"Yeah, I do," Titus snaps. "There's one in my rider. I get a massage three times a week at home after we wrap. But a massage therapist means they take it seriously and don't give handies. A masseuse is what we're having here. Big difference."

"Lance, isn't that what you had before you got divorced? A masseuse?" Tony asks.

Lance nods uncomfortably, taking a lot of shit from these guys for being the money man.

"Lance and his ex-wife had a masseuse that would come over twice a week and give his wife a massage, then give Lance one," Elmer explains to me. "About a year ago, his wife found out that he was getting a blowjob at the end of every massage, and then she divorced him and took half his money. That sound about right, Lance?"

Lance nods. "Pretty much. She got the place in Miami and never has to work, so a pretty good deal for her."

"Was she hot at least?" I ask. "The masseuse."

Lance solemnly shakes his head. "No, not really. But my ex-wife is gorgeous. After two or three years with anybody, you'll start getting bored of having sex with them. It doesn't matter how hot they are. Just look at the women Tiger Woods cheated on his wife with. Or how Hugh Grant cheated on Elizabeth Hurley with that crackhead."

"Well, to that end, I brought you all here for research," Titus claims. "We want to open a massage parlor and a brothel in Cortez next year, so we need to study all the best places and learn from the treatments, the amenities, the ambience, and so forth. Berlin and Rio have taken the prize so far in terms of selection of beautiful women and professionalism on the brothel side. But I like a lot of the class in a place like this. Definitely want your notes later, so stay alert."

"Good, I knew it when we were picking out the girls. That situation only happens when they're properly suited," Tony says and wipes sweat from his brow, close to needing out of this heat chamber.

"I believe the Marquis de Sade wrote that," Titus says, "in order to know virtue, we must first acquaint ourselves with vice."

"How much do you tip the girls here?" Elmer asks. "I left my wallet up in the locker room."

"They'll come to get us one at a time here soon, and we'll stop by the locker room for a scrub down. You can grab some cash then,"

Titus explains. "A $200 tip will get you a hand job. Five hundred dollars should get you a blowjob, maybe $1,000 for you, though, Tony, with your weird-looking dick. Tip them before the massage, so they don't have to pause and ask what you want later on. It kills the whole vibe. Trust me."

"In Mexico, it wouldn't be more than $100 for a blowjob," Tony says.

"Well, we're not in Mexico," Titus proclaims. "And we want Cortez to make money, and we want girls there with exquisite taste. Can't do that for $100 when they could go over to Vegas for a thousand."

I try thinking of something witty to say to add to the conversation, but all I can think about is a pregnant Ruby, and for some reason, I ask, "Do you fuck the girls here?"

"Hey, we're just here for a massage and a blowjob, Melvin. Get your mind out of the gutter," Titus says, and we all laugh.

"Well, how much are you tipping?" I ask, thinking it is better than my last question.

"Me? Five thousand because I'm getting two girls, and they know I'm famous, and I rented out the whole place tonight, so I can't be cheap with it. But you just give your girl $500, and you're golden. Okay?"

I am both repulsed by and jealous of Titus. I nod in appreciation. Tony is about to pass out from the heat, and Lance has still barely broken a sweat. Both men are wholly wrapped up in whatever they are dealing with internally. Elmer is next to me and looks somewhere between the two emotions.

"I'm just here out of equal parts curiosity and pride," Elmer says. "Like looking in the toilet after you take a big poop. You know, we should start a whiskey business and sell just that brand in Cortez."

Tony nods. "That's a great idea."

"Did you know that George Washington was one of the largest whiskey distillers of his time? A real badass," Lance tells us.

I ask Titus, "So you're making a movie down here about the Marquis de Sade? Is that right?"

"It's an adaptation of his work, loosely. Inspired by a story of his but isn't about him." Titus seems unsure in his wording. "It's a story by de Sade called *Justine or, The Misfortunes of Virtue*, so it will be the first modern adaptation of his work. It also kind of combines it with his other story *Juliette, or Vice Amply Rewarded*, which was his final book that sent him to prison until he died."

"First modern interpretation since Pasolini," Lance says out of nowhere.

"First of this story, and it is an adaptation from the French Revolution that we've set in the American Civil War era, so not so modern, depending on how you look at it," Tony says before looking sorry for offending Titus. "But I get what you mean."

"Who is Pasolini?" I ask, hoping to get some bonding in quickly so we can leave the steam room and head on to our massages.

"Who was Pasolini?" Lance replies as condescendingly as a history professor. "He was an Italian neorealist film director. Made a movie version of *120 Days of Sodom* in 1975. It was banned, still is in some countries. Based on a de Sade novel. And, of course, Pasolini was murdered brutally before the movie even came out. They crushed his nuts with a metal bar, then ran over him multiple times with his own car, and then they set him on fire. Talk about a way to go."

"Why did they kill him?" I press on for more details like a stupid child. Lance grins, presumably hoping I'd ask.

"Well, the night he was murdered, he was on his way to meet someone who was extorting him so he could pay them to return film cuts of the movie they'd stolen. The movie adaptation of the Marquis de Sade novel. They had taken the film reels of the final cut. That is the movie that ended him. It was his final film, and he died for it, and you've never even heard of it, so he died for nothing." Lance completes his interlude and goes back to silently meditating while staring at the opposite wall.

Tony wipes more sweat from his face. "Does this sound like the kind of project we should be producing?" I can tell that Tony has asked this before but also that he's only half-serious.

"I regret it every day," Titus answers smugly. "But it is a film that must be made."

"What's it about?" I ask, realizing I am the only one uninformed about the project.

"You don't know anything about the Marquis de Sade?" Titus inquires.

"I know the word 'sadism' comes from his name. Not much else," I say.

"Sadism for a good reason. His mind was twisted enough," Elmer says, apparently an expert. "De Sade was perverted to the extreme: pedophilia, incest, rape, necrophilia, you name it. He was infamous during his own time because everyone in France had friends and family that he had abused, but for years, his family could buy him out of trouble by paying off his victims. Money buys peace, same as today. His book *120 Days of Sodom* had stories of four powerful men raping their own daughters and then brutally murdering them and other children over the course of four months. Shocking for any time period."

"His life was fascinating," Titus says, unable to contain his enthusiasm for the subject. "His father was friends with Voltaire. He went to the same school as Robespierre. He was a prisoner in the Bastille until right before it was stormed. He was sentenced to the guillotine, but two days later, Robespierre was executed, and he was freed. When he published *Justine*, our project, Napoleon threw him back in jail. He escaped prison a few times. Can you imagine living when they would just chop off people's heads? De Sade was a wild man. One who wished for depraved control of everything. There's something to be learned in his stories, whether it's good or bad. We shouldn't just ignore his work because it was extremist or offensive."

"He was no hero, it sounds like," I say.

"No," Lance says. "He was no hero, but who of us is?" Even while being pompous, Lance is still more profound than I meant to be. "I always found his work simple and repetitive, but I believe in Titus and his vision to elevate it."

"But he was a lucid and disturbing storyteller," Titus says. "And if you were in high school, wouldn't you want to go see a movie based on a book that was banned as soon as it was published? Sounds dangerous and erotic and like something your parents would say no to, right?"

"That's a good marketing ploy," I say.

"Don't forget," Tony says, now using his towel to wipe sweat from his face and body while breathing heavily, "Marquis de Sade was a proponent of free, public brothels as a way to deter crime. Still a great idea." Tony smiles and gets a few laughs. "Look, I've gotta get out of here, guys. I'll tell the ladies that I'm first." And with that, Tony leaves the steam room and begins his journey to a magical massage.

"Can't stand the heat," Titus says, smiling.

"Have there been other movies about Marquis de Sade?" I ask.

"Yeah, Philip Kaufman made *Quills* in 2000," Titus answers quickly. "Is pretty good. Michael Caine, Kate Winslet, and Joaquin Phoenix are in it, and Geoffrey Rush plays de Sade in his final years, though it isn't very accurate."

"Europe in the 1780s is a hard period to make very interesting," I say.

"What about *The Libertine* with Johnny Depp?" Elmer asks, showing his lack of film knowledge.

"Complete unwatchable garbage," Lance replies. "I could barely sit through it."

"Didn't they light that whole film with candles to make it more authentic, though?" I ask, trying to take some of the heat off Elmer.

"Still sucked," Lance answers quickly. "And didn't even look good. *Barry Lyndon* was also lit by candlelight but looked incredible."

"But still, that one is boring as hell too," Elmer says. "I don't know why you think people want a period piece, especially taking the story and setting it in New Orleans in the 1860s. That's my two cents, about eight months too late."

"You've heard my spiel about *Dances with Wolves* already, yeah?" Titus snarls at Elmer.

"About a dozen times." Elmer laughs. "We'll see what people think of it. I liked *The Count of Monte Cristo*, though it isn't just two hours of torture and rape."

"The Marquis de Sade was fucked up," Titus admits. "But his art still has a place in our society. It's like a steam room: it can be uncomfortable, but it's cleansing. Plus, it turns me on, and it's really hot."

"Tell the computer guy more about the movie," Lance implores Titus, obviously referring to me as the one needing to be informed while also implying it isn't worth remembering my name.

Titus is happy to indulge. "Basically," Titus says, "there are these two sisters who are orphaned, Juliette and Justine. Justine tries to be Christian and moral and upright, but she is mistreated, abducted, raped, and abused at every turn. Meanwhile, her sister, Juliette, embraces vice and works her way up through society by not having any morals. There's a lot more to it, but simply put, it's going to make *The Passion of the Christ* look like *Bambi*. This girl goes through hell, and nobody ever comes to save her. There's no such thing as redemption. It's all fatalism in the end."

"Maybe, just maybe," says Lance, "it may be serendipitous that a sadistic tragedy written during the French Revolution should be adapted to be told with a modern perspective and set during the American Civil War in the South. If done correctly, it's all rife with symbolism. That's why I've helped pay for all this. I trust you to tell this story, Titus."

Titus appears genuinely touched by this, but nobody can tell tears from sweat in this cell.

The door to the steam room opens, which causes a snakelike hissing sound of fresh air escaping into our space. A woman instructs Elmer to follow her, and he does so without any inclination of remorse. Now it is just Lance, Titus, and myself boiling in a room of hot steamy air.

"You guys good? You need to step out for some air or water?" I ask, hoping they'll agree we should get out of this wet inferno.

"I'm good. This is cleansing, good before a massage," Lance answers earnestly, and I start wondering if he's a ridiculous specimen of a threat.

"So a story set during the French Revolution—you are setting during the American Civil War in the South? That's right? Why?" I ask Titus, trying to forget about wondering how rich and unnerving Lance might be.

"I just did," Titus says. "The debauchery and violence of today existed two hundred years ago just as it existed five hundred years ago. I think there is a compelling parallel." Titus closes his eyes and leans his head back against the dripping wall behind him.

"Okay, so why am I down here?" I ask.

"Let's enjoy our massages. Enough talk about work already. I want to relax," Titus says. "We'll all go back to eat and play poker at my place after this, and we can talk shop there." Titus implies this massage respite is too holy a place to utter our intentions out loud. "So you and Ruby are dating now after my New Year's Eve party, huh? How is that?"

"The porn star that's been hanging around Sequoia? Damn, she's hot. How'd you manage that?" Lance asks.

"Right place, right time, I guess," I tell them.

"She has a very impressive, uh, body of work," Lance says with a shit-eating grin.

"I got her pregnant, and it looks like we're keeping it. You're the first people I've told." It seems shocking to them both.

"Well, congratulations. That's amazing," Titus says genuinely.

"Wow," Lance responds. "Well, good for you, kid. I love that scene where her and three of her friends have a reverse gangbang with some guy for his birthday."

"Yeah, that's a good one," I respond, indignantly.

"I like the one of her getting fucked while riding a train somewhere. In the scene, it's supposed to be some random guy she just met, but I'm sure that was staged," Titus says. I am wearing a fake smile, but inside, I'm fuming and hate this line of discussion, but Titus continues. "I love public scenes like that, but congrats on getting her knocked up."

One at a time, the women we chose earlier are each to come in and lead us to a shower room with a table where we are told to lie down on our backs and then our fronts as they wash, scrub, and clean our every crevice before drying us off with towels and taking us to our private massage rooms.

Lance goes next, and now, it is just Titus and myself in the steam.

"So," Titus says, "you got yourself a nice stay-at-home trophy wife now? Someone to make you dinner and give you back rubs and say nice things to you?"

"Yeah, she doesn't do any of that," I say, and the two of us laugh. "She has basically moved in with me, though. Her and her dog."

"What kind of dog does she have?"

"It's some sort of small poodle. It's really old, so I assume he's going to die soon. She loves that dog; I think she will be destroyed when it finally goes. I've been trying to convince her we should get a puppy to help ease the transition."

"That's a good idea, actually. I heard the Dog Whisperer say something about that on an episode once. He'd have a pitbull or something, and when one got to the end, he'd get a pitbull puppy. The way he explained it, you get a puppy while the old one is still around so that the puppy can learn from the older one and pass wisdom and mannerisms along. So in some ways, your new puppy is just carrying on the torch. It's a touching sentiment."

"Kind of like Paul Newman to Robert Redford, and then Robert Redford to Brad Pitt."

Titus chuckles. "Exactly. You get it."

"You have any dogs?"

"No. I had a golden retriever, Max. He died about five years ago." Titus bows his head as if this is the one topic that could make him emotional. "I don't think I could ever have another dog after Max. Plus, I am always traveling for work, so it wouldn't be fair to a dog if I don't have the time to invest in it. Now I just watch shows like *Dog Whisperer* and enjoy them vicariously."

The door opens and the air hisses again, and two women lead Titus out to his scrub down.

Now it's just me and my thoughts waiting to go last for a massage from the girl I chose when I walked in here.

It is clear Titus wants something over me to compromise me, knowing that I've had access to Oscar's laptop and potentially had enough time to see what was on it. Titus understands that information is the highest currency of leverage, and I assume he wants to keep me close and do shady things together more out of assured mutual destruction than out of some bond of trust or something. Either way, it'll take more than allegations of a happy ending to compromise my career.

I'll get the massage and a happy ending but won't feel guilty about it at all. This is a service and unemotional and not bound to some sort of moral deliberation. I need to jerk off nearly every day anyway, so this one will just be done by someone else's hand. Plus, this morning, Ruby yelled at me and hit me in the chest to angrily wake me up because she had a dream I cheated on her, so timing-wise, the crime fits the punishment, and I am happy enough to be initiated as one of the gang and get some tension relief.

My brunette comes in and takes me for my wash and scrub down and then to the massage room. I give her a $500 tip before we get started, and it's worth every penny.

CHAPTER 9

After our massages and another round of soaking in the Jacuzzi, Titus's driver in the SUV takes us all back to Titus's place, or rather, the house he's staying in here in town for the next few months during the film shoot. It's an old plantation home with classic columns painted white and a red clay-tile roof, all partially hidden from the road by large oak and maple trees, which are fully blooming in advance of the approaching summer. It's a different vibe from his Los Angeles home, but it is still huge and beautiful, and the backyard is lush with vegetation.

Titus has converted what was once a large dining hall into a poker room with two big round tables covered in green felt with classic brown-leather armrests, though we're using only one of the tables. The walls are covered in oil portraits of the family that presumably once occupied this house for hundreds of years.

An old white-haired butler, who presumably came with the vacation rental, keeps quietly appearing in the room, bringing us whiskey drinks and an assortment of appetizers, which so far consist of shrimp cocktails, Cajun sausage puffs, and oysters. There's also a four-cheese spread. I like three of the cheeses, but I hate the fourth.

That's life, I guess, and the first-world problems you deal with at a mansion with a private chef: three cheeses out of four are delicious. We each have a small table conveniently arranged next to us to house our small plates of food away from the card game.

There's also a pretty young woman milling about the room in a tiny two-piece swimsuit, though her bottoms are wrapped in more of a thong than a typical American swimsuit. Her name is Sparkles, and it is apparently routine for these guys to have at least one young woman at each game for eye candy and recreation. She's wearing a lot of makeup and high heels. She's toned like she regularly works out, and her breasts are big and barely contained within her thin bikini top. It's explained to me that you can ask Sparkles for a massage in a back room for $100. Then, once back there, you can offer her more money for sex. Her presence is mainly atmospheric, and it is a nice distraction during poker to look up and see her shaking her body to the music in search of our attention.

The game is Texas Hold 'Em with a $200 ante and no limit. We're each taking turns as the dealer. We're three hands into the game, and Elmer is shuffling the cards and preparing to deal. The playing cards are of a higher quality than I have seen before. The backs of the cards have a metallic ink that gives them a bright sheen, and the design is a hypnotically symmetrical take on the classic bicycle cards to which I am accustomed. The cards have an embossing that I can trace with my fingertips in an oddly satisfying way.

On the first hand, Lance won by raising too much before the flop, so we all dropped out. During the second hand, both Tony and Titus went all in, and Titus won with a full house, which made Tony have to buy back in for another five grand.

Titus already has a stack of chips twice as high as the rest of us, and Tony is already twice as drunk as the rest of us. This makes him even more unpredictable, which makes him impossible to read.

Elmer deals out two cards face-down to each of us, at which we all furtively glance before trying to read the reactions of the rest of the group. My cards are a jack and queen suited, both diamonds.

Sparkles pulls out her large breasts and shakes them while smiling at me and blows me a kiss from across the table.

Lance calls the blind. Titus raises $500. Sparkles puts her breasts away and slowly walks around the room, showing off her ass now.

"Coming out strong," Lance says to Titus.

"I saw you scratch your ear. Must mean something." Titus winks and smiles, all too charmingly.

I call the raise, and so do Elmer, Tony, and Lance. These are the first decent hole cards I've had, and everyone is in the hand still.

Elmer deals out the flop: an eight of clubs, ten of diamonds, and king of diamonds.

The butler comes through and refills our drinks and takes away the empty appetizer trays. "Steaks should be out in fifteen minutes, gentlemen."

"Wonderful, thank you," Titus tells the butler as he exits the room, heading back toward the kitchen.

"Damn, Titus," I say. "Massages. Poker. Steak. Whiskey. You sure know how to treat a guy."

Titus chuckles. "I've had practice," he raises his glass, so we all follow suit. "Cheers, fellas."

We all say, "Cheers," back at him and take a sip of our drinks.

Tony is first in line to make a bet, but he checks to Lance, who bets $700.

Titus calls.

I call.

Elmer folds.

Tony calls.

"Tony, you're impossible to read. You're so drunk, even you don't know what you're doing," Titus says astutely.

"We'll see who's laughing when I have all the chips later," Tony says with all too much confidence.

I need either an ace or a nine to make a straight or a diamond to catch a flush. Theoretically, I could hit an ace of diamonds and have a royal flush, so there's no way I can fold now without regretting it later.

Elmer deals out the turn: a five of clubs. Not what I needed.

"So how's dating a porn star?" Elmer asks me.

"It's fine," I respond in a way that lets them know I'm done with the topic.

"I think Drake had a baby with a porn star, so you're in good enough company," Tony tells me.

"Thanks," I offer back. "So who's turn is it?"

"It's to Tony," Elmer answers. "Congrats on the pregnancy. That's huge. I'm happy for you. It might calm you down a little."

"I've done some porn. I'd be interested in doing more, though," Sparkles jumps into the conversation with a coy, flirtatious smile.

"I know, sweetie," Titus says. "Now, try not to interrupt us again. The men are talking, okay?"

Sparkles makes a sad face, but I don't think her feelings were hurt one bit, as she goes back to her seductive solo dancing.

"She seems like she's good for you," Elmer continues to me. "Better than your ex-wife anyway. Remember how miserable you were when you were with her?"

"What's the story there?" Titus asks me.

"We met in college," I say. "I thought we were in love, but she was always cheating on me. We got married, and less than two years later, she left me for someone else. That's about it."

"Where did you go to college? And where'd you grow up? I hardly know anything about you," Titus says to me.

"Grew up and went to school in Indiana. Studied communications. Thought I wanted to go into public relations until I saw what that was like. My first job was interning for Elmer, actually," I say.

Elmer nods and fills in the rest. "Kid was a whiz with computers and hated being around people, so I suggested he should set up his own shop and consult for me instead. That must have been fifteen years ago." Elmer sighs and nods like he's remembering the good old days.

Tony looks at his hole cards again as if he's forgotten what game we are playing. He checks and raises his glass to me before finishing it in a single gulp. "Congratulations, Melvin. You landed a girl that millions of guys jerk off to every day. You're already a winner in my book, pal." It's hard to know if he's being sarcastic or genuine.

Lance bets $1,000, and Titus folds. It's my turn, and I still only have king high, but I call, and Tony calls. There are three of us still in to see the river card.

"So much for that scratching-his-ear tell meaning anything," Elmer says to Titus.

"I am sure it meant something. We'll see when we see his cards," Titus says, confidently.

"Hey, Titus," Lance says. "You know that Britney Spears is an anagram for Presbyterian?"

"What? What the hell does that mean?" Titus asks.

"I just mean, not everything has meaning. Some things are just odd. Sometimes I scratch my ear."

"Tide comes in. Tide goes out. You can't explain that," I say, and the others smile at my Bill O'Reilly impression.

"Yeah, exactly," Lance says, looking vindicated.

Elmer puts the final card down, and my chest inflates as I finally have something. The ace of clubs is the river card, which gives me an ace-high straight. Not good enough for the size of this pot, but I'm here, so now I just have to outplay a drunk Tony and an eccentric Lance. However, it's hard to out-bet someone with all the money in the world. There's a possible club flush on the board now, but they'd have to be extremely stupid or lucky to walk into that on the turn and river.

Tony goes all in, and Lance folds. I guess we'll never know what Lance's ear scratch meant. Lance shuffles all the folded and burned cards together to bury his secret.

I look at Tony's chips and back at mine, trying to do some quick math. He's playing bold and aggressive now, but given how much he's been drinking, I feel good about calling, which would put me all in now too. So I call.

With all our chips in, Tony and I flip over our cards. Mine show an ace-high straight, and sure enough, Tony caught the flush, having stayed in with a ten and jack of clubs.

"What the hell are you doing staying in after the flop with a ten and a jack?" I shout at Tony while he pulls the chips back into his pile. It's beyond frustrating. I try to play smart poker, but dumbass rich people don't care one way or the other if they win. They can just throw money at things and cross their fingers.

Tony quickly stacks his chips and begins shuffling the cards. It's his turn to deal. As he organizes this, he gives me a grin that I don't like one bit. "Are you going to buy back in, Melvin?"

"I don't know. I don't have any more cash on me."

"I'll front you," Titus quickly retorts. "Call it an advance on your next assignment. The night's still early, and I haven't even told you what it is yet." Titus walks over to another table to count out more chips and brings me $5,000 worth.

I try turning the attention back to Titus and away from my personal life. "So what about you? Are you and Sequoia dating now?" I can tell this hasn't been asked out loud before by the other men's reactions and their eyes darting over to Titus for a reaction.

"Dating is a strong word. She does seem to enjoy a more hands-on directing approach, though. If I could just convince her and Isabella to double up on me, I'd be a happy man."

I catch Lance and Elmer's expressions as a collection of scrunched foreheads and eye rolls. Titus is in his own world and has insulated and sheltered himself enough to think this is a reasonable goal. There is no other reality in which a man would expect this of two famous actresses, both working on his movie, but in Titus's reality, it shimmers as a compelling possibility.

Tony finishes shuffling and begins dealing our cards as the butler returns with a cart full of plates, which he passes out to us individually. The steak looks and smells fantastic, and we all thank the butler as he efficiently leaves again once we all have our food.

My cards are shit, so I toss them back to Tony and go to work on my steak. Tony folds too and takes a bite of his food while Elmer, Titus, and Lance battle it out.

"I need you to go to San Diego," Titus tells me.

"Sparkles doesn't need to hear all this shop talk," Tony says, handing Elmer the deck and standing up. "Will one of you take over dealing? I'm going to go get another massage. Have the guy cover my steak in tinfoil. I'll finish it after."

"You'll take about three minutes," Lance jokes. "I don't know if there's time to get tinfoil."

Tony winks at us and mocks a fake laugh. He takes Sparkles by the hand and leaves the room.

"San Diego. This is the job?" I ask.

"Yes. Lance's plane can take you and Ruby back tomorrow. You can drop Ruby off in LA. Then you go down to San Diego. There's a woman there named Emily. I'll send you her details. I slept with her a couple of years ago, consensually, and now she's sending me messages out of nowhere saying that she had a baby and that it's mine."

"And she's threatening to go public? Wants money? What?" I ask.

Titus nods. "At the end of the month, if I don't respond to her settlement and child support offer, which I'm not planning to do. I'll give you a mouth swab from me. I need you to take my sample and compare it to the child's DNA and see if it is somehow my baby so I can get ahead of this. And I need you to do it quickly."

"Couldn't the court order a paternity test? Why the cloak and dagger?"

"Yeah, they could, but if it is somehow my child, I'd rather find out myself first before the court does. Or preferably settle before this ever goes to court and becomes public record." Titus waves his hand like this is all too obvious and I am asking the wrong questions.

Lance folds his cards and starts eating his steak. Titus and Elmer go to the river card and begin betting and raising each other, but I'm more focused on Titus.

"You know, I'm not like a private detective. And I don't have a DNA lab handy. This just isn't really my bread and butter. Wouldn't you want someone who handles this kind of thing, like Fred?"

"Titus trusts you, Melvin," Elmer tells me. "I'm sure you can lift a strand of hair from a baby. Its hairbrush or something. It's a simple task. A day or two at most. Fred's relationship to Titus is pretty well known, so he could be called in to testify someday. You're less of a known entity."

Elmer and Titus flip over their cards, and Elmer wins. Lance begins scooping up all the cards to shuffle and deal.

"Okay," I tell them, unable to think of anything more profound to say. "I'll come up with something. How sure are you that the kid isn't yours?"

"I'm positive. I pulled out and came on her stomach, I remember. I guarantee she just wants some money or some press." Titus seems disgusted by the whole notion.

"I'll be her baby's daddy," Tony says as he reenters the room with a big smile, laughing at his own joke the way only the drunk can.

"Almost four minutes, Tony. That's not bad," Elmer jokes. "We didn't have time to grab any tinfoil."

"We'll put you on the budget for the film, something PR related. What title should we give you?" Lance asks me.

"It doesn't matter what you call me," I say. "You can call me the rabbit, for all I care."

"I'll be with you on the plane tomorrow. We'll figure it out. I'll head down to Mexico after dropping you in San Diego. We should try to be wheels-up by noon tomorrow if we can. It's going to be a long day," Lance says while dealing out our next hand.

"So," I ask Titus, "before I go, how are you giving me this saliva sample? Are you just going to spit in a ziplock bag or something?"

GIRLS' NIGHT OUT

I arrive back at our hotel room a little after midnight, and Ruby is wearing a clay face mask and the tiny silk robe I gave her on Valentine's Day.

Ruby gives me the most gentle peck of a kiss on my lips so as not to smear her face mask.

"Hey, babe," she says. "I was about to take a bath. You smell drunk and like cigars. Did you guys have fun?"

"Yeah, we played poker, and I lost some money, but it was interesting. Fun in some ways." I sit on the bed in front of her and put my hands on her waist. She doesn't need to know about the massages. Ruby is speaking to me without looking up from her phone. "What are you up to there?" I nod at the phone she is fixated on.

"Oh, I'm playing *Animal Crossing*. Isabella and Sequoia play it when they're waiting around on set. I'm addicted now."

Ruby locks her phone, puts it on the TV stand, and falls onto the bed next to me, and I put my arm under her neck as we lie down together on top of the blanket.

"How was your day? Did you girls go have a nice dinner somewhere?"

Ruby tells me about the food they had at the restaurant and how the three of them had a fun day together. Ruby tells me how both Isabella and Sequoia have been getting harassed by Titus, and she recounts stories about him that she'd been told over dinner.

Stories about how when we were all in Cortez for New Year's, he had raped Sequoia and was still making her sleep with him through intimidation about hurting her career. That she was afraid of him, but he was so unrelenting.

How Sequoia is supposed to be back at Titus's house later tonight too. How he'd threatened to ruin her career if she said anything. How he was working on Isabella now and trying to have his way with her next through the same means. How he describes himself as kinky, but how that actually means he is physically abusive and gets off on hurting her and making her cry while still being careful not to leave any marks on her skin.

Titus sounds like the character in a violent porno or a horror film the way she tells it. I ask why they don't tell their agents about this, and Ruby gets mad at me for blaming the victims and reminds me of the part about Titus threatening them and him being a famous movie star and a powerful man.

"The man is a monster. You should not keep working for him." Ruby stands and heads toward the bathroom to wash off her face mask and take a bath. "All men are the same."

"Some men are assholes, babe, I know. I'm sorry. We're both on this movie's payroll, so remember, it's not just me. We could both not work with him ever again, and it'd be fine with me. The thing in San Diego is unrelated, though; it's for a different client. It'll only take a night or two."

"The thing in San Diego, it's really not for Titus?" She has her best innocent puppy eyes trained on me.

"No, babe, it's not. I promise."

She just replies with a "Hmm" as she turns on the water to fill her bath and closes the bathroom door.

When she emerges from the bathroom, I am nearly asleep, drinking a glass of wine while the TV plays comedy specials. A new one with Whitney Cummings has just started.

Ruby takes my wineglass and, in a fluid motion, pours the remaining wine onto my side of the bed, staining the sheets and pillows. "You really put on Whitney Cummings?"

"I just left it on the same playlist after the last comedian; it isn't like I was trying to offend you. I didn't realize you care what I am allowed to watch."

"You did this on purpose. You know how I feel about her."

Ruby can act out and be a bitch here and be degraded on camera for money, but my listening to a comedian means I hate women because of the patriarchy. She is automatically and continuously the actual victim, at least in her mind. Meanwhile, she can claim she's a feminist a few weeks after I shoot a video of me peeing into her mouth in the shower simply because it's her choice and she's making money from it and enjoys it. Feminism can be whatever she wants it to be. Either way, she's the victim, urine is sterile, and comedians can't be controversial. And don't worry, I drank three liters of water in preparation for the golden-shower scene because no one wants the urine to look yellow and gross in one of those types of videos.

It takes over an hour to calm her down. By the time she falls asleep, I have a piercing headache and think about how I should have brought some of my homemade chloroform with me to New Orleans.

CHAPTER 10

FILM IS AMERICA'S third largest export. If California were a country, it would have the fifth largest economy in the world.

Over ten million people live in Los Angeles County, and at least half of them are from somewhere else originally. It is the land of transplants and implants. Home of life coaches preaching how to be happy and prosperous even if they themselves aren't. It is a place filled with snowflakes pushing their dogs in baby strollers and virtue signaling on social media about their blind support of whatever liberal flare is in vogue at the moment, all competing for who can either be the biggest predator or the biggest victim.

LA is filled with tragic souls that go by five pronouns and have ten food allergies and a dozen self-diagnosed mental health issues, like the human versions of spoiled, inbred miniature poodles that have barely even been outdoors and are always desperately seeking to be offended. It's hipster men wearing thrift-store clothes at specialty coffee roasteries complete with twirled handlebar mustaches like they're off-duty army lieutenants from World War I.

This is a city well known for the vanity and self-centeredness of its occupants. Yet, it is also a combat zone for those fighting to be seen as the most sensitive resident. Far from the strong-willed determination that brought tough people west by horse and buggy, it's more common now for the citizens here to be self-diagnosed as a highly emotional person: someone easily triggered and constantly the victim who needs to be tiptoed around in order not to be offended. This is the only thing that's suitable to enable. Bullying and fat-shaming are wrong, and being as big as a house is brave. Conformity to some all-encompassing patriarchy is feared to such an extent that everyone acts and dresses the same to be different. Having a unique gender identity is just as good as having a personality. Historical social norms have been replaced by an imaginary fantasy land where everyone is admired and loved for who they are, and the children who are born into this are all but helpless.

Many who move to Hollywood are, at first, looking for fame and fortune, or at the very least, they want attention. Few achieve it, and the rest are left fighting to get their attention elsewhere. Some end up dressed up as superheroes on Hollywood Boulevard to take photos with tourists for tips. Some get addicted to drugs and become homeless. Some move back home—back to where they started. Some turn to sex work, and some get into porn.

Viacom, AT&T, CBS, Comcast, Disney, and News Corp—those six companies control 90 percent of mass media in the United States. For reference, in 1983, the same percentage of the media was controlled by fifty companies rather than six.

The cost of marketing and prints makes international theatrical distribution of any film cost at least $60 million, which makes it less likely for studios to fund or give wide release to any movie that doesn't have a big budget, famous stars, or recognizable brand or does have anything too radical. If you were a studio executive, would you prefer to spend $60 million promoting a film that cost $100 million to make or a movie that cost $10 million? Of course, bigger-budget movies end up making more money, so it is much more likely to be profitable by banking on big-budget movies.

This is why the types of films that get greenlit now are all franchises, sequels, and anything with existing intellectual property, like toys, games, or action figures. Even something based on a book has a built-in audience and therefore would be more likely to get produced than some random, low-budget, indie screenplay. This is also why they remake great classic movies that were big hits and ruin them rather than remaking movies that weren't done correctly the first time.

It used to be that more independent movies could break through, get distribution, and be seen. In 2019, indie films made up only 11 percent of box office receipts, meaning big-budget films take up a bigger and bigger piece of the pie. Mainstream movies are less about cinema and art and more about broad appeal and commerce. These big-budget movies are the most profitable ones for the studios, so they don't adequately consider funding the smaller niche projects.

Once a film does get released, exhibitors take half the gross. So to even be able to get that $60 million for marketing and prints back, your movie has to gross $120 million, and that is just to break even on the marketing budget. Digital releases have changed this somewhat, but you can appreciate why the trend has been fewer movies with bigger budgets that are more broadly appealing. With more consolidation of ownership and less creative options, most studio films become more and more homogenized. Superheroes and known entities get funding. New ideas don't. Also, it's worth noting that the international box office used to account for 50 percent of revenues and now accounts for 70 percent, meaning that being broadly appealing becomes even more of a fiduciary responsibility.

Luckily, someone like Lance can put up the initial $15 million to get something like Titus's movie moving, and the film will get distributed through a studio with a three-picture deal with Titus. Somewhat similar to George Clooney getting to create a passion project like *Good Night, and Good Luck* through Warner Brothers by agreeing to be in *Ocean's Twelve*.

HONG KONG

Lance, Tony, Ruby, and I board Lance's private jet and head to Los Angeles, where we drop off Ruby. I kiss her, order her a car back to my house, and tell her I'll be back in a day or two. We're quickly back on the runway and into the clouds.

"Hey, Melvin, we'll get you to San Diego in the morning," Lance tells me. "Tonight, we're going to Tijuana."

"What for?" I ask.

"More research," Tony says. "For Cortez. Have you ever been to TJ?"

"Yeah," I say, "I went to a bar there one night and got so drunk I thought I handed a girl my business card and told her to call me, but the next morning, when I woke up and checked my wallet, I realized I had given her my credit card."

"Honest mistake," Lance says in a way that assures me he's done exactly the same thing. "Gentlemen need a place they can go and be themselves. That's what Cortez is all about. Hell, even Robert Kraft got picked up at some seedy massage parlor in a Florida strip mall because sometimes a man needs something."

"Prostitution is like cheese," Tony says. "It's just one of those things that have been around forever."

"I don't know if cheese has been around forever," I say, chuckling.

"Sure it has," Tony says overconfidently.

"Criminalizing prostitution increases the risks for sex workers and makes it harder to stop underage prostitution and sex trafficking, yet we still criminalize it," Lance explains, reasonably. "It'll exist no matter what, so we may as well regulate it where we can, and our club should be the best example there is."

Tony falls asleep impressively quickly, and Lance and I keep chatting, as Lance explains to me how they all met and know each other.

As we descend for landing, I wake up Tony. He snarls and growls at me with dark, black, angry eyes, and I can finally picture him as an awful, fat, drunk swine of a man to women, though my response is a quick slap to his face to put him in line. He is genuinely surprised by the slap, and it does as intended. I don't need these guys. They need me, and they know it.

We land in Tijuana, check into our hotel, go to a casino, play blackjack for a while, and get acclimated. We have dinner at Caesar's Restaurante Bar, where the Caesar salad was supposedly invented. Lance and Tony suggest I take a Viagra to get ready for Hong Kong and tell me it will be a long night. Tony is doing cocaine and offers to share, but Lance and I turn him down.

Lance hands me a blue pill, and I chew it up. He undoes a button on his shirt, so there's now more unbuttoned than buttoned. "Eleven p.m.," he says. "That's when the third button comes undone. By 9:00 p.m., you should always have the second one undone."

"What happens at midnight?" I ask, like a student learning about manhood well past my time.

"By midnight, you shouldn't even have a shirt on anymore, kid," Lance replies, sagely.

Hong Kong is the name of one of the famous gentlemen's clubs in Tijuana. It's well known to horny young men from Southern California as a quick jaunt for blowing off steam, but I've never been here before tonight.

We walk into the club, and I'm initially taken simply by how large it is. There are tall ceilings, two floors, and several sections of different performances by naked women and other women dressed in lingerie. The second thing to hit me is the smell. Smoking is still allowed indoors here, and despite the large air conditioner units, it is a smokier building than you'd find in the States. There's also the unmistakable smell of years of beer spilled on the floors and cheap cologne.

There are a few bars, so we order drinks and do a lap around the large building to find a table. One counter has two women on it completely naked and covered in foam gently wrestling and touching each other. There's a woman on another stage getting a toy put inside her by some random patron. I can't tell how many women work here, but they're everywhere, and most of them are in their twenties and reasonably attractive.

You can drink and smoke and do drugs here without anyone caring. If you pick one of the ladies out, you can tell her you want to go upstairs, and she will lead you to the back door. There are security guards and cameras around the doors, and you give a one-dollar bill to the doorman who's dressed like a valet in a black vest. He will get a robe for that dollar, put it on the girl, and open the door.

The girl will hold your hand to lead you out one door onto the street and directly into the next door, which is an adjacent hotel the club owns. You can rent a room by the hour or for an entire night. The girl will come prepared with her own lube and condoms, and for $100, you can do just about whatever you'd like to her.

After this, you can go back down to the club and have a drink, and depending on your energy levels and the combination of drugs you're on, you may want to repeat this process a few times before leaving for dinner or whatever other obligations debaucherous libertines like us in places like this have to go back to when we are done.

After Lance and Tony have been gone for a while, a skinny, young Mexican woman named Chelsea comes over, sits on my lap, introduces herself to me, and asks if I'd like to go upstairs with her. I tell her yes, and she grabs my hand and leads me to the back door. She's dressed in thin, black lingerie, black fishnet stockings, and high heels. She has a pretty face and speaks decent English.

I give the man wearing a vest a one-dollar bill, and he provides her with a robe. We step out one door onto the street and into the next door to the adjoining hotel. We ascend the stairs and pay a receptionist for a one-hour room rental. I'm informed that there are some bigger, nicer rooms available to rent overnight, but I opt to start with a basic one-hour room. Once inside our room, Chelsea goes into the bathroom to take a quick shower and clean herself. While she freshens up, I remove my jacket and shoes and sit on the bed to disrobe my socks and shirt.

Chelsea reappears with a towel, drying herself off. She looks even more petite without the lingerie on. She tosses the towel on the sink counter and joins me on the bed, helping me out of my trousers and into a condom. She appears to be in no rush, and it may just be her professionalism, but I genuinely feel like she is attracted to me and wants to spend time with me. We begin in the usual ways. She starts by going down on me for a few minutes and proceeds to ride me with near-constant eye contact. I get on top of her. She is vocal, and by the noises she makes, I am convinced we are both enjoying it.

Then she gets on her knees, and I go from behind. After a few minutes of this, I ask her, "En el culo?" I touch her asshole with my thumb to make sure the request is clear.

She nods and says, "Sí, papi."

Still in doggy position, I slowly work my way into her ass and gradually speed up. She's less vocal now but still grunting, and it is less clear if she's enjoying it. I pull out, and in a sly, fluid motion, I peel the condom off and slide back into her.

I can't tell if she notices what I've done, but she hasn't stopped me, so I continue. For some reason, my desire to please her dissipates, and I begin to think that her only purpose here is to use her body to please me. Her comfort no longer matters, and for some reason, this excites me even more. I go harder and harder until I finish.

SHIT SANDWICH

In the morning, I find Lance and Tony in the lobby of our decent hotel, which is several blocks away from Hong Kong, and we grab breakfast together and catch each other up on how our nights went, what we liked most about the club, our victims, and how we could perfect certain aspects in the Nevada ghost town. Lance leads the meeting in a way that makes me think he must be a big investor with Titus in Cortez, which makes sense. Lance leaves us for two hours to get his blood transfusion and returns with a much higher energy level.

We take a quick flight up to San Diego, where Lance and Tony drop me off and wish me luck. I have the name and address of the woman claiming to have Titus's offspring, so I leave the airport in a rental car, and Tony and Lance fly off to whatever their next stop is.

I rent the car at the airport under the name Melvin Ritkin on my own credit card like a naive, or hungover, amateur. I stop by a spy shop in town and pick up a couple of gadgets and some gloves, paying with cash before heading over to a cute La Jolla neighborhood and parking down the street from the subject's home. Her name is Emily, and she works as a nurse. She has a lovely house, more put together than I expected. While I wait for her to leave the house, I ponder how many famous people probably have secret illegitimate children but have managed to keep it under wraps.

After a couple of hours, I see Emily exit her house through the garage with her baby in a stroller, and they walk down the sidewalk. As the garage door opens, I hold down a clicker on one of the gadgets I purchased earlier, and it manages to scan the code for the garage. Emily is pretty and, from here, doesn't look like the scam-artist type, but they never do. Still, I wonder if the baby might be the result of Titus and her having a one-night stand. The garage door closes, and once they are far enough down the sidewalk and out of sight, I put on black nitrile gloves, open the gate, and sneak up to the garage.

I have to be quick. If I'm seen breaking in by a neighbor and the cops are called, there will likely be evidence from neighboring homes' security cameras that would catch my face or the rental car's license plate, which would trace back to me. Knowing how I could get caught is key to making sure I don't, but I still get impatient and make the wrong move sometimes, like anyone. Life is just about as much risk mitigation as you can manage.

The smoothest way to break into most people's homes is like this: through their large, sliding garage door, if they have one. You simply need a small device called a code grabber. Most spy and surveillance shops sell these, or you can find one online for less than $30. It works by intercepting the signal of a garage door or gate opener, so you have to be sneakily nearby when the actual opener is used. Once they are gone, you can use the same duplicated code signals to open their garage anytime you want, as if you've cloned their clicker.

I go in through the garage and quickly find my way to the nursery. There's a small, soft hairbrush for the baby, and I pull a bundle of hairs off it and put them into a paper envelope. I snag the child's tiny toothbrush and put it in another envelope.

I do a quick pass through Emily's bedroom and the living room. The house has baby toys and contraptions scattered throughout, but otherwise, it is an immaculate and comfortable home. The framed photos show Emily and her baby smiling in various settings, and there's one photo of Emily and Titus with their arms around each other. That seems unlikely for a one-night stand, but I assume half of what Titus tells me is bullshit.

I leave by the garage and use my clicker to close it and hide any evidence of my visit, aside from some missing hair and a misplaced toothbrush. I grab one plastic bag from their trash can outside and toss it into the trunk of my rental car. You can learn a fantastic amount about someone by digging through their trash. I doubt anything in the garbage will be helpful for the paternity test since it's all mixed together, but I do imagine I could get more of a sense about Emily and the baby's lives by looking through it all.

I take the rental car and drive the two hours up to Los Angeles, drop the trash at Fred's office to hold on to, and return the car to the LA airport. I go to the laboratory that Elmer suggested and drop off the DNA samples. While I'm at the lab, I purchase a full

STD panel for myself to be safe after the risky escapades in Mexico. Going home and seeing Ruby sounds nice, but first I need to go back to Fred's office and dig through some trash.

◆ ◆ ◆ ◆

A week later, my phone rings, and it's the lab. It hurts to pee, and it has for a few days. At least, it stings slightly through the tube where the urine flows, not a piercing pain but undoubtedly unpleasant. They tell me that I've got gonorrhea, that I should come in for treatment today. I tell them I'll be right there and ask about the DNA results. The man on the other end of the phone says they confirmed the genetic code from the sample matches the baby's sample. The baby is Titus's biological child. I ask them to fax only the DNA results over and give them Elmer's fax number since he actually still has a device that can receive those.

I call Elmer to tell him the news and let him know to expect a fax with the official details.

Elmer calls Titus and breaks the news to him. Titus calls his lawyer to yell and scream for a bit. An hour later, we're all on a conference line together. Titus rants for ten minutes before Elmer decides to talk. When dealing with upset artists on a phone call, it's always best to let them get every one of their complaints out first so they feel heard before you chime in with possible paths forward.

"Well, the good news is that we're going to get out in front of this and maybe even keep the lid on it," Elmer says calmly. "Sure, it would've been the right thing to do if she'd just told you the truth two years ago when she first realized she was pregnant. The best option now is to agree to her child support requests and have her sign an NDA. She isn't asking for much, and I think negotiating will just drag this out and won't be good for anyone. If we do this right and have a little luck, no one ever finds out about this. She's had two years to shit on you in the papers and she hasn't."

Titus sighs on the other end of the line.

"All things considered, this could've turned out a lot worse," Elmer continues. "It isn't your fault. She should've been up front, but at least we aren't finding out about this from TMZ, and she isn't trying to cancel you or anything. I can think of a dozen ways this could've been much worse."

Giving bad news to clients is an art form in Hollywood, and Elmer is a pro at it. He just packaged this news as a shit sandwich and gave Titus a new perspective to view it all in. Even though the baby being his child was Titus's worst-case scenario in his own mind, Elmer was able to explain it in a way that made it seem not so bad.

A shit sandwich is the only way someone like Titus can receive lousy news from agents, managers, and lawyers. He's been coddled and surrounded by yes-men and kept in an echo chamber where everyone thinks he's the most incredible man alive, and they constantly remind him of that. You have to squeeze the shitty news in between two compliments or rationales for their mistakes. That's what makes it a sandwich. For example, "None of this is your fault. In fact, it's her fault for hiding it until now. You need to pay the child support and agree to her terms. It's disappointing. But again, this isn't your fault, and it could be way worse. You're paying for this one-year-old's college tuition. You're the good guy here if you stop and think about it."

This isn't to be confused with a praise sandwich, which is just the opposite. In that case, you shit on someone, praise them, and shit on them again. It's much more gratifying, but you can't do it to your own paying clients.

"Plus, you have the chance to be a part of the baby's life now, if you decide to, so that's a positive," Elmer adds as food for thought.

"I don't want to be a part of the baby's life," Titus barks back viciously. "I'll sign the checks, and that's it. I don't want to hear the baby's name or the mom's name ever again from any of you. Got it?" Titus doesn't wait for any of us to answer. "This is unbelievable. Let's get her to sign an NDA this week. If she ever talks to the press about this, the payments stop, and I sue her for damages. That's final."

The lawyer ends the call by saying he'll call Titus directly to discuss next steps and draft up the paperwork. I go back to my laptop and make an invoice for reimbursing my costs for the rental car and testing the DNA, and I send it off to Elmer.

I go get a shot of ceftriaxone in my butt cheek to treat the gonorrhea, and I start to wonder how I'll break the news about the disease to Ruby, who I have had sex with this week and is undoubtedly now exposed to the same damned bacteria.

I can already imagine her yelling at me.

DIRTY WORK

I type "Daniel Castillo" into my private search bar and click the return button, always taking screenshots of the top three pages of results for posterity. I keep track of what they used to look like in comparison to what they look like after I've finished my crusade. Each new tactic I employ against Dan's name online won't necessarily cause a ton of damage by itself, but over time and with enough effort, his online brand will be nearly impossible to repair. Think of it as compounding interest, the same as an investment account or physical exercise. Over time, these minor additions make all the difference. The easiest way to eat an elephant is one piece at a time.

It's almost July, and the time has come for me to start hitting upload on all my separate Dan projects. Within the next day or two, he will know that someone is smearing his name, but at this moment, he still has no clue this is all about to happen, and I savor this with sinister nostalgia—the calm before the storm. I've planned out three solid rounds of allegations and accusations and have constructed multiple calls for his complete cancellation. The first round of material needs to go up tonight, so I begin going through my checklist of reputation destruction, all organized in an Excel spreadsheet simply titled "Dan checklist."

The first thing I do is launch the website www.DanielCastilloIsAFraud.com and set a few other domains to redirect to it, including DanielCastillo.com and others I had managed to purchase. Having his full name in the URLs will help them show up higher in search results for his name. I populate the website with the first three blog articles written from Fred's perspective. There's a contact section for other victims of Dan's to reach out with their own stories and connect to each other, and there's a section with a complete timeline of documented lawsuits against Dan and a detailed analysis of each case and verdict, all vetted by our lawyers.

Then I launch the first episode of the short docuseries we've made. There are three episodes, and I plan to publish one a week along with shorter clips from the episodes. I create social media accounts on each platform with the handle @dancastillofraud and schedule the first dozen posts and video clips the designer mocked up. I set up ads on those accounts to gain followers and send traffic to the blogs and video views to the first episode. Each episode will get at least two million views from the paid media within forty-eight hours of upload, and that kind of perceived traction is what I am counting on. There are a few dozen sockpuppets I've had growing for the past couple of months with myriad interests and audiences. I schedule those accounts to also share and comment on the initial content, and I pay a colleague in Ukraine to begin launching thousands of bot accounts to do the same for the next few months.

We're less than an hour into the campaign, and the ads are approved, views and clicks are coming in, and actual people are starting to share and comment. Now I send out an email blast and a press release that have been carefully worded to only include citable facts and evidence proven in courts of law and released publicly in court transcripts. If you fundamentally write the article for them, lesser journalists will happily regurgitate your findings. They need to publish news about something, and this reeks of controversy. The press release is centered on the newly launched web series. It is pitched as another true-crime channel that casts serious doubt on whether Dan Castillo should still be working in the entertainment industry rather than behind bars.

I send out another email to a handful of smaller entertainment publications where I think I can get traction. You never start by pitching someone like *The New York Times*. They'd fact-check too critically, and the whole thing could backfire. First, you get the story published in smaller publications, and you upstream it from there. The more placements your story gets, the more credibility it acquires and the stronger the allegations will become in search results for Dan's name. This is all for the public campaign. The stuff that Dan can and will trace back to Fred and me. The docuseries features Fred and other notable fraud victims of Dan's, and we make no effort to conceal who financed and promoted the series or these blogs and social accounts. Fred knows he may be questioned at some point, and we've rehearsed his responses with the legal team.

Once the initial press articles come out, I will update Dan's Wikipedia page to include a section with an objective account of his legal battles, referencing notable sources that I engineered. Weekly, I will repeat the above processes for new articles, videos, and social posts and ads to promote them all. This public phase alone will hurt Dan and might be enough to satisfy Fred's initial request, though it's not a satisfying enough conclusion for me.

The subsequent phase is more sinister and hopefully won't have any trace of Fred's or my own involvement. The fraud claims can be backed up and can't be labeled as libel. Still, sometime next month, I plan to sneak into Dan's office and plant some child pornography on his computer. Then I will start sending out anonymous claims alleging he is a predator and child molester. I'll use some of the photos I got from Oscar's hard drive and a few other people I've investigated to make it look like he's been downloading and soliciting content like this for years. Fake chat histories will be fabricated, screenshotted, and shared on social media by other anonymous accounts. If I can allege something with soliciting a minor across state lines, that'd be a federal crime and a home run. That's my best-case scenario, but I don't want to have any of the evidence be disputable, so I need to think it through.

That's the initial plan, at least. For now, I need to make sure the fraud story sticks and get at least a few small publications to share it. This is a marathon, not a sprint. The next phase will require a lot more obfuscation.

Ruby comes home from shopping and puts her bags on the kitchen counter, filled with clothes she just bought. She's silent for a few minutes, but she's got an intensity about her that worries me. Ruby pops and asks me who Chelsea is and why I followed her on social media and liked her photos after the New Orleans trip.

It takes me a minute to remember Chelsea from Hong Kong and that I'd followed her online after the unplanned pit stop with Lance and Tony in Tijuana. I remind Ruby that she was the one who suggested I should cheat on her if that gets my fantasies fulfilled, and since the topic is already brought up, I throw in the bit about having an STD and needing to wait another ten days before we have sex so I don't give anything to her. And that she should go get tested too.

I don't know how I should expect her to react at this point in our relationship, but she springs into action like a tornado and begins packing several bags to go stay at her apartment. She packs up the products she had in my bathroom, along with most of her clothes, jewelry, and electronics and Frankie's things.

"Where's my watch? I can't find it. My Chanel watch, where is it?" She looks genuinely panicked, and I have no idea where her watch is.

I shrug. "I don't know. I don't remember the last time you wore it. I'll help you look."

Ruby hurriedly checks every drawer and cabinet in the place, and I rummage the couch cushions and closets to see if it had been dropped somewhere. Ruby finds her watch on the floor behind the nightstand on her side of the bed, tosses it into her purse, and calls herself an Uber to leave.

She goes to the door, carrying three heavy bags, a purse, and a leash that's attached to Frankie's collar, and tells me I need to unfollow "that dirty whore," and demands I unlike all of Chelsea's photos. Ruby slams the door, and her and Frankie are gone.

For a moment, I feel grateful.

Generally, when we argue, she refuses to leave, as she seems to prefer screaming at the top of her lungs until she's exhausted and has been thoroughly apologized to. In this instance, I breathe a sigh of relief that I got the STD conversation out of the way and go to take a shower and catch up on some work.

CHAPTER 11

RUBY WAITS UNTIL my full ten-day contagious period ends before coming back over to my place. She goes and gets tested for STDs to confirm I didn't give anything to her, which, thankfully, I somehow didn't. She comes back with Frankie and more bags of her things and lists out the other women on social media I should unfollow so she doesn't get jealous again, and I oblige her shallow request. She even specifies comments and captions with my exes I had posted years before and says I need to delete those too. I consider pushing back but don't foresee any possible benefit from the argument, so I relent, unfollow, and delete.

I finish my work early one day and go into town to meet with Ruby and Miles on the rooftop of The London Hotel in West Hollywood. Miles is an assistant to some big real estate mogul in town. He is gay and looks like he may have been a cute twink at one point, but now, in his late twenties, he has a face full of acne scars he coats in makeup, and when Miles stands, he is much taller than the average man or woman, especially in this outfit. I have no doubt he would make an excellent volleyball player, given his height.

I arrive at lunch, and they are already seated and waiting. Ruby is dressed in tight jeans and her Pornhub letterman jacket that boasts how many subscribers she has on the sleeve. Miles is wearing fishnet stockings, a black skirt, and high heels and proceeds to tell us he had sex last night with a woman for the first time in his life. Miles is usually into Asian twinks, so this was big news. In the weeks since I have met Miles, he has changed his pronouns from he to they to her and back to he and is now cycling through them based on however he feels that day.

I am not sure whether Miles is gender fluid or still finding themselves, but we're happy to call them whatever they prefer.

I'm only sure about how close Miles and Ruby are and that seeing Miles always makes Ruby happy. They grew up together, moved to LA around the same time, and have remained best friends ever since, now both in their late twenties. The weather is perfect, and we all laugh and enjoy the conversation as we ask for more details about how Miles ended up sleeping with a woman for the first time after only being with men his entire life.

"Pussy is amazing," he explains. "I can see why straight men go broke over it." Ruby and I laugh. Once the check comes, I pick up the tab, and Ruby and I go home and watch a movie together before bed.

❖   ❖   ❖   ❖

My phone rings at 3:00 a.m., and it's Elmer. Ruby is back to regularly sleeping at my place again. She's in bed next to me with her belly showing at almost six months pregnant, and Frankie is in his place curled between Ruby's feet. I slide my legs out from the sheets carefully so as not to wake either of them, and I pick up the phone and go outside to see what's wrong. Elmer never calls this late with good news.

"Herb, something's happened. Lance just called me and said they need us in New Orleans right now."

"What happened?"

"Well, it's not good. I'm on my way to the airport. Can you be at LAX in thirty minutes?"

I wake up Ruby to tell her I have to go. She asks why, and I shrug and tell her something terrible must have happened in New Orleans. I throw on a jacket, grab my laptop bag, and head to the airport. It's early enough that there isn't as much traffic as usual. The LA airport is eerily calm—the employees and TSA security guards are the main occupants.

Elmer waves me down and hands me a plane ticket while whisking me toward the security line.

A few hours later, we're descending into New Orleans, and Elmer gives me the details he'd gotten from Lance.

One of the actresses in the movie had overdosed on heroin that night and is dead. Not only that, but her body was found by Titus at his rental house in New Orleans. The same house where we all played poker.

Isabella, who had been playing Justine in the movie and who Ruby knew was physically and emotionally turned off by Titus's advances, had been in his home and died of a heroin overdose that night. The circumstances, as Elmer recounts them, are shady at best.

As Elmer tells me the details, I get a tiny whiskey bottle and a coffee from the flight attendant and pour myself a strong early morning concoction for what promises to be a long and miserable day.

By the time we arrive at Titus's spot in New Orleans, the sun has risen. The police and paramedics have already come and gone for the most part, and only a few emergency responders and rolls of police tape remain.

They took Isabella's body and pronounced her dead at the scene. A high-powered criminal defense lawyer in New Orleans was called and arrived in time to sit in while the police questioned Titus and got his initial statement. Photos of the scene had been taken, and the remnants of the heroin supplies found near her body were already photographed and taken into evidence.

The level of Isabella's fame means that within the next couple of hours, there will have to be statements made to the press. Pretty much within two hours of her family being notified. The nature of damage control for a situation like this is malleable and hardly prescriptive. Would there be implications that Titus was involved with Isabella sexually? If so, and she was found dead at his house, he might be suspected of enabling or supplying her with the drugs. Some may suspect even more mischievous foul play, such as his having killed her or drugged her because she didn't want to sleep with him. These and other possibilities begin swirling in my head before we ever walk into the house or speak to Titus himself.

The movie studio has insurance policies against actors for situations like this, so certainly, Lance and Titus will be investigated for their part by several capable investigative teams and agencies. Legal and insurance concerns aside, there will also be accusations and questions in the press and in the court of public opinion.

We walk into the house, and there are a few investigators still present. One introduces himself as Detective Barre. He asks for our names and personal details, including where we were the previous night.

Elmer and I tell Detective Barre we are on the film's publicity team and we just flew in after learning about the tragedy and would be preparing statements on the studio's behalf. I give Detective Barre my name and business card, claiming my identity is one Melvin Ritkin and crossing my fingers I've done enough legwork for the identity to hold up when he looks into me.

Upstairs, we join Titus and his local attorney, as well as Lance, in a sort of closed library room that offers some privacy. Titus looks like a wreck. He's wearing pajamas and a robe, he hasn't slept, and he has clear signs of panic resting on his face. Lance is pacing around the room, while Titus and the lawyer are seated in two chairs by a coffee table. Elmer and I sit on a couch opposite them.

"Elmer, I'm sorry about this." It seems odd that the first words Titus utters to us are an apology for making us fly down here.

"It's going to be okay, Titus." Elmer always reassures that everything is okay as a perpetually soothing father figure. "Just tell us what happened."

"I've gone through it with the cops several times already. Yesterday, we shot Isabella's final scene in the movie, and she was going to fly back to LA in a few days. We celebrated, and she wanted to keep partying, so I invited her over. We had sex, and then she got up and left the room. I thought maybe she was taking a shower or getting something to eat. I didn't think about it. By the time I got dressed and decided to look for her, it was past midnight. I found her on the couch downstairs with a rubber band on her arm and a needle, and she wasn't moving. She had stuff coming out of her mouth, and when I touched her, she felt cold and wooden, so I called 911. That's the whole story."

"I know Detective Barre," the attorney pipes in with a New Orleans drawl. "Good man. He already told me that it looks like a straightforward accidental overdose to him. Her family has already been contacted, and her publicist will send an announcement out within the hour. All of them think it was an accident too."

"What about where she was found?" I ask the room. "Does anyone know that she was here with you? Assuming that the press will find out, how do we handle that? There will be assumptions that you gave her the drugs or that it's your fault somehow. Even if the police don't charge you, this is going to look pretty shady."

"Yeah, yeah, I get it," Titus interrupts but doesn't seem sure about what else can be said.

"Look, I think we'll know a lot more in another day or two." The lawyer is trying to wrap things up. "Maybe you guys should stay in town for a few days while we work this out. We can meet tomorrow and talk and give Titus a chance to decompress."

I ask Elmer to book us at the same hotel the film crew is staying at, and we head there and unpack.

Ruby calls me as I step out of the shower of my hotel room. She starts off cheery and laughing and tells me she just got off the phone with Miles and he had a threesome last night with a man and a woman.

I cut her off and painfully break the news to her about her friend, Isabella. Immediately Ruby is crying and asking me what happened. I tell her the basics, just about it being an overdose—no mention of Titus.

She asks me how Sequoia is handling it and says she needs to be with her. The three of them had gotten closer lately, and this could not be happening.

Hearing Ruby cry should break my heart, and I feel like I should be holding her just as she wants to comfort Sequoia, but all I can focus on is the work that will need to be done over the next few days in order to shape the story of how Isabella died. I suggest Ruby fly in to join me, as this may take a few days and having her close may provide her some comfort, and she will get to be with Sequoia. She agrees and says she'll see me tonight, that she will book the next possible flight to New Orleans and ask Miles to take care of Frankie.

I get dressed, go down to the lobby bar, and order an entire bottle of tequila.

"I've got something I'd like to show you." Some stranger has placed himself next to me at the practically empty bar, and he's smiling at me through a thick scraggly beard and thick glasses.

"Are you coming on to me? Maybe let me have a few more of these first."

"My name is Pat. I'm the sound mixer on this movie and on the last three pictures Titus was in. He likes me. Thinks I like him. I have some files up in my room that I think you'd be interested in hearing."

UNLIKELY EVIDENCE

We're up in Pat's hotel room, and it looks like he's been living here for months, which I guess he has been while in town working on the film. Most of the crew on these projects is hired locally, but certain key positions are flown out from LA because they often work together. The desk area is overtaken with hard drives, memory cards, monitors, and sound-mixing equipment.

I still have my bottle of tequila and am taking small swigs from it.

"So what are we doing up here?" I'm tired from traveling and from the lack of sleep and exhausted from being a cleanup monkey for Titus. Just cut to the chase.

"Give me your cell phone." Pat holds out his hand, so I confusedly give him one of my cell phones, which he promptly turns off.

He puts both of our phones in the hotel room's microwave and closes the microwave door as if he's about to cook them. A man as paranoid as me. He turns back to me, finally feeling safe.

"Sometimes actors will forget to turn their mics off during the day between shots. Sometimes I'll get some juicy stuff on tape that no one even knows is on tape. I've got files of Titus and other actors from all my past shoots. I've never done anything with them, like blackmail anybody, but it feels nice to have, like insurance, you know?"

I nod. "Okay, I think I see where this is going. Do you have something with Titus and Isabella on tape you want to show me?"

Pat sits at his desk and starts clicking files on his laptop and opening audio software. He turns back to me more seriously. "The last few months on this set, I've gotten a handful of pretty cringey conversations where he didn't know that her mic was still on. Same with Sequoia."

I pull up a chair beside Pat and sigh. "What kind of conversations?"

"Him hitting on her aggressively and inviting her to go out or go to his place. Him saying he could help get her some part she wanted. He must either assume that I'm not recording or that I don't care. Either way, the guy is a freak."

"I see. Anything about drugs?"

"I don't think so. I'll give you copies of all the tapes, but the one from yesterday is why I brought you up here."

"Why are you telling me all of this? Why not go to the police?"

"I know you work for Titus. I want to make money the way you make money. Just want to learn from the best."

"So you want money for keeping this quiet?"

"No, you've got me all wrong. I just want to learn from you. You know what kind of audio I might have on other celebrities. I'll help you out, and maybe someday, you'll give me some tips or kick something back my way."

I can't tell, but I think I believe him. "If this is as serious as you say, again, why wouldn't you give this to the cops? Someone's dead."

"I know what you are. And like I said, it can't hurt to have you owe me one. Plus, she's dead anyway, and what's one dead actress, more or less?"

He tells me that after shooting Isabella's final scene yesterday, his master recorder captured Isabella's lavalier audio, and Titus didn't realize it. He goes into her dressing room and pressures her into coming over again.

Pat plays the audio, and on it, Titus says all she has to do is spend one more night with him and some big role in some big studio movie is hers. She relents and says okay.

A man's nature can be shown in how he treats a woman in private, like how you can tell someone is an idiot when they fake throw a tennis ball to trick a dog. A decent man may treat a woman like a queen when they are alone together, while an insecure one may act forcefully, demanding, or abusive.

I give Pat my business card and tell him I do owe him one. He gives me copies on a thumb drive of all the tapes he has on Titus and Isabella and returns my phone from the microwave, and I go back to my room.

I order room service and wait for Ruby's plane to land so I can go pick her up at the airport. I open my laptop and read the outpouring of grief on social media over Isabella's short-lived career.

What's one more dead actress, more or less?

COVER-UP

Ruby and I go for a subdued morning walk around the French Quarter. We meet with Sequoia at Café du Monde, and she immediately collapses into Ruby's arms as they embrace in a long hug. Both of them start crying, and I back up for a moment to give them space before I hug Sequoia and tell her how sorry I am about Isabella. I then excuse myself so I can meet with Lance, Elmer, Tony, and Titus to talk damage control.

We all meet at a harbor and board a flamboyant yacht. I am introduced to a captain and a few crew members. I can't exactly tell who owns or rented the vessel, though I suspect it's either Lance or Titus.

As we embark, I hear bits of Titus laughing and yelling into his phone and laughing again. "Bobby. Baby. You know I'm an opportunity whore, but this is too much." He smiles while he listens to the other end of the line. "What's that? Say that again. I'm sorry, I'm on a boat. I can barely hear what you're saying. Oh, is that right? All right, piss off. I'll call you later tonight."

As the boat is guided out of the marina, I sit by Lance and ask about the binder he's examining. It looks like something you might have in school for a big project. He shows me, and each page is laminated with a photo of a young Latina and some basic stats about each one. I first assume they are actresses, but he explains they are virgins in Brazil and that for $50K plus visa fees and flights, he can fly any one of them up to the States in order to deflower her. My eyes pop wide as he says this, and I move seats to leave him to his browsing in solitude while I digest what he just told me.

I take a seat next to Tony, who seems strangely at home on the water, though he's in a suit.

"I like the way you operate, kid."

"How's that?" I reply.

"You get it. The same way Lance and I get it. You know how to control things behind the scenes and keep your face and name out of it. I respect that."

"Oh, thanks." I feel like telling him he has no idea. That Melvin isn't even my real name. But I know better.

"People like Titus are the ones that get the fame and glory, but they're also the ones who are stuck knee-deep dealing with shit like this Isabella fiasco out in the press. His name is on the line here. Not ours. Definitely not Lance's. This whole movie could get shelved or tank, and it wouldn't even show up on Lance's radar in terms of the money."

"That's true," I agree, though I don't feel the slightest bit sorry for Titus or his fallout from his part in Isabella's death.

"You know, one time I went to a Cubs game with John Cusack, and right before we got to the stadium, he put a full-on ski mask over his face so that he wouldn't be recognized when he walked in. Even though the man is adored in Chicago, he still didn't want to bother with being recognized, and I think I can understand that a little bit, not that I act or anything. But I can get the need just to go out and be anonymous and not have to smile and put on an act for your fans and sign autographs and take pictures with them and all that shit. I don't know how they put up with it."

"Poor guys," I say, and Tony smirks, but it's clear he doesn't like my reaction to his story.

Once the boat is out in the Gulf, we all light cigars and are served tropical drinks by the crew. If you saw us, you'd have no idea that someone we knew died last night. Luckily, we are far from any cameras or sycophants out here on the open sea.

I start giving Titus the third degree. Though I don't tell him about the audiotapes since I don't want to get Pat fired or lose a new source, I do imply everything I know from listening to the tapes, and he doesn't seem as shocked as I would like. "Titus, come on. You know you look suspicious here. Tell us what really happened. We're all on the same side, but I need to know the truth. It'll just be another day or two before the media starts reporting that you were involved."

Titus shrugs, unfazed. "I figured she liked getting high before sex, so I got her some heroin. She liked it, and we did it a few times the past couple weeks. I guess maybe this batch was bad. It must have been mixed with fentanyl or something."

Elmer and Lance look at each other and then at me.

"So you didn't do any last night? Just her? You bought it, gave it to her, and she's the only one that took the lethal dose? Don't you see how that's suspicious? The police are going to try to find out where she got those drugs," I say this with as much conviction as I can muster, though I'm starting to feel like him getting caught wouldn't be the worst outcome. Involuntary manslaughter or something. It could at least ruin his career.

Titus puffs on a cigar. "This was just a tragic accident. Elmer, we should put out a joint statement with the studio today. Let me know when you've got it ready."

"Social media and gossip mags already have photos of you and Isabella together, along with photos of the ambulance at your house here. Rumors are already circulating. What are we supposed to do about that?" I say rhetorically rather than as an honest question.

"What are you asking me for? This is your job. I don't care what you do. Tell some reporters that she left a suicide note." Titus suggests all this flippantly, but I think he's thought this up for me ahead of time.

"What does this do for the movie?" Elmer, of course, brings up the dirty business of business. "There's only a week left of shooting. How will you finish without Isabella?"

"Her last scene was shot already. That's why she was going back to LA. We may end up needing a pickup shot or two, but we can fake it with her body double. We canceled the shoot for today, and I'm planning to say something to the crew before we start shooting tomorrow."

"I hate to be the one to say it, but this could be great for the movie," Lance says something for the first time the whole boat ride since telling me about his binder full of Latin virgins, and he seems pretty excited about the ordeal. "I'll bet good money that she'll win awards for her performance in this movie when it comes out, post-humously. Just like Heath Ledger did for *The Dark Knight* after his overdose."

Titus perks up even more and smiles at Lance while Elmer and I look at each other with a fair amount of concern.

"To be honest," Lance continues, "this might be the best thing that could have happened to this movie. It just might give us the edge we need. Cheers, boys."

We raise our glasses and toast our good luck that some sweet, troubled, and easily manipulated young actress was good enough to finish shooting her scenes before dying.

Controversy and tragedy sell. Newspapers never write about the planes that land.

"Fuck, I hope this wins an Oscar. I figured by the time I was thirty-five that would have happened," Titus says. "For fuck's sake, Spielberg was only twenty-eight when he made *Jaws*."

"Well," Elmer says, both ironically and reassuringly, "you never want to peak too early."

"Tony, do you remember the day Isabella agreed to sign on to the picture?" Titus asks, apparently getting nostalgic.

Tony grunts and shakes his head.

"You were there. We all had lunch at some rooftop restaurant in West Hollywood. I forget which one," Titus continues. "Anyway, we finished lunch, and you were talking to her agent, so she and I walked over to the side of the building overlooking Sunset Boule-vard, and I pointed at the billboard of my last movie, with my face right in the center. And I said, 'With this role, that could be you. This could be your calling card. Your chance to really shine.' And she agreed. I had hoped from the beginning that I'd get to sleep with her. I just didn't think I'd be her last."

I can picture the lunch and the conversation. And I can imagine Isabella being charmed by the billboard and agreeing to be in his movie that day.

None of it is surprising in the least.

DEATH OF AN ACTOR

As is true in any career, sometimes people in the film industry die while they're in the process of making a movie. After that, their career and that film's legacy are both viewed in a new light. River Phoenix was only twenty-three when he died of an overdose. At the time of his death, he was shooting a movie called *Dark Blood*, which just couldn't be completed without him, so it was shelved.

In 1983, while shooting *Twilight Zone: The Movie*, Vic Morrow and two children died on set because protocols weren't being followed and explosives caused a helicopter to fall on top of them.

Brandon Lee was shot by a prop gun with live ammunition while filming *The Crow*. After his tragic death, a rewrite was done on a scheduled sequel to his movie *Rapid Fire* where Lee's character's name was changed to John McClane, and that became the third *Die Hard* movie.

Sometimes the shroud of mystery around an actor's death creates an atmosphere ripe with wild theories and allegations. Natalie Wood's death on a boat with Robert Wagner and Christopher Walken is notoriously fishy. She was shooting a movie called *Brainstorm* at the time, and they were able to finish her final scenes by using body doubles. The marketing for the film's release touted it as "Natalie Wood's final film" to sell more tickets, which worked.

Paul Walker's face was superimposed over other actors in order to finish his scenes for *Fast & Furious 7* after he died in a car crash.

Chris Farley was going to be the voice of Shrek and had already started work on the movie before he died of an overdose. That version of *Shrek* was more like a high school character than what was rewritten for Mike Myers.

As Lance implied, Heath Ledger won an Oscar and a Golden Globe for *The Dark Knight* after he died. Even though it wasn't his final performance, it was one of his last roles, and that emotional connection can't be separated from what you feel when you watch the film. The awards were almost a way to commend his entire career while an opportunity still existed to do just that.

CHAPTER 12

"**O**KAY, EVERYONE. QUIET down. Titus would like to say a few words." The assistant director helps corral the film crew to a central area of the warehouse-sized studio they are shooting a scene in today. There are several different sets built and decorated to look like interiors of 1860s New Orleans homes, with lights and equipment everywhere around them.

Titus climbs onto a type of small square-shaped wooden crate that production crews call an apple box to make himself taller and speaks loudly to the team that has gathered. "Listen, everyone. I know you're going through a lot. Isabella had a gentle and loving soul, as you all know. She was always approachable and loved helping others. Our hearts and prayers go out to her family."

There are sobs and tears scattered throughout the film stage. For as little as they seem to love Titus, they did all apparently love Isabella. The sense of loss and sadness on set is palpable, and no one but Titus seems to know what to do.

Titus carries on, appearing as empathetic as anyone. "If any of you would like to speak to a grief counselor, talk to Mary Beth, and she'll connect you with one. I think of this crew as a family, and we've spent a lot of time together. I don't want to try carrying on as though nothing happened, but we only have four more days of shooting, and we can't extend that without crashing the budget. If anyone is uncomfortable finishing principal photography this week, just tell Mary Beth. You'll still be paid for the full shoot, and we'll arrange some sort of replacement. We'll start after lunch today on scene twenty-six. And of course, if anyone would like to talk to Lance or me about any of this, don't hesitate. Just let us know. Let's all take the rest of the morning to compose ourselves and try to power through this. Thank you."

The speech seems to go over well. Titus begins a procession of hugging various employees and feigning a semblance of shock and sadness as he nods and says things like, "I know, I can't believe it either. She was too young."

Pat, the sound mixer, gives me a nod, and I look over to Lance and Titus to make sure no one saw Pat and I acknowledge each other. I go to find Ruby to check out of the hotel and head to the airport and back to Los Angeles.

On the way to the airport, Ruby hands me her phone. On the screen is a thread of tweets about Isabella's death, as though everyone rushed to post on social media to prove they were one of the first to know. A generation of headline-skimming digital Paul Reveres that appreciate being known as in the know.

While we're on the topic, it must be established that public mourning may be one of the most despicable social trends available, though widely employed by everyone who thinks the world needs them to chime in online when anything tragic happens. Honestly, what kind of person feels it's necessary to say something like, "I supported so and so for x amount of years and am more hurt than anyone by this." It is selfishly cringeworthy yet familiar now to be so self-absorbed that each situation needs to be about you. Mourn in silence, and don't be a douchebag who makes someone else's misfortune all about you on social media. Especially in the entertainment crowd Isabella ran in, this is the expected public commentary.

While searching her name online, I see dozens of such tweets from familiar names grumbling about how this news impacts them.

For the PR response Elmer is leading and I am assisting with, a short and straightforward condolence statement should suffice publicly. Privately, we try to help raise questions about anything other than Titus's involvement. There are always fanatical and dubious people who post their own suspicions online, but we either don't address them because we don't want to lend them credibility or we minimize them by labeling them simply as conspiracy theorists. If you can mark something as a conspiracy theory, the vast majority of the public will be happy to instead believe our narrative as reported in the mainstream news.

It's late when we land in LA, and for once, Ruby and I aren't fighting at an airport. She is sad and just wants to be comforted, so I do my best to make her feel loved. I hold her hand and kiss her cheek and tell her everything will be okay. Miles is nice enough to pick us up from the airport and take us back to my place, and he brings Frankie so Ruby can immediately cuddle with her geriatric mutt.

Once we're home, I go straight into the bedroom closet where my safe is and place the recordings that Pat gave me inside, next to copies of other hard drives and memory cards I've acquired over the years, including Oscar's.

Ruby drops her luggage and sits on the bed. "What is that?" she asks right as I zip up my computer bag.

"Just dirty laundry, babe. It's nothing."

A FUNERAL

Isabella's funeral is held in her hometown, a suburb outside of Dallas, Texas. It's on a Saturday, and Ruby and I are invited due to them being friends. We flew from New Orleans to LA on Wednesday, and from LA to Dallas on Friday.

Sequoia is invited as well, but no one else from the film is welcome, as we notice when we enter the church and take our seats. The service is private, while Isabella's fans are relegated to leaving flowers and photos and burning candles outside the gates of the property.

It's the first week of May, and the weather in Dallas is perfect compared to what it will be like in the coming summer months of grueling heat and humidity. Isabella's mother never stops crying the whole time and is being comforted by Isabella's father and other close family members.

The arrangements are refined and somber, and the pastor's speech about life and death seems to deliver on its intended goal of making the audience consider the random, fleeting nature of our short time on this planet. He quotes Psalm 144:3–4: "Lord, what are human beings that you care for them, mere mortals that you think of them? They are like a breath; their days are like a fleeting shadow."

Ruby had once told me her oldest sister had stopped talking to her once she got into the sex industry and they hadn't spoken since. She hated that sister. Or at least, she said she did, and she said it often. The rest of her family still loved her and treated her the same as far as I could tell. I'm unsure what her dad must have thought, but that isn't my place to presume, and I never heard too much about him.

Isabella and Sequoia, however, knew Ruby from school and became closer friends with her in LA, well after knowing what she did for a living. They never once made her feel ashamed or looked down on or less than. Ruby is friendly but doesn't have a lot of friends, so the few she does have, she holds close and dear. I don't think she realized how much she loved Isabella until she was gone.

This was the family they chose, and they lost a friend and sister.

After the service, we proceed to the grave site. More psalms are quoted, and Isabella's body is lowered into the ground. As this occurs, Ruby grabs me tightly and sobs into my shoulder. I hold her close and try to give this beautiful, pregnant dream girl of mine as much comfort as I possibly can. Across from me, I see Isabella's mom doing the same on her husband's shoulder, and I wish I could tell them something to give them some explanation, but I can't.

After Ruby and I let go of each other, Ruby finds Sequoia, and they hug and cry together for several minutes. I slowly walk back toward our rental car to give them some space as they console each other.

All I can think about is how the public will never know any of the questionable details about Titus's involvement in her death. Isabella's parents walk by me, and I give them both a handshake, hoping I can say something helpful to them. A day hasn't gone by that I haven't thought about the older couple at the hotel in Tulum, when I froze up instead of delivering a proper condolence.

"I will always remember how much she really loved *Animal Crossing*. You should know, none of this was your fault."

Isabella's parents both look at me in astonishment before walking away.

Ruby and I have dinner with Sequoia, and I listen to them tell stories about the good memories they had with Isabella. The weather is agreeable, so we sit outside, and the moon is in the waxing crescent phase and looks like a distant space banana, though that could be the drinks making me think that.

At some point during dinner, all three of us have a good laugh and a good cry in Isabella's memory. Though I barely knew her, I try to appear emotional from the heaviness of the situation.

The next day, Ruby and I fly back home to LA, and I continue to subtly maintain the narrative of Isabella's death simply being the tragic result of hidden addiction and depression. I send off fake quotes from nonexistent friends and colleagues that give the impression that all the telltale signs were looming in plain sight. That this was inevitable, regretful, and horrible.

Then I go to my safe and gently remove the hard drive with the materials I need. They include garbage from Oscar's files, as well as stuff from a few other perverts. I gently place the hard drive in my computer bag like it's a bomb that might go off at any moment. I place a T-shirt over the top of it before closing the bag, as if keeping it from sight will somehow shield the evil it contains.

"I've got to go out for a while. It's for work."

"It's not for Titus again, is it? Isabella's death is his fault, and you know it. That man is a monster. The movie is over; we shouldn't have anything to do with him anymore."

I know she's right, but also she isn't.

"The movie is done shooting, that doesn't mean that it's over. But no, this isn't for him, I promise. This is something else. Take a bath and try to get some sleep. I'll be home in a couple of hours. Okay?"

She shrugs, grabs her phone, and walks away to draw herself a bath.

SPY SHIT

It's the middle of the night, making this either the most ideal or the most idiotic time to break into Dan's offices in the LA neighborhood of Century City. Before working with Titus, most of my skills were focused on the digital world, with very few forays into the physical space, and now I am breaking and entering a small office complex on a Sunday night like it's just another day. In my computer bag is a hard drive with enough illicit content to send a dozen creeps to prison for a decade or two. Needless to say, if I get caught, I am fucked.

First, I disconnect the phone line. Just like you see in Hollywood movies, most basic alarm systems send alerts through a phone line. So by disconnecting it, I prevent the alarm from being sent to authorities, though on-site, the alarm may still sound. Next, I disable the alarm itself by using a four-digit code I observed while staking out the location for the last few days. All I needed for this was a pair of binoculars and some patience. By having this code, I technically didn't need to disconnect the phone line, but I like to be extra careful. After disabling the alarm, I don my gloves and a ski mask and break into a fire exit door. I take the stairs up and remove my ski mask, as I know from my homework that there aren't any active cameras inside past the first floor.

I find the door to Dan's company on the eighth floor, and it's obvious where his desk is, as it's the only one. The office is tiny, cluttered, and decorated with concert posters on every inch of the walls. I sit at his desk and power up his desktop computer. Once the machine is on, it takes a simple brute force attack by my thumb drive about fifteen minutes to break his log-in code. This is an old-school method of hacking that works through all possible variations of encryption keys until it finds the correct one, but it works, and I have access to everything.

I'm not interested in taking anything off Dan's computer. I am here solely to plant damning evidence in a way that can't be traced back to me. I plug in another hard drive and begin installing a script that will backdate questionable search queries and download histories going back to whatever year he purchased the computer. I hide a handful of new folders where he will never notice them. The folders are filled with photos and videos of children performing illegal acts that I had confiscated from other monsters. In this case, most of the content is from Oscar's laptop, and I think he actually might have filmed some of it, though I haven't had the stomach to sit through and deeply analyze the videos like the police will be forced to.

Adding the files takes about half an hour, then I power his computer back down and slink out the same way I entered. The online histories now on his device include the username and password for a dark web site for child predators, where authorities will be able to verify his past downloads, uploads, and messages.

Whereas I once justifiably felt morally neutral, I am now beginning to feel a proclivity for this sort of terrorism. I run everything back over in my mind and reassure myself I didn't make any mistakes. Now, all I need to do is give the cops a reason to pull a search warrant. On my way out of the building, I rearm the security system, reconnect the phone line, and leave without a trace.

When I get back home, Ruby is asleep. I return the wicked hard drives to my safe and quietly go to my desk. I take my laptop out and begin sending predrafted, encrypted emails that include fabricated screenshots of messages between Dan and underage girls, along with a series of claims about him being a pedophile and, most likely, a producer of child pornography. I also include links to the online forums that Dan has been frequenting, according to the information I just planted, and to the first phase of verifiable allegations that recently came out about Dan's business improprieties, to give the new allegations even more credibility. I hit send, and this info goes out to a dozen journalists and tabloid websites, as well as the police.

I'm still self-assured that none of this can be traced back to me. I close my laptop and crawl into bed next to Ruby.

CHAPTER 13

I T'S ONLY BEEN a few weeks, but there are already multiple stories circling in the media alleging all manner of crimes committed by Daniel Castillo, and each report at least mentions his past of being a confirmed con artist. These reporters were doing their research on groundwork I had laid out carefully for them. If you control the narrative, you control the story. If you control the story, you control the outcome.

The police receive anonymous tips implicating Dan in various illegal activities, some of which cite the fake screenshots of his chat histories I sent out and that were later posted and reposted on social media.

Then one day, I find out Dan's office was raided by the police, and they found all the files and search histories I knew were there. Dan was arrested, charged, and held without bail awaiting his trial. I immediately went and bought Ruby and I some ice cream to celebrate. At least, I knew I was celebrating. Ruby had never heard Dan's name once, so she just assumed I wanted to be sweet and picked us up ice cream spontaneously.

The search results for Dan are now occupied with salacious stories that he'll never surmount, even if he were to be somehow found innocent by a jury. The district attorney already has all the evidence needed to send Dan to prison.

I follow the indictment with an unhealthy amount of excitement. Another couple of weeks go by, and I read that Dan's wife of eleven years has divorced him while he's still in custody awaiting trial, and his fate is all but sealed. Even if his charges miraculously got dropped now, there's no way he's washing this shit smell off him after all this. I don't feel bad for him or his wife. I was hired to do what I did, and from my perspective, he got what he deserved.

Creating a movement isn't nearly as easy as latching on to existing trends. There is already outrage in society over entertainment executives preying on women, and everyone can get on board with tarring and feathering a pedophile. You must use power plays that lean into whatever the latest source of outrage is in order to create your own opportunity to pervert the news cycle.

It's like how one stand-up spot of Hannibal Buress talking about Bill Cosby drugging and raping women was recorded, uploaded, and somehow caught traction, and Cosby was prosecuted as a result, though later released on a technicality. What if that clip of Hannibal's stand-up spot was recorded, uploaded, and caught traction because someone engineered it to happen?

Sometimes you just need to nudge things in the same direction they are already headed.

HAPPILY EVER AFTER

Ruby makes the most beautiful and excited mother to be, and she stops wearing porn-related clothing altogether. Her belly is showing now with a sizable bump, but she carries it well. Her cheeks are a bit more flush, and she's somehow even more emotional but still sweet. Our fights have become less and less frequent and much less hostile.

When we have an issue, we talk through it. The baby likely has a lot to do with us both maturing, simply because we know we have to.

One day, I bring up the idea of marriage, and Ruby laughs it off. Everyone she knows who had ever been married ended up divorced and bitter, including her parents and myself. We don't need to get married right away just because we're having a baby together. We can live together and raise a family, and getting our relationship governmentally certified is not substantially relevant enough to make our commitment to each other a matter of record.

We love each other, and we will most assuredly love our child, and that should be enough, she says. In spirit, I agree with everything she says about why we shouldn't get married, and I promise not to bring it up again. In fact, I feel a sense of relief, as planning a wedding, inviting people, and putting on the pageantry for us to maintain the same living situation and plans for our future just seems like a horrendously taxing ordeal.

My own opinion regarding marriage is not so different. I subscribe to the notion that marriage is a construct invented around ten thousand years ago, when agriculture and land ownership both took hold as dominant forces in civilization. In order for some male landowner to know that his land would be passed down to his offspring, he wanted to ensure those were his offspring and the woman he chose to procreate with would not be sleeping with anyone else, which, in essence, sounds like, "This land belongs to me; therefore, you must belong only to me as well."

Ruby didn't exactly seem convinced by my ownership theory of marriage, but she nodded along as I told her about it and shrugged as if it were just one more reason she was right about not wanting to ever get married.

Today, I decide I will surprise Ruby with tickets for an afternoon ride in the Goodyear blimp for two hours. There are several rows of seats, but I rent the entire airbus. It's not luxurious, but it is a beautiful view and a memorable experience that not everyone gets to enjoy.

Right before we need to leave the house to get to the takeoff site on time, Ruby returns home from the salon and has some takeout food she picked up for us. My meal comes with french fries, and Ruby helps me eat every last one of them. She likes to eat healthy but never passes up a chance to eat my fries.

After eating, I grab my wallet, phone, keys, and sunglasses and start to open our front door to get us on our way.

"Want to grab your flip-flops?" I ask.

"They're called slides," Ruby says.

"All right. Do you want to grab your slides? Are you ready?"

"Yes, I'm getting them. Stop rushing me," she snaps, irritably.

Frankie is smelling a dark bowling-ball bag I had set on a chair. I grab the bag, and we leave Frankie at home while we head to our afternoon excursion.

Once we finally get there, we are quickly loaded onto the blimp and our seat belts are fastened for takeoff. The pilot and copilot introduce themselves to us, and slowly, we ascend over the city.

Moving slowly through the sky like a floating bubble helps illuminate the serene simplicity of Los Angeles from above. We float over the South Bay beaches of Manhattan, Hermosa, and Redondo and both point and smile at things we notice and recognize.

I remember that Ruby got her hair and nails done that morning, so I make a concerted effort to compliment both of them several times, as she often gets upset when I don't notice or say something about them. The nails are plastic, long, and white, glued onto her natural nails, so I don't have a genuine opinion or understand the need for them, but I tell her I like them. In truth, I have never understood why some women get fake nails glued onto their natural fingernails, but I haven't ever actually tried to understand either.

"I had a dream last night that we had a threesome with Miley Cyrus, and it was great," Ruby says out of nowhere, and now I'm glad I complimented the nails, in case that's what prompted this admission from her.

I make a frown and tilt my head back, indicating that I'd like to hear more about this dream.

"I think she would be the perfect person for us to do it with if we ever did that. To be clear: I'm not into the idea, but if it was her, I could be." Ruby winks and kisses me on my cheek.

"If we both want it badly enough, we'll just manifest it," I say.

"Okay, Daddy. Maybe she'll sing at a random Christmas party we're at again this year." She gives me another kiss but this time on my lips, and it lasts long enough that afterward, when we slowly look at each other, our eyes are dilated from a mutually delivered cocktail of dopamine, serotonin, and oxytocin.

From up here, Los Angeles is as beautiful in appearance as it is ugly in nature.

"Do you have any new thoughts on baby names? Have you come around to the name Boudica?"

Ruby snorts and laughs at me, giving me a look like she's happy about everything in life right now and knows I'm only kidding.

"It would be such a badass name for her. Think about it."

"I like the name Alicia," she says as I put an arm around her and my other arm cups her belly. "The only Alicia's I've known were really nice."

"Oh, all right. I like that."

"Me too." Ruby smiles and holds my hand. "You know what would be cute? Once Alicia is born, we should do little picnics with all three of us at the park or the beach. I would like that, I think."

"I'd love to. Let's do that." I kiss her and think about what a great day it's been. "Oh, I almost forgot. I got a present for you." I snag the bowling-ball bag and put it in my lap. Luckily, Ruby hadn't asked why I brought it on this flight.

I open the bag and produce a tiny poodle puppy. I gently pick the animal up and hand it to Ruby.

"I got us a new family member," I tell her.

Ruby holds the puppy close to her chest and it licks her face. "I love him. What's his name?"

"This is Roscoe. Do you think Frankie will like him?"

"Oh, I think Frankie will just love him." Ruby begins to cry tears of joy as she looks into Roscoe's brown eyes, and I give her a kiss. "I love you, Herb."

CHAPTER 14

IT'S MID-SEPTEMBER, AND it has been a happy and dull four-teen months since Ruby and I spent a nearly perfect day floating around in the Goodyear blimp. Our little family has settled into a friendly, middle-class-type lifestyle. We named our baby girl Alicia. She has red hair just like her mom and smiles and laughs at everything she sees. Her cheeks are as rosy red as her hair, and her playfulness makes me imagine what Ruby must have been like as a pure, innocent little child. Alicia is a happy, healthy, joyful baby girl, and she is perfect.

Alicia was born on October 24th with no complications. Ruby had a C-section so she wouldn't "ruin her vagina," as she put it, and she was pleased her daughter was a Scorpio for some reason.

Roscoe has grown into a sweet one-year-old puppy and acts in many of the same ways Frankie had.

Two months after Alicia was born, Frankie had a series of seizures that left him unable to walk and then unable to eat. Within four days, Frankie went from being functional to not, and we were forced to take him to a vet to put him down. Ruby hugged Frankie as he took his final breaths and closed his eyes. We embraced and cried for hours.

We went home to Alicia and Roscoe, who both demanded our care and attention, but for three days, Ruby couldn't stop sobbing, so I handled the bulk of their care. After those three days, Ruby snapped out of her despair and focused her love on the living.

Ruby created new social media handles for herself using her real name rather than her stage name and has left her more famous accounts dormant. We've joined the ranks of new parents who post photos of our precious child at least once a day for the rest of the world to see and like.

We've settled into a three-bedroom home we bought in the Valley, which is a more suburban, family area north of LA. We have a small backyard with a pool and are in a good school district approved by Ruby.

Before Alicia was born, Ruby called her agent and permanently retired from porn to be a stay-at-home mom, which made me happy even though it forced us to combine more of our finances. We decided to keep separate bank accounts and have one joint account for paying the bills, mortgage, and car payments. With Ruby's loss of income, I set aside a separate weekly allowance for her to keep living around her same level of spending as before.

I handled some boring, pedestrian accounts in the past year for work, nothing very exciting or memorable. A few people needed to get damaging news articles pushed down in their online search results, and I charged them hefty fees for simple campaigns I was able to manage without much time or effort. I took a break from my catfishing shenanigans to spend more time with Ruby and Alicia. Plus, with Ruby's flair for jealous rage, I wasn't sure how to explain having over a dozen fake dating profiles if she ever discovered them, even if most of them were profiles of fictitious women. None of them included photos of me, but I still didn't want to need to explain any of it.

Ruby only has a sense of what I do for work, and I have never told her any of the filthier details about my career. I had been saving up money from my biggest clients and built up enough of a nest egg for us to be sure we would be able to provide Alicia everything she could want in life.

About six months after Dan was convicted and sentenced to fifteen years for possession and distribution of child pornography, I read in the news he had been beaten to death by another inmate while taking a shower in prison. I still had Google Alerts set up to receive any mention of Dan, and when I read the news of his death, I felt an awful pit in the middle of my stomach. The headline described about as much as the article. There was neither any mention of the other prisoner's name nor any explanation for how it happened. I had presumed Dan would be in some sort of protective custody or isolation given the nature of his alleged crimes. It is well known that child predators and rapists often receive a brutal version of selective justice while incarcerated in American prisons.

The combination of guilt, regret, and the awful tragedy of the loss of human life of any type made me feel a cold emptiness for weeks. All I knew about him was either manufactured by me or stuff I found online while researching him. I saw one post where he said his favorite movie was *The Professional*, which I also love. I deleted and shut down any websites and social handles we had created to attack Dan. I deleted the web series and erased all the online evidence I had distributed while destroying his reputation. Even after deleting my portion of Dan's allegations from the web, plenty still remained that had fed off my misinformation. His memory is already shaped, and anyone who wants to learn about him will find only the results of the lies I manufactured.

When the project to destroy Dan officially ended with his murder, I felt a real sense of hollowness, like that mission to defeat him as directed by Fred had given me purpose, and now, I was left back wandering my shallow and absurd projects without any sort of worthy adversary. This was a selfish response to the false motive for someone's murder being slightly my fault, but it is how I felt all the same. I felt like I had lost my sparring partner and had to shadowbox alone now.

I had never met Dan, and I wondered if I had met him in person and shook his hand and looked him in the eyes and talked to him, would I have employed the same strategy? I wondered if I would have been just as ruthlessly effective in getting others to hate him if I knew him as a person and not just as a caricature on a screen or the spineless con artist described by my trusted colleague, Fred.

Ruby would see me as a monster if she knew my role in those activities, and so for days, while I wallowed silently, I did not tell her what was upsetting me and causing me to lose sleep. I continued to keep any talk of my business to a minimum to avoid having to defend these secret missions.

One night, I lay in bed next to Ruby while she slept, and I stared at the ceiling for hours thinking about Dan's wife and Isabella's mother crying at her funeral. Dan's wife had divorced him even before his trial, and he was murdered shortly after being sentenced. If she were to learn the truth now, she would probably hate herself for having turned her back on a man she likely loved for years. I stared at the ceiling all night, thinking about Dan and his wife and what they may be doing together now if I hadn't gotten involved in their affairs. I also thought about what Isabella would be up to now if she hadn't ever met Titus or possibly hadn't ever moved to LA in the first place. Then, once the sun came out, I got up to make coffee and breakfast and put on a smile for Ruby and Alicia as though nothing in the world was wrong.

Fred was the only person I could be frank with about how Dan's death made me feel. This isn't the kind of thing you talk to a therapist about. We discussed it only once and agreed to never bring it up again, given the implications if the news were to ever get out.

Fred wasn't exactly jubilant about Dan's murder, but he didn't seem dismayed about it either.

Alicia and Ruby are the only two innocent, constant, positive things in my life. Everything else is the destruction caused by me opening my laptop. Because of Alicia, I also get to behold a new version of Ruby. The selfless mother. Caretaker. Guardian. From the day our baby was born, Ruby made Alicia the number one priority in her life. I put in my share of sleepless nights and feeding and changing diapers and the rest, but I was also out working a lot while Ruby stayed and gave Alicia the kind of attention only loving mothers can provide.

She was perfect, and so was our daughter. And so was our puppy.

TEST SCREENINGS

Titus's movie *Justine* has been edited and screened for various studio and marketing people over the last few weeks, as well as random audience test screenings, where members of the public are shown the film and asked for their opinions of it. I'm called in along with Elmer to watch the latest cut of the film with Titus, Tony, Lance, and a handful of studio execs I have never met or seen before.

The studio's screening room goes dark, and the movie begins. I hadn't ever taken the time to read the script, and I hadn't seen any of the dailies or previous edits, so everything in the film is new to me aside from the one scene I watched them shoot on set. The cut doesn't yet have any musical score, which makes some of the scenes feel overly slow and depressing.

The story is just as dark as Titus had promised. With each scene, the debauchery and criminality increase until the viewer is desensitized to both. The two main characters are Sequoia, who plays the role of Juliette, and Isabella, who plays the role of Justine. Each time I see Isabella on screen, it causes my stomach to churn knowing that these scenes were filmed during her final days and that off-screen, she was being intimidated, drugged, and sexually abused by Titus. There are scenes of men pressuring and abusing her character that ironically parallel the actual end of her life in a disgustingly accurate way.

Throughout the film, Isabella's character attempts to hold on to her virtue but proceeds to be falsely accused, imprisoned, and repeatedly raped by men with power. Meanwhile, we experience glimpses of her sister's good fortune: Sequoia's character embraces a life of vice and continues to rise in the ranks of society until she wields a position of power herself. The film is literally dark as well. The lighting is from candlelight, and it feels like I just spent two hours in some creep's dungeon, watching as he has his way with Isabella's character.

In summation, the edit is beautifully shot yet hopelessly pretentious. There are long sections with too much dialogue, followed by brutal scenes of torture and rape, and repeat. The story is bizarre enough, but having it set during the American Civil War rather than the French Revolution somehow brings in overtones of slavery and racism along with the misogyny and sadism of the original work.

The acting is probably the film's best quality and saving grace, though the cinematography is beautiful as well. The plot is an awful gruesome mess filled with the sort of extreme heartache that can only serve to shock or depress an audience while sating the director's obsession for including gratuitous violence and sex. For the graphic sex scenes, they used body doubles that were actually porn stars who looked similar to the actors, like in *Nymphomaniac* by Lars von Trier, complete with closeups of penetration. I had known about this during the shoot and was glad Ruby wasn't actively involved in the production, as that would likely have haunted me.

When the movie ends, I'm not sure what to think of it, but the top brass in the room already have set opinions. An executive starts yelling at Lance that they'll need to recut it themselves. That the studio is taking over. Titus's version is a train wreck, he says. "It just doesn't make any goddamn sense. It's torture porn. There's no way this can get an R rating. This is obscene, and I told you a dozen times the gang rape by the priests is out. The test audiences hated that. One lady threw up in her seat and then stormed out. We gave you a chance to edit this into a watchable movie. Now it's our turn. We need to at least get it down to an R, or this never gets released. I'd rather eat the $60 million from production than put our studio's name on this obscenity."

"You saw the script before we shot the movie."

"We've had five different test audiences watch it, and they all hated it. It's confusing. They don't know what it's about other than the torture." The executive's face is red, and he's grinding his teeth.

In some ways, I agree with Titus and feel sympathy for him, at least in his arguments for the film's artistic merit. I find that most art created by and for the younger generation is about being performative and proving wokeness in order to be applauded for effeminate, progressive, and supportive positions. It takes some audacity to make something you know will upset people. Empowerment doesn't mean what they think it means, and great art rarely comes from a mindset of appeasement.

Titus, Lance, and the executives continue to argue while Elmer and I find our way out to the parking lot.

THE STUDIO'S VERSION

A month later, we see the studio's new cut of the movie. Certain grotesque scenes have been pared down or removed to achieve the R rating, and somehow, the narrative structure of the plot itself makes a bit more sense while somehow being even more vaguely bizarre. Certain long monologues have either been cut or incorporated into voice-over. The studio had a new score done, and that by itself makes the film feel more grand and polished.

It's like if you took a Terrence Malick or David Lynch film and tried to have Disney make it more of a broad, family-friendly, commercial project in the editing room while still having the same fucked-up ending with Justine physically and emotionally ruined.

The decision is made that the film still can't be commercially successful but can possibly win awards if marketed correctly. Elmer and Titus hire me back on retainer to do all I can to get the movie some good reviews for opening weekend and possibly get the film nominated to award shows. There is undoubtedly a difference between art that receives critical success and art that achieves mainstream box-office success. Somber stories that make the audience feel dirty can still win awards more easily than comedy or action films, despite their respective quality.

An R-rated film will never have as much chance of getting a massive box-office gross as a PG movie you'd bring the entire family to or a PG-13 movie that has broad international appeal. A film like *Justine* needs critical success because that is all it can ever hope to achieve.

Sometimes critics and the public aren't expecting or aware of the fact that they need to see something new over something trite and formulaic. Personally, I love the movie *The Cable Guy*. But when it came out, it got many bad reviews from critics who were walking into the theater expecting Jim Carrey to be like he was in *Ace Ventura*, and they were upset it was something darker. Even great critics, like Roger Ebert, have been guilty of this, and his review of *The Cable Guy* falls right in line with that strange preconception. Roger Ebert also shit on the movie version of *Fight Club* when it came out, so nobody is perfect, and taste is subjective.

If you search, you can also find early negative reviews of lasting pieces of art by Picasso and Beethoven that seem almost comical when viewed in relation to how the general public feels about those works today. Consider also that *Blade Runner* had terrible reviews when it came out but is now considered a classic. *The Chicago Tribune* published a scathing critique of the novel *The Great Gatsby* when it was released. Nevertheless, those early reviews substantially impacted public opinion and those creators' potential commercial success during their lifetimes.

With this likely in mind, Titus invites me back into his stuffy office in his Hollywood Hills home, and along with Elmer, Lance, and Tony, he directs me to come up with a way to ensure a certain amount of positive reviews. I am tasked with concocting a strategy for propping up the appearance of critical adulation and am supposed to translate that into a shot at getting the film some awards. Money is no object, they tell me. Neither is morality. I am off leash and expected to do whatever is necessary to help save this movie when it goes out wide.

It is from my recent boredom with work and lack of sleazy projects that I am excited to collaborate with these slimeballs and Elmer and put my skills to no good use for them again, so long as Ruby does not find out.

Being told by these men that morality is inconsequential, I take it to heart, absorb that notion, and throw whatever ethics I have left into the wind.

"Sure," I tell them. "No problem."

HOW TO WIN AWARDS

How would you imagine the major awards shows operate? Meaning, how do you personally think winners are decided for significant entertainment accolades like the Emmys or the Oscars? You might assume each voting member has one vote and the nomination and voting processes are a transparent and straightforward majority rule, but you would be wrong.

The awards shows themselves would like you to believe that everything is strictly handled in an egalitarian manner. In reality, there are countless examples and stories alleging corruption, bribery, and blackmail behind the scenes. The nomination process is based as much on politics and marketing as it is on merit and talent. If you have enough money and power, you can almost certainly guarantee you will be nominated. If you apply enough pressure, you can practically ensure winning the all-important trophy as well.

As far as the voting process is concerned, people vote for any number of reasons. They may vote for a project they worked on or that a friend worked on. They may vote against someone because they don't like them personally or because they hold some petty grudge against them.

First, I will need to tackle film reviews, as the elitist judgment of art does hold sway over Academy voters as well as the general public. I will have two weeks to travel around the country to as many prominent reviewers as I can convince before the premiere. After that, I will turn my attention to the Oscar voters.

Like the film critics, many of these voters can be bought or extorted into submission. I'm tasked with replicating my efforts on a more significant scale to get Titus's film nominated and voted for in as many categories as possible at the Academy Awards.

There are over nine thousand active voting members in the Academy of Motion Picture Arts and Sciences, and there is no way to manage that many votes by force in secrecy, but I can at least sway a few dozen of the most influential members and convince them to convince others that if we win, they win.

Voting irregularities in the major award shows have been detailed by many. Even Stephen King has weighed in on the topic in a *Washington Post* opinion piece. Of the fifty or so films nominated each year for the Oscars, many voters watch only about half. These shows are always rigged, whether I'm involved or not.

Our criteria for choosing reviewers to strong-arm include the reviewer's cachet, the publication audience, and how persuasive their opinion may be on other reviewers. More importantly, it is based on the likelihood we'll be able to bribe or blackmail them. As far as the strictly online and YouTube amateur critics, they will take their leads from the legitimate critics. Most people just want to imitate, and only real, educated journalists are to be taken seriously.

We lock in on twelve film critics who seem important enough for me to have the luckless duty to extort in person. So we begin by sending each of them digital screener copies of the film for review purposes, and once they click our link, we own their devices. It's the same type of phishing attack I employed on Oscar on Christmas Eve when I first met him. With unfettered access to a person's digital life, it is reasonably elementary to find weaknesses to exploit.

The critics we identify are spread out in Charlotte, Miami, Boston, New York, Chicago, and LA. I save as much dirt as I can find on each critic, creating a portfolio of blackmail materials. I book my flights and head first to Charlotte, North Carolina. The negotiations and extortion start off rocky, as each critic puts on a front that they have ethical standards. But in the end, I am able to convince them, one by one, they will be better off on my side than against me.

PART 3

CHAPTER 15

B y the time I get to Chicago, film critic Evan Hawke has received our rigged digital screener along with my follow-up texts sternly suggesting we meet in person. Evan is the eleventh reviewer out of twelve I intend to have in my pocket. The first ten went smoothly. I quickly divulged what dirt I had on them. They each readily agreed to my demands without much fuss.

I don't send them any details ahead of our in-person meetings, as I don't want them to have evidence of my demands. The protocol is that we meet for drinks or dinner, and I spring it on them. By now, I have my threatening speech honed down to a compelling piece of forced propaganda, and I am starting to realize critics may actually be used to some version of this dance for many films a year.

When I searched Evan Hawke's devices, there was evidence of infidelity, offensive email threads, and ostensibly, some indication he had possibly written glowing reviews for films he despised in exchange for money in the past. I send him the name of a restaurant and direct him to meet for some nice dinner and extortion in downtown—par for the course.

Evan shows up right on time. It's late November in Chicago, so the climate is brutally cold. We each give someone our coats and are given a ticket in exchange for our apparel.

We sit across from each other and order drinks. I show Evan some printouts of his financials and his text exchanges with his mistress.

"So this is really happening. This is what you do? You blackmail critics for good reviews? Did you work on *The King's Speech* too?" Evan jumps right in with a joke like he isn't taking me too seriously. "What if I'm recording this conversation? You'll be locked up, and this movie may never come out."

I place three pages in front of him, each printed with information found on his devices. "You've taken bribes in exchange for good reviews in the past. I can release all this information about you and your affairs in the next hour to the press if you don't play ball, and we can go down together," I warn him.

"Yeah? And I can tell the press about your release plan for *Justine*. I'm sure that will hurt more than just you. The studio has how much money sunk into this project? More than you or I will ever earn, I'm sure."

"Well, it would be a shame if we called each other's bluffs, so why don't we skip the foreplay?" I say and continue with a speech I've been practicing on the road the past couple of weeks. "Reality isn't what dictates our choices, but rather, it is our perception of reality that does."

"Very deep. What's that supposed to mean?" Evan says just as our drinks arrive.

The waiter asks if we're ready to order food, but I shoo him away.

"You think we're not on the same side here, that we don't have the same interests. In reality, we do share the same interests. You write a good review, and we stay on the same side. Then we both win."

Evan looks at me in anticipation for more as we both take gulps from our drinks.

"You ever hear about this island off the coast of England in 1914?" I don't wait for his answer, as I'm sure he hasn't heard this story before. "It was a small island with only a few hundred people: French, English, and Germans. And there was no way for them to get news of the world outside their island except for a British mail boat that came every sixty days or so."

Evan is smirking now, enjoying the tale, and we both take sips of our drinks.

"Well, one day in September, that mail boat came and gave the residents the news that the English and French were at war with the Germans. Not only that, but they had been at war for six weeks. During those weeks, those people on the island had all been living as friends and neighbors and had no idea they were actually enemies until they were told what side they were on and what that meant. That's why I am taking the time to let you know that we're on the same side and that this movie's critical success ties into each of our mutual successes. Do you follow?"

"I follow: you're the British mail boat, I'm the French, Titus is the English, and the truth is the Germans. It reminds me of the Juneteenth holiday, and how from January 1st to June 19th, there were African Americans still in slavery in the Midwest because the news hadn't gotten to them yet that they were free. News travels slowly sometimes, and I can appreciate you flying out here in person to do this. I don't want you to start posting dirt on me. I have heard who you are and what you can do. You've got a nasty reputation."

In addition to keeping Evan's secrets hidden, I offer him $20,000 via cryptocurrency in exchange for him writing a glowing review for *Justine*, and after two more drinks, he relents. Payment is to be made to him once the review is published. I get his account information to send him the crypto and say we'll be in touch.

"I already watched the movie the other night," he says. "I have no idea how I'll spin that garbage as something decent."

"You'll figure it out. Watch it again and find something positive in it. I'll leave you with one last anecdote: I worked with a guy once here in Chicago, and he told me he was offered the first CMO role at Amazon when the site was still new, and he turned it down. Said, 'You're going to sell books online? Good luck.' Don't make that guy's mistake. Don't be so shortsighted."

"I'll figure something out. You'll get your review, don't worry."

PERCEPTION IS REALITY

Reviews matter. Whether it's on Google, Yelp, TripAdvisor, Rotten Tomatoes, or Amazon, we can't help but trust the averaged opinions of others to inform where we go and what we spend our hard-earned money on.

There is a measurable and direct correlation between customer reviews and a product's long-term success. If your store or restaurant has an average four-star rating, your foot traffic will be substantially higher than if your rating drops to a three or lower. This can be particularly frustrating for small businesses, as negative experiences instigate most consumer reviews, and it's less common for people to post a review about a good time they enjoyed.

In the same way, you may consider several options for a product on Amazon and read countless reviews before deciding which to buy. Movie reviews have always been a crucial component in opening-weekend gross. There are now more platforms with more options for content than ever before. People must be convinced a movie will be worth their time and give them some sense of satisfaction. No one has patience anymore, and the studios have decided we no longer need stories with any ambiguity or subtlety.

Today's audience is better at detecting bullshit than any generation before, and we like to think we're sophisticated enough to smell out where some big business is trying to manipulate us. But in general, we aren't. In the past century, propaganda campaigns for big tobacco and big oil affected millions of people. The same tactics are now used to various ends, just on newer mediums.

RELEASE STRATEGY

After I get enough critics on our side, we will need to start jury tampering with the Academy members by bribing and blackmailing them in the same way we have with the critics. Everyone is hiding something, especially in LA, so I don't predict anything will be more complicated with the voters than it was with the reviewers. Anyone can be manipulated, no matter how smart they think they are.

Given that the film's subject matter is so controversial, I also make sure that some ultraconservative Christian groups and radical feminists are sent details about the movie along with an explanation for why they should be outraged and marching against it, all in an effort to drum up some backlash before the film premieres.

Controversy sells tickets, so long as the critics like it. If some group is putting out press releases, holding picket signs, and going on talk shows saying the movie is immoral and hurtful to women and they attempt to ban the film, it will only cause more press and more interest from audiences who wouldn't have heard about the movie otherwise. The backlash gives you free press, and nearly any press is good press. This is a tried-and-true tactic, and it almost always works.

Within a few days, there are numerous articles about the self-contrived controversy surrounding the plot and source material, and now, every news outlet is talking about the movie because of me. They're talking about the aspects I want them to talk about. They aren't concerned with how Isabella's body was found at Titus's rental home while shooting the film. They don't question whether the movie is any good. They're quoting top critics as though it is a foregone conclusion the movie is brilliant. The early reviews from established critics are all glowing. It's only the far-left and far-right agendas that are taking issue without needing to first see the film.

The *Mona Lisa* wasn't nearly as famous as it is today until it was stolen in 1911. That's when everyone was informed how important it is and how valuable the painting is to our society. It became something we all can agree is excellent and priceless and vital to our culture because we were told as much. You have to lean into the controversies while deflecting them all. This can be a tricky balancing act, but you can help steer what the public sees as controversial or essential about a work of art with enough skill and preparation.

With only a few weeks left before the film is released, I have one more critic to coercively seduce into writing a positive review. The critic in question is a famously eccentric academic based in Los Angeles in his late sixties who is widely admired: Roger Jenkins. Once Roger is on board, I will be able to move on to researching and hacking a few dozen Academy members to begin tilting the scale of awards in our favor. This is critic twelve out of twelve on my list.

FELONIES

Tony insists on joining me for my meeting with Roger Jenkins.

Roger is, arguably, the most influential film critic in LA, and Tony said he and Titus have a bad history with him. I tried to talk Tony out of joining the meeting, as I've already successfully convinced every other critic on our list.

Despite my efforts, Tony insists, and so we ride out to Roger's house in the Pacific Palisades together in Tony's car. When we arrive, I feel on edge about the new dynamic and worry Tony may randomly throw a verbal grenade into the conversation and blow up any opportunity we have to convince this man.

I've read many of Roger's reviews throughout the years and think of him as an educated and rational man, so I am hopeful the conversation follows the same path as the rest of my critic crusades.

Roger is separated from his wife and has two college-aged kids away at school in different states. In digging through his files, I couldn't find any compromising emails, texts, or photos, despite searching for hours. Pretty vanilla type of person on the outset, though I did find enough of his income and tax information to make a convincing case for tax fraud, so that is the leverage of the day. Anyone can fool the IRS until they get audited, and I decided to run this audit myself.

We arrive, and there is a gate from the road leading up to Roger's house. Tony rolls his window down and uses his knuckles to hit the buzzer on the gate.

"Hello?" a voice answers through the speaker near the gate keypad.

"It's Tony and Melvin," Tony answers for us both.

A moment of silence passes.

"Okay, you were supposed to be here ten minutes ago. Come on in," squawks back through the speaker, followed by a beep that suggests we have been approved for entry.

The gate opens, and Tony drives us uphill to find Roger waiting for us dressed in khaki pants and a busy tucked-in polo shirt. We park at the top of the hill, near the front door and next to Roger's SUV in a large circular driveway that still has a basketball hoop from before his kids moved off to college.

We park and step out of Tony's car. Roger doesn't shake our hands, invite us inside, or anything. Things are immediately tense, and it's obvious Roger thinks we are wasting his time, and he does not like Tony at all.

The driveway leads up to the front door and off to a small garage on one side with two garage doors catty-corner where the basketball hoop is. A large retaining wall provides a sense of seclusion in this large, private, uphill cul-de-sac, as the retaining wall is taller than any person and made of concrete. The house itself is not huge but is nice. It has a classic craftsman style, and I imagine the small backyard is probably lush with trees and grass and much nicer than the driveway to which we've been relegated.

"You call me out of nowhere saying we have to meet, so I'm wondering why you're here," Roger says, turning his back to us and opening the back hatch of his SUV. There is a bag of golf clubs in the back of his car, and he pulls it out and stands it up on the porch near the smaller garage door before turning back around to face us.

I step in. "My name is Melvin Ritkin. We're here to talk about your review for *Justine*. I believe you got the digital screener?" I say in as respectful a voice as I can manage.

"I watched it last night. I'll write the review this afternoon. It's obscene garbage. Too bad. Maybe if the film had been directed by a woman, it wouldn't be so filled with abject domination that reinforces objectification and violence against women, and the characters might seem somewhat realistic." Roger looks pleased with himself and excited to write a review shitting on Titus and Tony, though he seems indifferent about whoever I am.

"Show him the papers," Tony directs me, and I pull out the folded printouts of Roger's tax information from my pocket.

"What papers?" Roger asks as I hand them to him, and he slowly unfolds and studies the information printed out in his hands. "I don't understand. Where did you get these?"

"They're your tax documents," Tony explains. "Compared with the side income you actually received and where you've squirreled it away. The IRS would probably have a field day with you if they saw this."

Roger flips through the documents, reading each paragraph carefully until he lands back on the first page. "This is hysterical. And with this, what? Is your intention to blackmail me into writing a good review for this movie? And probably any other movie you work on? And you'll keep this to yourself? Did I get that right?" Roger laughs dismissively and hands the papers back to me. I fold them and return them to my pocket.

"That's about the gist of it," Tony says.

"I don't answer to anyone except my editor. You guys have lost touch with reality, and you're living in some bad movie," Roger taunts us. "Tony, get a grip. You and Titus are honestly the only pricks in town stupid enough to think you could pressure me into this. Maybe this guy too, I don't know. This method to extort me is as shameful as your movie."

"The movie sucks because the studio didn't give Titus the director's cut," Tony tries to argue.

"I don't think that's why it sucks," Roger leans in.

"It doesn't suck. It's just misunderstood," I say, trying to calm some nerves.

"Okay, for instance, why did he set this story from eighteenth-century France to during the Civil War in New Orleans? That makes no sense. Can you explain that to me, please?" Roger asks.

"I think it's so it would have the backdrop and symbolism of slavery. It's a commentary on racism and misogyny that has parallels with today." Tony makes a more succinctly compelling argument than I ever heard from Titus.

"That," Roger retorts demonstrably, "choices like that where you're shoehorning a cause into some preachy esoteric parallels rather than just telling the story in the most entertaining way. That is why people won't get it or love it. At best, this movie will be forgotten in six months."

"You can pretend to be the one person in Hollywood with integrity, but we both know you're as much of a hypocrite as anyone. Tax fraud is a pretty serious crime," I tell Roger, trying my best to sound intimidating.

Roger doesn't flinch or look the least bit worried about us. "So is extortion. It's a felony, and as soon as you two leave here, I'm calling the FBI to report this. I'm sure there will be some investigation, as I doubt I'm the only person you've attempted to hack and blackmail like this. I'm excited to see what skeletons the feds unearth on you bunch. I'll take my chances with the IRS."

"Now wait a minute," I say, pleading for the first time in my dozen such pitches.

"No, you've had your minute. Now you fucks go and get off my property, or I start calling the authorities while you're still here and add trespassing to my complaint." Roger looks pleased with himself as he riles himself up. He's confident and feels in charge here, on the front steps of his home.

The conversation has hit a stalemate, and I don't like the idea of him calling the FBI and instigating an investigation into me or my identities. This hasn't happened before, so I'm not sure what to do. Generally, I can find a way to convince them. But not Roger. I didn't even get a chance to tell him about the small island during the Great War and the British mail boat. For a moment, I think about what Dan's final moments must have been like, being beaten to death in prison for something he didn't even do.

Before I realize the consequences of what I'm doing, I pull out my to-go bottle of homemade chloroform from a jacket pocket and casually spray some onto my handkerchief. Roger doesn't see it coming, and within a moment, I am behind him and cupping my handkerchief over his mouth and nose.

"Hey, does this smell like chloroform to you?" I ask with a smile. Roger flails his arms up for an instant, and his body goes limp. I softly set him onto the ground and take a step back and a few deep breaths.

"Fuck." I shake my head like I can't believe Roger made me do that to him.

"I didn't know you had that, you've been holding out on me, ha-ha. Quick thinking. Good job, kid. 'Does this smell like chloroform to you?' That's great. I love that." Tony pauses while conspiring a new plan, his wheels spinning.

Knocking Roger out cold was never part of the plan but something instinctive, as the conversation was quickly devolving and it felt like the only acceptable solution. I thought it, and I did it. There was no deeper reason.

"As long as we're not on any home security cameras around here, and we don't leave any fingerprints, we might have a chance here," Tony says with a renewed optimism, looking around for any cameras planted in corners up above. "Have you touched anything? Aside from him?"

I shake my head. "A chance of what?" I say, genuinely concerned about what is going on inside Tony's head while I do a quick scan around the property to also look for cameras, as I think I'm decent at spotting them. There either aren't any, or they're sneakily placed.

"We kill him. Make it look like an accident. You did half the work already by knocking him out. It's either that, or we go to jail."

CHAPTER 16

MY FIRST INSTINCT is to tell Tony murder is a bit of an extreme means to a good movie review, but I decide against it, and instead, I ask, "What kind of accident?"

"We'll just put his car in neutral and roll it toward him and crush him against that retaining wall. It looks steep enough to get up some speed. It should kill him fairly quickly. By the time his gardener comes and finds him, at least. It should look like he had just gotten his golf clubs out of his car and was going to check the mail but forgot to put his parking brake on."

The simplicity of the plan makes me consider it's not the worst idea. Tony's quick creativity is both worrying and impressive.

"They'll investigate this. I don't know if they'll buy this as an accident," I say.

"It's how Anton Yelchin died. It happens. Here, put these on." Tony produces a pair of gloves from his jacket pocket and hands them to me. He produces another pair and puts them on himself.

"What if it's not his gardener that finds him? What if it's his kids or ex-wife or something?" I ask, trying to sound like a decent human who is resisting this plan just to mitigate any chance some vengeful god may decide to strike me down on this very spot.

"Come on, you gave me the background search on this guy. His kids are in college out of state; the ex is in Aspen. No need to try getting on some high horse now. This is happening."

"We texted him about coming here to meet him today—what about those texts? Cops read that, and we're the first and only suspects they've got, no matter how convincing you make the accident look."

"That's why you're here. Delete the text."

I put the gloves on and try following Tony's lead, as he looks pretty determined. I grab Roger's phone, and it wants his Face ID to access the device. I swipe it with Roger's limp forefinger and point the screen at him. His dead face with eyes closed does the trick, and I'm in. I delete our exchanges and return the phone to his pocket.

Tony looks around, calculating the source of the staged accident.

"So you came with a perfect plan and two pairs of gloves?" I ask, insinuating premeditation.

"I'm always prepared, but I'm not the one who brought chloroform. That's another level of preparedness." Tony picks up Roger and carries him like a child in his arms over to the wall in question, fully lifting him so Roger's feet don't drag or leave any trace of movement. Tony props Roger up on his feet and leans him back so his body is resting against the wall, with his sunglasses still on like Bernie from *Weekend at Bernie's*.

"Come over here and hold him."

Again, I do just as Tony instructs. I walk over and grab Roger around his torso like I'm giving him a tight hug from behind. I'm not comfortable with the idea that we are about to commit the worst of crimes, but a thought pops into my head, and I chuckle.

"What?" Tony asks after hearing me laugh.

"A critic that couldn't stop being critical. He was even critiquing the way we were blackmailing him."

Tony belts out a deep belly laugh as he gets a screwdriver out of his trunk and uses it to remove the front and back license plates from his own car.

"Hey, take your time. This guy isn't heavy at all or anything. Hoping I can rub some of my hair, fabric, and skin cells all over him before we do this."

Tony ignores my comment and keeps unscrewing. "Maybe this way, we'll avoid being noticed on any security cameras nearby on our way out. We'll go to the park by my house to put the plates back on, and I'll drop you off there. We're going to need separate alibis," Tony says as he casually tosses his license plates into his trunk and returns his screwdriver.

"Haven't you ever seen any detective show on television? They'll grab copies of every security camera within a mile and will see us pull in with the plates on. I'm sure there are a handful of home security cameras just on this block. Your windows are tinted and we might get lucky, but we have just as much chance that they get the plate on the way in."

"The best detective shows were the ones before there were cell phones. They just had to look around and figure stuff out, they couldn't just use texts, security cameras, and cell tower information." Tony seems to have forgotten we're about to kill a man and wants to discuss this instead.

"Yeah, well, I don't disagree, but you just brought up cell towers. Both of our phones are here in our pockets. This plan is a leaking ship, and you're plugging holes with chewing gum." I'm starting to already regret what we're absolutely about to do.

"Do you have gum? I could use some." Tony breathes into his hand to smell his breath and makes a disgusted face.

"No, I don't have any. Look, I love *Columbo* and *Magnum P.I.* as much as anyone, but they're not the cops that are going to be investigating this." I readjust Roger's body in my arms, as he's getting too heavy on my left.

"All right," Tony says. "Moment of truth. Hold him against that wall and don't let go of him until you have to. We need the car to hit him straight on so it crushes his ribs into his lungs."

Tony closes the back hatch of Roger's SUV, goes around to the driver's side door, opens it, adjusts the steering wheel just so, and puts the car in neutral.

Tony walks to the front of the car and gives one solid, violent push to make the car roll backward at a bobsled's pace toward Roger and me, and it occurs to me that we are carrying out this crime as though it were just some banal ordeal. More of an afternoon exercise than anything.

I position Roger's body in as much of a standing position as I can manage, tight up against the wall and facing the back of his car. I slowly begin taking small steps away from him and loosen my grip holding him up until I am just pressing one finger against his chest with all my strength to keep him from toppling over before the impending SUV impact.

The steep incline of the long driveway gives the vehicle enough time to pick up momentum as it plummets toward us. Roger is set squarely in the middle of where the back of the car should land, and I am in the same vicinity and know I'll have to wait until the last moment to move.

The backside of the large SUV barrels toward Roger and me, still gaining speed, and just as it reaches within a few feet of us, I jump out to the left and narrowly avoid being hit myself. Roger's body begins to slump forward, but the car does its job and hits him first in the face, which rockets his head back to hit the wall and doubly concuss him.

There is a loud thud and smashing of the car against Roger and the wall. The first sound is a violent, metallic explosion of the glass on the back of the car. There is a rough crackling, surely of Roger's rib bones breaking and puncturing his lungs. Roger's eyes open, and it looks like he sees me and raises his eyebrows as if telepathically asking me what happened while blood pours down his smashed skull.

Then Roger looks down and sees the damage his car has done. He can't speak, and his eyes and mouth are both as bloody as the top of his head. I stand, look away, and walk toward Tony's car, unable to watch any longer.

There is a faint coughing that sounds painful followed by soft moaning that lasts longer than you'd wish any of your enemies to endure. Any sort of quicker and less painful means of death would have been humane compared to this.

Tony walks over, inspects Roger, and walks back over to me.

"He's a goner," Tony says, matter-of-factly. "That car was moving faster than I thought it would. Let's get out of here in case anyone heard that."

ALWAYS CONTROL THE NARRATIVE

I wake up in the middle of the night, needing to pee, and check my phone to find a recent text from Titus that says he needs to see me right away.

I respond to the text that I can be there in half an hour.

The sky is still pitch black when I show up at Titus's LA home. The same home I had come to on Christmas under false pretenses. When I arrive, Tony and Titus are waiting for me with the front door open, and we go to the backyard and have coffee and cigars. Tony is dressed in a dark suit, and it's hard to tell if he's been here all night or just arrived. Titus has on a white hoodie and Gucci sweatpants and looks like he hasn't shaved in several days.

It's obvious Tony already told Titus what happened the day before with Roger. That Tony and I had collectively murdered the man over a review and staged the crime scene to look like an accident. The news of Roger's death was already on the internet before

I went to sleep, but just as Tony predicted, the media coverage described his death as a tragic accident.

My guess is they want to make sure I'm not halfway to cracking up and confessing to the police about Roger's murder or a host of other revelations. Still, both of them seem as calm as I've ever seen them, and I would probably be much more worried if this meeting were held on a yacht instead of in a backyard. Falling off a boat and drowning would just be another strange coincidence for a day in the life of Tony. The backyard of a movie star, however, surrounded by dozens of home security cameras and a manned gated neighborhood entrance feels like as safe a place as any to agree to keep this secret locked away nice and tight.

We sip our coffees and light cigars while exchanging pleasantries. Before our conversation touches anything interesting, one of the staff brings a man with a large musical case onto the back porch. The music man shakes our hands, introduces himself, goes into the courtyard, and takes out his instrument.

The man sets down a cello a fair distance from us, and after a moment of tuning, he proceeds to serenade us with a twelve-minute cello solo as the sun also rises. I just assume this is the sort of thing Titus regularly spends his money on. The cellist finishes and speaks to us for a few moments. For a hired musician, he is as pretentious as you can imagine, and I can't wait for him to leave, despite thinking his performance was oddly satisfying.

The cellist is thanked again and shooed away from the property. Our coffees are refilled, and now, we can have a decent conversation. The subject of murdering a film critic isn't explicitly broached, but it is implied with "How are you dealing"-type questions. Titus fills me in on the marketing timelines for *Justine* and the upcoming premiere, and he thanks me for the early reviews I've secured. Then, right as he's thanked me for one task, he begins talking about how I need to start applying pressure on Oscar voters now.

"Have you guys ever heard of the cobra effect?" I ask.

"Was that a Wesley Snipes movie?" Titus asks me back.

"No, it's Sylvester Stallone," Tony says smugly.

"No, it's a phenomenon based on a made-up story about the cobra population in Delhi, and how the government offered a reward for cobra skins. Instead of eradicating the cobra population, people began farming them to make money off breeding and then killing them. As the story goes, when the government stopped the program, there was no more money to be made in farming cobras, so the farmers just let them out in the wild, and so the program ended up multiplying the problem in the end."

Tony and Titus puff on their cigars, suggesting I should continue a bit more until they grasp the point I'm trying to make.

"It's like, 'the road to hell is paved with good intentions,' you know? It's also called perverse incentives, and it just means the solution to a problem is worse than the problem itself."

"What's your point here?" Tony asks.

"I mean, we've gotten away with some shit by lucky problem solving, but I don't know how much more time we have before our luck runs out," I say, almost begging. "Tony and I just killed someone. You got the good reviews; that's a win. If we start going after Oscar voters now, that's just more people that could cross us and more situations like yesterday that could lead to the feds opening an investigation. If any investigation gets started, they can probably find out about the stuff we've gotten away with until now. Like the cobras."

"I see," Titus responds and takes a long puff on his cigar. "I know what happened yesterday wasn't easy. Not some small hiccup. Tony says you kept your cool, and that's all you need to do. Nobody is going to suspect either one of you, and if I ever get questioned, I am a decent actor, you know. As for the Oscars, I hear you. We just need to be more discreet, is all. The plan hasn't changed, and neither has your fee. In fact, I'm bumping it up another 40 percent as a token of my appreciation for yesterday."

"I handle all these bribery meetings myself from here on. You guys just need to help me set up the meetings." I say this to make it clear I think yesterday's fiasco was the result of Tony joining me.

"Fair enough," Titus says. "There it is."

"I feel like I didn't really wake up today," I say, without even understanding what I mean.

"What the hell does that mean?" Tony responds.

"I know what you mean," Titus says, presumably knowing enough for all of us.

THE PREMIERE

Ruby and I receive our invitations to the film premiere of *Justine* at Grauman's Chinese Theater on Hollywood Boulevard. After everything I've done for this film, this premiere invite and my exorbitant fee are the least they can give me. Ruby spends the day getting her hair and nails and everything else manicured. She buys a new dress for the event, and I get a new tuxedo. We have a babysitter we trust and relax some knowing Alicia is in good hands.

We arrive at the premiere in one of a long line of limousines. The big stars will arrive last, so we are among the first to unload and take photos on the red carpet. None of the press recognizes me, nor should they, but Ruby is recognized almost immediately. She and I take pictures and questions for a few minutes, and Ruby undoubtedly looks excellent in every shot.

A reporter with TMZ is a massive fan of hers. She takes his questions and tells him about our relationship and that we have a baby together. Our private lives will be a matter of public record by the time this reporter gets back to a computer. Far from how I usually operate. Regardless, I'm proud to be seen with Ruby by anyone who cares to know that we're together. My name here and elsewhere is Melvin as far as most anyone knows. If the need ever arises, I can always change my name again, after all.

By now, there have been a plethora of positive early reviews of the film circulating, so despite whatever gut reaction the audience has, I expect them to expect artful and strange and enjoy it simply because they have been subconsciously primed specifically to embrace that opinion.

Even Ruby enjoys the movie, which makes me think it's not as bad as some of us had feared. In a scene with Isabella near the end of the movie, I glance over at Ruby. Tears are dripping down her cheek, and I hold her hand.

When the movie ends, there's a standing ovation, and the audience claps for much longer than seems necessary or warranted. Internally, I assume all credit is due to my efforts and not so much to the film's actual quality.

◈　◈　◈　◈

Two weeks later, the movie gets a wide release and is a relative success, both critically and financially. The film makes enough money to recoup investments by the studio and financiers within six weeks.

Other reviewers we hadn't blackmailed end up regurgitating what the more respected critics we had bribed said. People like to pass others' ideas off as their own instead of taking the risk of having an original thought, pretending to see deeper meaning in a movie that is reportedly brilliant. The papers are saying it could win an Oscar for best picture. It's all absurd.

I shut down my laptop as Ruby opens the front door and returns after hanging out with Miles for a few hours. It's clear she's in a good mood as she wraps her arms around my neck and kisses me. She goes to check on Alicia, who is deep in the throes of a much needed nap.

"How was your day, babe?" I ask as Ruby returns and plants herself on the couch next to me. Roscoe jumps on the couch and settles into her lap.

"It was really good. Miles says hi." Ruby takes off her shoes and earrings and removes her Chanel watch and hands it to me. "Would you mind putting this in your safe? I don't think I'll wear it again for a while, and I don't want to lose it."

"Yeah, no problem." I stand, go to the closet, open my safe, and place her watch inside before locking it back up. "Hey, I need to go handle some stuff tonight. I'll be home late."

"What stuff? I didn't know you were going out tonight." Ruby looks disappointed but not upset.

"Just work stuff. You know I can't talk about it. You know the kinds of things I do." I hope the explanation will keep things brief, but she keeps pushing.

"You know, I don't understand much about what you do really. I get some of what you do online, but I don't see what you have to go out all night for." She's asking perfectly reasonable questions, but I need to find a way out.

"I don't think you'd want to know, babe. It's better this way. Someday soon, when I retire, I'll tell you anything you want to know, but I think you'll like me more if you don't know the specifics."

She crosses her arms and makes a childish pout.

I give her a kiss and walk out the door.

◆　◆　◆　◆

Three hours later, I'm entering the Hong Kong gentlemen's club in Tijuana. I've messaged with Chelsea a few times recently and am back here to see her again, just like a self-destructive addict.

I book her for three hours and rent the nicest adjoining hotel room for us. By the end of the night, Chelsea and I are naked in the Jacuzzi together, and her head is resting on my shoulder. I'm not drinking or on any drugs, but somehow, I'm convincing her and myself of some fantasy scenario where we could run away together and she wouldn't have to work anymore.

Chelsea says she would love that. I don't tell her about the type of work I do or the fact that I have a daughter and a girlfriend waiting in bed for me back in Los Angeles.

SHARING PASSCODES

It's Christmas Eve once again, and I've been out handling last-minute present shopping. When I arrive home, I find Ruby standing next to my desk with my hard drives and memory cards lined up in front of her like a mom who found unsavory items in her teenage child's room. It feels like a nightmare from the first moment. The hard drives and memory cards are from my safe.

The ones I was sure no one would ever see.

The safe was meant to shield my dirty deeds, like a morality Faraday cage, and the prospect of Ruby finding out the truth of my dark soul has never been a serious consideration.

I'm an idiot. Plain and simple.

I had shared my debit card password with Ruby on more than one occasion out of convenience, just as one would in any serious relationship, and now I realize how lazy I was to use the same four-digit passcode on the safe in my closet. I use a different code for my phone and other devices, but for some reason, my safe had the same entry code as my debit card. This is what transparency will get you. And a lack of planning. This is the cost of love and virtue and trust.

"What is this? What is all of this? Please tell me what the fuck this is. I went into your safe to get my watch and found these." Ruby is rapidly demanding, and she is angry in a way I've only seen her while drunk in the first weeks of our relationship, though it is clear she is far from drunk.

My heart begins to race, and I have a gut-wrenching need to hide the hard drives. I take one step toward them, and Ruby steps right in front of me, blocking my access to my dirty secret files.

"Tell me, Herb. What the hell is all of this, huh?" Closer to her face now, I can tell she's been crying.

I can tell she has viewed the contents of the disks.

"Did you already see what's on those? You know what I do for work, babe. That's all stuff I've confiscated or held on to for blackmail. It isn't mine or anything." I'm trying to speak gently enough to make her forget everything she's seen—as if that's possible—but I know it's all over.

"I saw your files about the film critics. And Roger. What the fuck? Did you kill someone?"

"Of course not, babe. Let's sit down and talk." I want her to move away from the hard drives so I can grab them and run away, but she refuses to budge.

"And the videos with Oscar and Titus. They should be in jail. Why the fuck isn't Titus in jail? Who the fuck are you?" Ruby picks up a flower vase filled with roses I bought her and hurls it into the next room with all her might. It shatters, and the carpet is bathed in water and flowers. I try to touch her, and she pushes me away. Somehow, Alicia doesn't wake up and start crying from the exploded vase, and I am relieved at least over that. Roscoe is awake but hiding under my desk to shield himself from the rage.

"Babe, calm down. I'll explain whatever you need me to explain."

"Don't tell me to calm down. I don't even know who the fuck you are. What kind of sick perverted lunatic are you?" She's crying now, and it's breaking my heart. I expect her to throw a few more things, so I am on the lookout for anything within arm's reach.

"You know what I do for work. You don't ask for specifics, but you know that this is what I do. I find awful shit, and I cover it up. Most of those files are just evidence for blackmail. It could be our retirement package. I was going to tell you everything. I wasn't trying to keep secrets." I'm hoping she isn't as angry as she appears and we'll be making up soon, but I have never seen her so upset. The tears continue running down her face, and seeing her cry is the most nauseating aspect of the situation.

Ruby pushes the space bar on her laptop, choking back sobs. "And what about this one?"

The audio recording I had gotten from Pat, the sound guy, begins playing. The terrible conversation between Titus and Isabella is forced on my ears once again. It sounds even more predatory this time, and Ruby's face keeps streaming with tears as she looks at me while the audio recording plays through to the end of the conversation, when Isabella finally agrees to have sex with him again. It's audio from the day she died.

"That man is a monster, and all you do is cover for him, which makes you just as bad, if not worse. I made copies of all this shit already, and I don't know what I'm going to do with it. I think you should go stay at a hotel tonight, and I'll be gone in the morning with Alicia. I don't ever want to see your face again, or at least for a while. I don't know if I want you near my baby. With all of this in our house, you could go to jail for a long time. All I have to do is show a divorce lawyer one of these videos. I doubt it matters that you stole it off other people's computers. That might even make it worse. You're a monster."

Ruby's tears and words are making me begin to cry too. I can tell she means every word she says and she wishes she didn't. I am a bit skeptical that she was able to copy every file, but I was gone for hours, and it's certainly possible. She is handy enough with technology to have done what she claims.

"Babe, please," I beg.

"Get the fuck out, or I'm going to scream until I pass out. You want me to wake up Alicia? Do you want one of the neighbors to call the police?"

"Babe, I'm..."

Ruby's eyes tighten, and she looks at me like she hates me. "Get the fuck out of here before I start screaming, and I won't stop until you leave. If you need to pack a bag, go ahead and do it. You've got two minutes." She glances at her fancy watch.

I decide she's right and serious, and I quickly pack up two bags as she stays seated at my desk, sobbing. I pack one bag with clothes and the other with the hard drives and equipment. She gives me a searing stare while I grab the hard drives from in front of her.

I hope she'll get over this with some time and that she didn't actually make copies of everything. If she wanted to, she could likely prove what happened to Roger, Dan, and Isabella. She'd crush me with the truth if any of that ever came out. And so I pack my bags, kiss Alicia on the forehead, drive to the nearest hotel, and text Ruby the details of where I am.

She doesn't respond. Seconds later, I receive a notification that she has stopped sharing her location with me.

CHAPTER 17

AFTER A GRUELING evening desperately trying to fall asleep, I finally doze off long enough to have some horrifying dreams. I leave my hotel room as soon as I'm awake and showered, driving the short distance to our house while attempting to clear my head of the nightmares with my windows rolled down and the radio off. For the whole ride, I try to only consider best-case scenarios playing out: the possibility that Ruby might forgive me, and we might somehow forget about everything she's seen. Maybe she will just hand me a cup of coffee, and we'll take a long walk with Alicia in her stroller and figure out a way forward like evolved adults with a loose handle on ethics.

When I pull up to the house, the first thing I notice is Ruby's car is missing from the driveway. Again, I try to be optimistic and assume she's just taken Alicia to go look at Christmas decorations.

I go inside, and the sad reality is confirmed: Ruby has left me and taken Alicia with her. Most of their clothes are gone; the bathroom is devoid of Ruby's beauty products and Alicia's baby products. Ruby's jewelry box is gone from our bedroom. The nursery is missing toys, diapers, and bottles, and it doesn't look like a weekend's worth of belongings. It looks like she filled up an entire car and isn't coming back. Roscoe is gone, as is his dog food, treats, toys, and dog bed.

It's Christmas Day, and this is not at all how I imagined the day going. It's a sunny and perfect day outside in Los Angeles, and our Christmas tree in the living room has lights and ornaments and is surrounded by every present I bought and placed there. The bag of last-minute gifts I brought inside the night before when Ruby cornered me is still sitting by my desk, still filled with unwrapped presents.

Alicia was just barely two months old last year on Christmas, and I was so excited to watch her face and reactions to all the presents and cheer now that she was a growing and expressive one-year-old. I wonder where they are and hope Alicia is smiling and enjoying the day.

I attempt to call Ruby, but my phone says the call has failed, which means she has either blocked my number or her phone is off. Her phone is never off, so that can't be it. I try to send her a message on social media, but she's blocked my public "Melvin" accounts everywhere online, and I can't even find her profiles. I tell myself that she is probably just blowing off steam and she'll unblock me and call me within a day or two. If not, I will try calling her from burner phones and DM her from one of my less sleazy sockpuppet accounts. Finding her doesn't feel like an obstacle that will be difficult. I can't believe she would take our child and never speak to me again. No matter my potential crimes, I am Alicia's father, and that has to mean something.

In this era, you can block, erase, ghost, and forget someone for as long as you want in a way that is cold and brutally effective and could never have been done in the past without moving to another town, all because of our little machines.

Weeks go by, and I can't find where they've gone. Ruby's phone number has changed, her social media accounts have been deactivated, and none of her friends or family will tell me anything. I'm helpless and empty. I assume they went to live with Ruby's family in Texas, but I fear following her there will only make her more likely to expose my many secrets. I keep telling myself that with time, I will see them again. I have to. The alternative is unthinkable. Even just a few weeks without them has been constant torture, and I slide into a dark, alcohol-laced depression.

For the first few weeks on my own, I take the separation as severely as one can. I go back to heavy day-drinking. I buy some cocaine for the first time in years, finish it in one night, and have to immediately order more. Within a month, I slide down into an isolated, unkempt, irritable man who's too rude to everyone to be considered just eccentric or peculiar. I am a shadow of myself, and I have no healthy way to deal with my emotions, so I try to brainstorm ways I can hurt other people online to get my dark frustrations out.

To stay busy and have someone to take my anger out on, I go all-in on my part in digging up shit on a few dozen Academy members, and I meet with them one by one to threaten them. Either they vote for Titus and *Justine*, or I will make ruining their lives my sole purpose on this planet. I transform my depressed, depraved hopelessness over my lover and my daughter vanishing into volatile fuel for hurling ugly threats and accusations. It becomes my daily therapy, and the hard work quickly pays off as I am convinced that each voting member I meet with understands the implications perfectly well. In spite of everything, when I give in to being a monster, it makes me feel whole, even if only for a while.

When I finish my meetings and the Oscar votes are cast, I have no more seedy campaigns to run and am left feeling only my regret and isolation, as well as a burning need to know where Alicia and Ruby are and find them and apologize and find a way to be with them. Even if Ruby doesn't want a relationship with me, surely she will allow our daughter to see me and know her father.

THE OSCARS

It's March. It's been three months without seeing or hearing from Ruby and Alicia, and I am no closer to finding them. Our house is a vacant, sad mess, and I can even feel Roscoe's absence. The Oscars are always held six weeks after the nominations are announced, so I make a few final visits to producers and urge them to vote for Titus for Best Director.

Once my work commitments are dutifully completed, I take a trip to Texas and go to Ruby's mother's house and her sister's house, but no one will tell me where Ruby and Alicia are. They don't even invite me inside. I wonder if she has told her family or anyone else why she was mad at me or what I did. No one indicates they know the full details of why Ruby left me, but they seem convinced enough I am simply no good.

I return to LA and sit at my desk in our home in the Valley, hoping if I just stay there, sitting near the front door for long enough, I will be greeted by them returning home one day, as if it were all just a funny miscommunication.

With a sense of bored curiosity, I tune in and watch the Oscars for the first time in years. By the end of the night, I am stunned both by the results and how easy they were to manufacture. Titus's passion project, *Justine*, seen by some as trite, confusing, and unnecessarily graphic, closes out the night by winning three gold statues. The accolade for Best Actress is posthumously awarded to Isabella and accepted by Isabella's younger sister, who gives a touching and heartfelt acceptance speech about depression and addiction. Titus's director of photography wins the award for Best Cinematography, and Titus himself wins Best Director. It would be gratifying if it didn't piss me off so damned much.

The film's official marketing strategy has been in place for months and was run by the studio's marketing teams. I am not involved in promoting the film publicly, so I have nothing to do with that. Billboards and movie trailers are not my areas of expertise. I am on retainer as a marketing consultant, but my role's scope is known only to Lance, Elmer, Tony, and Titus, so the credit for *Justine*'s successes will be given to them. Titus will bask in his unearned adulation, as always.

I accomplished my goal. I pleased all the people I was supposed to please. Deep down, though, I know it was wrong, and I know nothing I have been through over the past year has been worth it.

All I want is for my family to return and life to go back to the way things were before. Before Ruby knew who I really was.

I shut off the television, line up some more cocaine, and pour more tequila into my glass.

I'll bet if Monty Brewster from the movie *Brewster's Millions* were a real person and I had worked for him, I could have gotten "None of the above" elected as the mayor of New York City, and I would have been incredibly proud of myself. Monty Brewster wouldn't have gotten any of his inheritance, and I would've ruined his life, as he probably wouldn't have enjoyed being mayor.

CORTEZ REDUX

Titus sends me an invite via text message to attend another party in his ghost town of Cortez. This time, the purpose of the excursion is to celebrate the Academy Awards wins. Half the town has been renovated since my last visit. It has hundreds of residents and a small-scale high-end tourism infrastructure. The clientele is strictly the rich and famous, and you will not find details about Cortez in any Nevada tourism brochure or website.

Ruby still isn't talking to me, so in order to have some company on the trip, I invite two girls I met on the Seeking Arrangements website to fly out to Cortez with me and keep me company. Seeking is a site that matches "sugar babies" with "sugar daddies." On the site, you agree to a specific allowance for the girls in exchange for companionship, which is simply a high-tech version of prostitution where the website acts as a connector and replaces the need for a pimp. It's like a dating website where it is understood the women are there to be taken care of. When things are more straightforward, such as on a site like Seeking, it is easier to negotiate certain things like not wearing a condom, staying the night, or having a threesome. It's all transactional, and none of the women seem the least bit offended by the situation. They made a profile and signed up for this, after all.

The two girls from the website I booked for the trip are nineteen and twenty years old, blonde, and petite. They are both California girls with hippy, free-spirit, flower-child energies about them, and they are easy to talk to. They're always wearing things like round sunglasses, tight flower pants, and tiny, cute, colorful shirts. They never get angry or upset about any of my statements, unlike Ruby, and that feels good for my heart health, if nothing else. They are eager to please and fun to be around.

The three of us hung out several times to make sure we got along well before I invited them to Cortez. As soon as they were naked in my bed during our first encounter, I saw they both had several small tattoos and each had both of their nipples pierced. They're sweet girls, but they're too young to know what they want. The younger one, Clementine, also has a nose ring and is slightly taller, but aside from that, they could pass as sisters. Rather than paying them each meeting like escorts, I am paying them a monthly allowance to cover their rent and bills, which works well for the three of us as long as I get to be with them a few times a month.

We've checked into our room in Cortez and are sharing stories and lounging in our robes before dinner.

These two are best friends who grew up in Los Angeles, and both are adorable and just as fun as I could hope for. In bed, they have no problem sharing and going back and forth. They will kiss each other but won't go beyond that as far as touching each other, which is disappointing. For my money, the hottest female-female-male threesomes occur when all three individuals are equally into each other and the girls will go down on each other or even be into kinkier stuff, like felching and such. I've been with these two young, skinny blondes a handful of times over the past two months, so I already know their limits going into the Cortez trip. All the same, I am grateful to have both of their company, though I would prefer if they'd be more involved with each other during the act. The grass is always greener, I suppose.

I am always curious to hear other people's tales of catfishing or any strange online dating encounters, so I ask the girls if they have any good stories from their escapades in online matching and sugar daddies. The first several they describe to me are not surprising. A man flew them out to San Francisco for a weekend once, and when he picked them up at the airport, they learned he looked much older than his pictures and was married and had kids. Even still, they spent a weekend with him at some fancy hotel while he told his wife he was out of town at a conference for work.

Another guy they met was fiercely violent in bed and hit them both until they bled and cried since that was apparently what turned him on, which reminds me a lot of how Titus was described by Isabella to Ruby and then by Ruby to me.

I'm continually surprised by how comfortable and open they are with me. Clementine casually mentions how she lost her virginity at fourteen at a rock concert on a bathroom sink counter to a twenty-seven-year-old man.

"The craziest one I've heard is from a friend of ours. We weren't there, thankfully," the older one, Blaze, tells me. "Our friend is twenty-five and said it was one of the most disturbing weeks of her life, but she made good money."

Clementine lies down on the bed to hear the story, and I settle in and pour us all fresh glasses of wine while I listen.

"She met some billionaire guy from another country. I forget where, but I guess Dubai because that's where he brought them. He paid our friend a bunch of money to act as the madam and bring like six or seven girls to Dubai for this one rich guy," Blaze explains. "So she invited six blonde, eighteen-year-old girls to Dubai. Private plane. They all had to be blonde, and they all had to be eighteen, and they were all from LA. So this guy, a Saudi prince or something like that, had each girl into his room one at a time, and once they got in the room, he would place $100,000 in cash in front of them, and he offered each girl the $100,000 to have sex with his German shepherd dog in front of him. Each girl was made this same offer, and every single girl said yes and did it and got the money."

"Holy fuck, that's gnarly," is all I can manage to respond with.

"The main girl told me that the whole weekend was, like, really traumatizing, but the one good thing was that the dogs came fast each time."

I just about choke and laugh at this last statement, but I manage to shake my head in disappointment along with them both.

After hearing this story about the dog in Dubai, I feel like I need a shower. Stories like this are why I had always hoped to never have a daughter of my own and have to worry about her experiencing such things. My daughter, Alicia, may grow up without a father and with a porn star mother. Surely, this would make a bad recipe for her to live the sheltered and charmed life I had hoped for her. She will likely experience all sorts of lessons and hardships that only a woman can.

Everyone has a price. Seeing the $100,000 in cash in front of them convinced every girl who got the offer to allow herself to be penetrated by some rich guy's dog until completion. Pretty, blonde, eighteen-year-old girls being defiled by a beast for some sick fuck's demented amusement overseas. And that's the way that the world goes around, I suppose.

After we shower, get dressed, and finish our second bottle of wine, we go downstairs and join the other guests outside for dinner. There is a long dinner table again, this time twice the length of the one from New Year's. Titus gives another speech, of which I don't believe a single word. So instead, I focus on Blaze and Clementine, and we get drunk over the fancy meal.

We leave dinner early and go to our room to have sex, and I fall asleep early.

Around 3:00 a.m., I wake up to pee and bring my phone with me to scroll and use as a flashlight rather than turning on the bathroom light and waking up the girls. While urinating, I scroll through the news alerts in my email inbox, and one of them terrifies me immediately. I finish peeing all over the floor but barely notice because I am too absorbed in the headline.

The article is from a Google alert for Titus, and it claims bombshell evidence has been anonymously shared with the press and police alike. The evidence, it says, is still being combed through but alleges that Titus, Tony, and Oscar are all likely guilty of a host of crimes. Elmer and Fred's names are even mentioned as possible coconspirators.

I can't believe it. Ruby must have actually turned over all the evidence she copied from my hard drives. In my wildest dreams, I didn't think she could do this to me. I thought she was bluffing. All the precautions I've taken in life around my privacy and security and how easily I've accessed other people's data crashes through my mind. It seems torturous that the way I end up getting hacked and exposed is by my girlfriend simply going into my safe because I used the same damned PIN as I did on my ATM card. It's tragically stupid, and I can't think of a clean solution.

The article doesn't go into much depth, but it lists possible connections to Isabella's death, Dan's false conviction and death, and the murder of Roger Jenkins. Any news before today had recorded these three deaths as accidents, and this is the first time it has been alleged foul play was a likely factor in any of them. I begin to panic. Everything around me slows down, my skin gets goose bumps, and I feel like my whole body is vibrating—but not in a good way.

It's 3:00 a.m., I flew here, and I am with Titus, Tony, and Oscar. Nevada police could show up any minute and scoop us all up at once. I feel like folding into myself like a dying wet spider, done.

I have to get the fuck out of here somehow.

OFF THE GRID

Blaze and Clementine wake up as I turn on a light and begin frantically packing my bags. They both yawn while covering their eyes and ask what's wrong, and I tell them to go back to sleep, that I have to do something but will be right back. They seem suspicious but tired, and they follow my direction to go back to sleep as I flip the light back off. I leave a little cash by the sink for the blondes to find the next morning, and I step outside to call Elmer.

He's here in Cortez too, and he answers despite the hour. He hadn't seen the news yet but looks it up while we're on the phone. He says he'll meet me outside by the big table where we all had dinner, and he emerges within seconds in classy old-man pajamas.

I tell Elmer this might be on me, that it was almost certainly my files being turned over by Ruby. I tell Elmer about how Ruby left me and explain to him the threats she made about copying my hard drives. How the exposer became the exposed.

Elmer tells me I should get out of town, especially if there's more shit that she's leaking. He'll deal with giving the news to Titus, Tony, and Lance. I should just get out of here. I can tell Elmer is disappointed in me and that he didn't know the extent of any of this beyond Isabella's suspicious overdose. It makes me feel like I let Elmer down, but there's no time for pity parties.

I tell Elmer about Pat the sound guy's files that would stir up long-ignored details about Isabella's death and that my files on the film critics would eventually make it clear we bribed and blackmailed our way into awards and good reviews. With enough digging, it would be evident that Tony and I killed Roger. It's possible,

I tell Elmer, that he could face questions, at least about Isabella.

Like a burdened father, Elmer puts his hand on my shoulder and says to me, "Just get out of here and keep running. There's no talking your way out of this one. We're probably all screwed."

Fuck.

Dan Castillo was in jail for content from Oscar's hard drive that's now in police and press custody, and he was killed in prison over it. Immediately, I can imagine being indicted on charges of involuntary manslaughter for Dan, planting evidence, extortion, and murdering Roger Jenkins. Now that they know to look for us, I am certain security footage will find Tony's car and a review of our cell phone records will put Tony and me at Roger's house at the time of Roger's death.

I toss my phone in a trash can and go in search of new transportation since the private jet isn't going anywhere with me tonight.

Leaving Blaze and Clementine in bed in Cortez, I steal a car from the employee parking lot. The car must belong to some poor fool who drove in from Vegas to serve these celebrities.

The car door is unlocked, and it's an older model that is simpler to hotwire. Under the steering wheel, two red wires control the vehicle's power and a brown wire connects to the starter. Getting a spark to jump the ignition happens about as quickly as you see in the movies, and I'm stirring up dust abandoning this ghost town and my coconspirators.

◈   ◈   ◈   ◈

It takes me a little over six hours to get back to Los Angeles, and I go straight to a storage unit I had rented years before to store go-bags for this sort of scenario. Going to my house or picking up my car both feel like impossibilities. I leave the stolen car unlocked near skid row in downtown and hop on a Greyhound bus down to San Diego with a backpack and a duffel bag. The duffel bag has in it, among other things, $20,000 in cash, fake passports, and some clothes.

It's noon when I arrive in San Diego, make my way through Chula Vista in a taxi, and find the border with Tijuana, where I cross on foot.

If you cross the border entering America, you are likely to be vigorously questioned and searched, but the process of entering Mexico from America is much easier, especially as an American. Of course, if you fly into Mexico, they will check your documents and forms and insist that all protocols are followed, but the land border has always been less strenuously guarded, especially when crossing on foot. I wear some aviator sunglasses and a hoodie up over the top of my head so security cameras have a more challenging time identifying me.

As I walk through the border center, the lines for the on-foot entrance to Tijuana break into two lanes. One lane is for Mexican nationals going back home, and the other lane is for non-Mexican citizens. The lane that non-nationals are supposed to take includes speaking to someone who may scan or stamp your passport, while the Mexican national line just walks straight through without having to declare who you are or where you're going. I walk through with the Mexican nationals with my backpack and a duffel bag, and no one asks to view any of my paperwork or identification. Within five minutes, I'm in Mexico with no evidence I ever crossed the border.

No one even checks my bags.

Becoming a ghost means not using credit cards that can be traced to your old identity. It means using burner phones, VPNs, and encrypted email accounts, but luckily, I already live like that. It may be more of an adjustment for others who are on the lam. The most difficult part is creating a believable new fictitious name and persona. The average person isn't going to draw up a fake birth certificate and Social Security number on the spot. You need specialists for those documents. I'll admit, having my alternate passport and persona prepared ahead of time is a significant benefit.

Getting a fake passport isn't terribly difficult on the dark web, but it can be too late if you wait until you need one to get one. I feel confident I can pull off the very tricky task of never being recognized again. My newest passport and identity is that of Walter Risdale, a thirty-eight-year-old from Scottsdale, Arizona. According to my new backstory as Walter, I ran a small landscaping business that I sold to retire early, move south, and live as an expat. Walter didn't attend college, and I think he should have a few tattoos on his arms and legs, so I'll get those somewhere along the road.

With the cash I brought over, I quickly find and purchase a car in Tijuana that should get me far from LA. I will find someplace south of here to hole up in for a while, far from my previous life and ongoing investigations. Not exactly my oligarch yacht delusions but close enough, all things considered.

My first destination is the Yucatán, where retired gringo expatriates don't stand out so much, especially if I grow my beard long, get some tattoos, and learn to speak Spanish. After a month or two, I will continue to drive south through Panama and take a ferry into Colombia.

I make a stop at Hong Kong and go inside to look for Chelsea. I wait around for over two hours, in case she is upstairs with a client, but she never appears, and I am unable to find her on Instagram or WhatsApp anymore. She has disappeared without me. I go back to my car in defeat and begin driving deeper into Mexico, heading first toward Puebla.

If you're ever driving through a foreign country where police corruption is the norm, which is likely anywhere south of the American border, bring some cash with you to take advantage of bribertunities. If I am pulled over for any reason in Mexico, with the threat of impounding my vehicle or taking me to jail looming over me, I can most assuredly offer the officer some money and get out of just about anything. Even if your Spanish is rough, the first and only phrase to consider mastering should be some form of "¿Podemos encontrar una manera de resolver esto aquí?" It's not too forward but gets the point across. It translates to, "Can we possibly find a way to resolve this here?"

Corruption is the law of the land, so I should fit right in. Before you judge the system here, consider that the average Mexican police officer earns less than $500 a month. It's not surprising they need to earn extra income that isn't reported.

After a few days of driving through thunderstorms and on toll roads, I arrive in Mérida, the capital of Yucatán. I am not stopped or asked by any police, federal, or immigration officials to review my documents on the entire drive, so I arrive unseen, except for a realtor who helps me find a house to rent for one month. Welcome to Mexico. The house I rent is about half an hour north of the city in a small beach town east of Progreso called Uaymitún, where I am isolated but still have access to the internet and other necessities for planning out the rest of my life. I begin growing out a beard and changing my appearance to fit my new personality as Walter Risdale.

I chose this as a midway point to stay for a month and gather my thoughts before heading farther south partly because it is reportedly safe here and partly because it is easy to remain anonymous out at the sparsely populated beaches. It is a well-known rumor of the locals that many of the Mexican cartel's families live in Mérida, and so they made deals with each other and the police to keep the city as a sort of neutral zone, where crime and cartel activity are not allowed. If you commit any crimes in Mérida, you are asking for a type of medieval discipline that only the cartels can provide, so I feel safe for now.

CHAPTER 18

YOUNG PEOPLE TODAY may blindly agree that the internet can solve most of our problems, but if you need a device and an app to help you meditate, you're missing the whole point of meditation.

After two weeks alone in Uaymitún, sitting alone on a beach drying out and meditating over my future with no smartphone but now equipped with a Mexican pre-owned laptop and burner phone, I finally receive an email from Ruby to one of my encrypted email accounts. It's the first word from her in months. At first glance, all I notice is that the body of the email itself is short, and it has no subject line.

She had blocked my phone number and deactivated her social accounts long ago, and I had gotten rid of my phone and deleted most of Melvin Ritkin's online presence. I guess email was the only way she knew she could still reach me.

I begin reading her note, and I have to stop and look away after the first sentence. I take several deep breaths and mentally prepare myself for the rest of the hurt with a healthy swig of mescal.

Her email simply informs me that she and Alicia are indeed in Texas and staying at her mom's house. She says that Alicia is happy and safe. She says that she is sorry for all the drama but that she did what she felt was right. That she misses me but that she can't be with such a horrible criminal, and that she hopes I seek professional help and don't get into too much trouble. The note ends by saying she has already applied for sole custody of Alicia and is likely to get it with my criminal allegations and disappearance.

I type back a quick email response asking if we can speak on the phone. I say she and Alicia are the best things that have ever happened to me, and I hit send.

I stare at the cheap laptop, hoping for an immediate response, and a few minutes later, one downloads into my inbox. Ruby doesn't send any phone number to contact her with or even respond to anything I said. She simply asks where I am now. It makes me imagine police standing over her shoulder, hoping I'll give myself away. If they were, surely they would be on board with a phone call so they could attempt to trace it.

I can't decide if she's playing me or not, so I simply respond to the thread with a one-word reply: Pineapple.

WHAT YOU READ IN THE PAPERS

Every once in a while, I manage to make myself go online and read about what has transpired since I escaped LA, but most days, I try avoiding the internet altogether. The news makes my stomach turn, and I have been throwing up enough just from detoxing from my short-lived cocaine relapse, as I haven't inhaled any since crossing the border.

Titus, Tony, and Oscar have all been arrested and charged with various crimes. Tony is charged with the murder of Roger Jenkins. Oscar is charged with soliciting minors, rape, and possession and creation of child pornography. Titus's charges range from conspiracy to commit murder to possessing child pornography and indirectly causing Isabella's death. Some newspapers have already pieced together enough of the evidence to all three deaths to make for gripping front-page headlines.

I'm surprised by how quickly everything has changed, and part of me is obviously glad they got what was coming to them while I got away. I had almost envied Titus, yet I always wanted to see him ruined. Tony and Oscar both deserve to have their lives stripped away as well, but I hope nothing impacts Elmer too negatively. Fred has been absent from the news, but I assume he's on a similar path as mine.

The Academy of Motion Picture Arts and Sciences publicly stripped the statue for Best Director from Titus for his part in Isabella's death. He has become the subject of a host of other accusations from other women and actresses who allege other past crimes by him, most of which involve intimidation and rape. Some articles focus on the evidence of bribery and blackmail against the film critics. There is widespread outrage and backlash, which includes boycotting *Justine* and the studio that produced it. It has been months since the film's theatrical run, which had already made a profit, so I don't see much point in the boycott. It's like focusing a movement that could potentially effect real change onto something like convincing people to stop watching Kevin Spacey's projects after he was canceled. At the same time, those same people still listen to R. Kelly and Michael Jackson songs because boycotting a movie and not watching it again after already seeing it isn't as hard as abandoning music that has an emotional connection to your youth.

An unknown coconspirator is mentioned in some of the articles and court documents, but none of my aliases are listed anywhere publicly yet. There is no doubt in my mind that the authorities back in America are after me.

BROKEN HOMES

Another week goes by, and I am approaching the end of my month-long lease in Uaymitún, so I have to decide where to go next. According to the maps, I could make it to Belize City in around seven hours of driving, plus another hour or two to cross the border. If I bring my cheap used car into other countries, I will likely have to declare the vehicle and obtain car insurance in each individual country. This will not be hard, but it will mean each border crossing should be on its own day rather than rushing through to Panama as quickly as possible.

I hardly sleep at all lately, and I talk to myself most days like I'm Tom Hanks in *Cast Away*. I am on the run and consider that there are only two options before me: I can either keep running and probably never see Alicia or Ruby ever again, or I can turn myself in and most certainly go to jail. Ruby would likely keep my name hidden from Alicia for a while either way. It may be ten years before she ever asks about me, and by then, Ruby could be married and just tell Alicia that man is her father. Still, since my name is on Alicia's birth certificate, it is possible my daughter could one day want to meet me, forgive me, and visit me either in jail or after my theoretical release. With the number of possible charges and overwhelming evidence tied to three deaths and other offenses, I am not confident I would ever gain parole.

Another option would be to kill myself, but I figure I can always do that later. I'm still in my late thirties, after all. Robin Williams was sixty-three when he ended it all. Anthony Bourdain was sixty-one. Hunter S. Thompson was sixty-seven. I remind myself that suicide can always be an option in another twenty-five years or so. That choice will always remain, but I still have a few better alternatives right now.

I love my daughter more than anything in this world, and despite Ruby turning me in, I can't help but still be in love with her too. That said, prison is hardly ever the right choice, hardly still at this moment.

So I decide to keep running.

Many nights, I wake up covered in sweat well before the sunrise, stirred awake by strange dreams and shaky withdrawals. I walk out to the beach and watch the sun being born, and I am relieved and calmed by the consistency.

In one of the dreams I remember having last night, the world was ending. A giant tsunami came for Los Angeles while I was trying to save Ruby and Alicia by taking them via Jet Ski to a spaceship that was preparing to launch. The spacecraft was apparently our only option for survival, but there were countless obstacles in our path to get there before it took off. The effects and explosions and sheer panic of the dream left me with little understanding of what it might mean, and I thought about it while watching this morning's sunrise. The whole ordeal seemed more like a Dwayne Johnson movie than anything that could signify a deeper subconscious meaning, so I brushed it off and made coffee.

In Mexico, I have tried to adapt to this slower pace and respect the local culture, but the ambitious and conniving American in me is taking a while to adapt.

Down here, there is enough humility and kindness to make up for the overwhelming lack of either back in Los Angeles, the city that will suffocate you in ego. Businesses in America make a business out of keeping people busy. The American attitude is geared to live to work. Let's have meetings about the meetings. We'd like to know that you're online on Slack at all times and using our project management apps and accounting for each hour of work. We will even hire professionals whose job it will be to make sure you are being productive. If you don't respond to an email within an hour, you may as well pack up and head home because you don't care enough about the enterprise.

As selfish and embarrassing as it is to admit, I begin to feel like I am better off alone. I'm more myself. Less happy but also more myself, and that seems like plenty.

Loneliness is good. It's also necessary. At least, that's what the lonely tell ourselves.

The truth in my heart is real self-hate over my indifference. It's a specific disappointment in my poor, pathetic, desperate, irredeemable soul. We never got to do the family picnics that Ruby had yearned for and for which I too now so desperately wish.

In *Understanding Media: The Extensions of Man*, one of the points that Marshall McLuhan makes is that most people think about driving and looking in a rearview mirror as an analogy for looking behind them and into the past. Many people assume there is little to be gained from looking into the past when we can be so thoroughly entertained by the present or dazzled by speculating about the future. McLuhan explains how you can see cars coming up behind you in a rearview mirror, which actually shows you what is coming. Looking back can always inform what is coming, so I look back often. I think about what has transpired over my life and what regrets I have from the past few years. I think about how much I miss my newly formed family, and I think about the trouble I would be in if I were caught now.

No one has asked me for any paperwork in Mexico, but if I continue driving south, I will assuredly have to use a fake passport. I'll have to risk opening a bank account somewhere to access my offshore and crypto funds. If I can change my personality and appearance enough to make my new fake identity work, I may be able to lay low and remain hidden.

Since my only real option is to continue south, I begin to draw up a route to take me to Colombia, through Venezuela, and into Brazil. If I stay long enough, have a steady income, and have no criminal issues, I could find a local lawyer to help me through the hoops of naturalizing in Brazil and becoming a citizen. Even though Venezuela and Brazil have extradition treaties with the United States, they will never deport one of their own citizens, so I mark getting citizenship in either country as my next primary goal, followed by renouncing my US citizenship. Getting there is step one. Naturalizing will likely take me a few years to complete.

I'll find some quaint beach town that's cheap and has tourism. I could start a smoothie and coconut stand on the beach or rent out Jet Skis by the hour to tourists. I could fish and sell my catch to local restaurants and families. I will do something that does not involve a computer. I will find a way to get off the grid permanently. I will attain a permanent sunburn and free my mind of my digital and legal spiderwebs.

Technically, I do have enough money and crypto stashed away in offshore and untraceable accounts to live comfortably in South America, but a person needs something to do. If I ever hope to become a citizen, I will need to show some source of income and check all the boxes as a contributing member of society. I should probably get plastic surgery done once I'm in Brazil to change my nose and chin enough so no facial recognition software ever picks me up. I should also either gain thirty pounds or lose about twenty. I haven't decided which, though overeating and gaining weight sounds more enjoyable at this moment.

The easiest way to eat an elephant is one piece at a time, so I set my sights first on getting to Belize.

CHAPTER 19

MY DRIVE TO Uaymitún took me around sixty hours from San Diego. It could have been quicker, I suppose, but I got lost several times. The toll roads were well maintained through most of Mexico and easy to navigate. However, the cities where I stopped to sleep each night were consistently jumbled messes of honking and aggressive driving where I always got flustered and turned around and made several wrong maneuvers that inevitably set my timetable back.

Uaymitún is a fifteen-minute drive from Progreso, the closest touristy beach town in the area. This means I can remain far away from Progreso's four-mile-long pier, the largest in the world, and the condescending gringos disembarking from cruise ships there. My goal is to keep away from anyone who might recognize or even notice me. I am not a tourist here. I am a Yucateco, despite my sunburn.

The drive from here straight to Panama City would take another forty-five hours or so. My car, an old Honda I purchased in Tijuana, is holding firm and was impressive as an investment decision. In Mérida, on my way into Uaymitún, I got the oil, brakes, and tires changed, and the car seemed capable of going another hundred thousand miles if I needed it to. I plan to stay two nights at each stop hereon to break up the driving and border crossings until I reach my destination. Once in Colombia, I intend to stay for a few months before crossing into Brazil.

I could make it to Belize the first day of driving, to Guatemala on the next. El Salvador, Honduras, Nicaragua, Costa Rica, and Panama would follow a similar pattern. In Panama, I would likely ditch the Honda, as there are no roads going from Panama to Colombia through the Darien Gap. I would have to deliver the car in a shipping container, which would likely cost more than the vehicle itself originally did in Tijuana. Once in Colombia, I could always acquire another car. Something cheap that could at least make it across another border or two.

If driving through Mexico as a foreigner, the biggest piece of advice you will be given is to drive during the day since cartel and crime activity are more common at night. In other countries farther south, if your Spanish or Portuguese is not excellent, you can invariably run into a host of issues, so I listen to a series of Spanish education lessons in the car during the drive to Belize, and I make an effort to practice almost every day while driving.

Most days, I wake up from nightmares covered in sweat at around 3:00 a.m., knowing I'll never get to go back to America and I'll probably never get to see Ruby or Alicia ever again. Alicia could be saying words by now, for all I know. There is a gut-wrenching feeling that only parents can know or imagine when your baby is unwillingly removed from your custody. I made my own choices, but I am pained by the pit in my gut anytime I remember she is growing up without me.

Most days in Uaymitún, I start the day by drinking a series of four margaritas by noon. That is followed by about fifteen beers and eating a torta, and I top that off with three mescals, which puts me to sleep by 8:00 p.m. each night like clockwork. The merciless mosquitoes leave my body covered in bumps each day. The kind of mosquitoes that will sting you through a shirt or anything else in their way. They have only one purpose, and that is to feed on you. As I grow accustomed to my new climate, I begin ritually covering myself in citronella spray, which helps some, but there's always some exposed part of my body that gets swarmed with bites. There could be three inches on my left calf left untreated, and that three square inches would later be the picture of chickenpox.

In Uaymitún, each day, I think about how all the pink flamingos on the swampy south side of the peninsula always have their heads plunged underwater as if they are trying to shield their eyes from everything above level. I know they are eating, and there is some purpose behind their submerged skulls, but they always seem happy to look down under the surface, and I can relate to that. I relate to the flamingos the same way I relate to the beach dogs that have no home but scour the hot paradise for food each day. I too need to be alone and outside and near the water. Always too wanting to be inside somewhere comfortable with company but knowing that being alone in the sun is what I truly deserve.

By the time I leave Mexico, I have tried to stay focused on getting to Colombia as quickly as possible.

In the span of five successfully uneventful days of driving, I arrive in Honduras.

THE SADDEST JERK-OFF

I check into a cheap hotel in the poorer side of town in Tegucigalpa, the capital city of Honduras, and try to relax for a while. I can't stop thinking about how much I miss my baby and how I will probably not ever get to see her again, whether I'm in prison or on the run.

I sleep for about an hour.

At 12:30 a.m., my eyes open, and I know I won't be able to go back to sleep.

I lie on the cheap, springy mattress and stare at the moldy ceiling, unable to sleep, and for whatever reason, the song "Two Piña Coladas" is stuck in my head, repeating with the chorus over and over. What is this fucking soundtrack stuck in my brain? The heat, isolation, and stress, along with the exhaustion of driving under the constant fear of being discovered, all must be combining to melt my brain.

I have been alone and stressed for months now, yearning for love and family. And for their sweet smiles. The gentle touch of a woman can go a long way to keeping a man sane, and taking her and his only child from him does exactly the opposite.

Once I am tired enough of staring at the ceiling, I decide that I should jerk off, hoping it will help me sleep. I search for threesome videos on a porn site on my laptop, and three different videos of Ruby pop up on the first page of Pornhub's search results, as my VPN says I am in America. Out of twelve video thumbnails presented, she is in three of them, and they aren't clips from the same scene.

Ruby's face in the thumbnail photos looks so sweet and innocent yet so sinister, and I miss that deadly combination she had been born with. Not just the sex but *her*. Everything about her and about our child who I didn't ever intend to abandon. In our time together, I had envisioned our future as us being just as wild and crazy in our old age but still together. Just a little grayer and more wrinkly.

I hadn't watched her earlier work with other guys since we started dating, but something makes me click on one that has Ruby's face in the thumbnail, and after that, I watch two more videos of her with three other girls sharing one guy. I skip forward on the last one and torture myself with a hollowness of longing and jealousy and rage.

She's riding the man in the reverse-cowgirl position while the other two girls watch from nearby, and she comes so hard and screams, shakes, and quivers in a way that forces him to pause, as if she is a fighter tapping out. I know she's not acting, and I know I never made her feel like that.

Her nails, tan, hair, and eyelashes may be fake but not the moans. That I can tell.

At the end of the video, the guy finishes inside her, and she says, "Oh, it's so warm," and I feel a tingling sensation in my back that seers with regret right before I finish on my hand and stomach. The whole operation ends up making me feel like a self-imposed cuck, a sad disgrace that will never feel the satisfaction any of those male performers had experienced. I finish with a dose of kinky taboo curiosity and a stronger sense of jealousy—equal parts titillating and shameful.

It was the saddest jerk-off session of all time.

I get up out of bed, clean myself off, and pour a drink. I start looking at the route to Nicaragua to try to get my mind off my lost family. But I can't. The more I try not to think about them, the more I'm forced to focus on them. My mind races through possible scenarios. I could set up a few dozen fake profiles on dating apps in the Dallas area and try to catfish Ruby for a chance to chat with her again. I could try sending phishing links to her email in order to get access to her cloud accounts and see recent pictures of Alicia. But Ruby is too wise to my methods, and I doubt it would be easy to fool her at this point, so I set aside my notions and decide to make coffee and start the day.

NICARAGUAN TRAVESTY

I stop for two nights in Managua, Nicaragua, and check into a decent hotel. I say decent only because there is internet and running water and a bed, and that is all I require. I haven't stayed at any actually nice hotels along the drive so I won't be noticed and have opted instead for third-rate places off the beaten path that I assume could also be rented by the hour by those who require that sort of arrangement. There is certainly no concierge here and no valet. There is no private parking lot, so I park on the street a block up from the hotel.

Each country you pass through requires its own currency for toll roads, gas, food, and bribes. Part of my routine has been to stop by a bank to exchange money either the day I arrive in a new country or the next.

One challenging aspect of starting a new, untraceable life is the absence of a bank account or credit score. Unless you're being set up in witness protection by the government itself, you won't likely have easy access to a fresh Social Security number and a fabricated credit history without stealing an actual person's identity. With my cryptocurrency and offshore accounts, I do have some funds I can access. For my crypto, in particular, I have a debit card in Walter's name that can't be traced to Melvin or Herb. To access crypto by debit card, most options require identity verification in order to have higher daily and lifetime transaction limits, but I have opted for unverified cards with smaller limits that only allow me to take out a maximum of $200 per ATM withdrawal per day, which has me making trips to every ATM I pass to make rent. Once I am able to obtain residency in a new country under a new identity, I will have more options for identification, bank accounts, and cards to access higher limits.

I will be relying primarily on the cash I originally brought over the border with me for the immediate future, and I simply exchange currency in each country. In nearly two months of being on the run, that $20,000 has turned into $12,000. The $8,000 spent so far has covered my car, food, and lodging.

I now have two duffel bags and a backpack, as I picked up an extra bag along with some new clothes in Mexico. The twelve grand in cash I have left is split between all three bags, squirreled away as well as possible. Once I get into the hotel room each night, I combine the cash in the hotel safe, if there is one. Most often, there is not a safe, in which case I just set the bags next to the bed.

Once I've checked in, I generally take around $500 and go to find the nearest bank to exchange it into the local currency and, if possible, the currency of the next country I'm headed to. This isn't always possible, but it makes the border crossing process much quicker if you already have the local currency.

Again, debit cards and credit cards are out of the question, so I can't pay any fees online before I arrive to temporarily import my vehicle or pay for my visa at each border. Having cash, the car title, and a believable passport helps make each border crossing as smooth as possible, but in my case, I can't help but constantly consider worst-case scenarios. I imagine federal police at any given border crossing shouting at me that I'm actually Melvin or Herbert and forcing me out of my car and into a small dank cell, where I'll await extradition for my crimes.

It's beginning to rain in Managua, and it's already dark out.

I park my car on the street near my hotel for tonight and tomorrow, pull out my bags, lock my car, and make my way to the sidewalk. I set the duffel bags down as I put on the backpack, put my keys away, and do my best to remember some of the key Spanish phrases for the hotel check-in. My beard is coming in nicely, my beer belly has grown in size, and I've gotten a few tattoos on my forearms and biceps of generic Mayan design, though I still think I need some more.

Just as I lift my two duffel bags from the wet sidewalk, I am greeted by two skinny young men speaking so quickly I can hardly understand one word per sentence. They are possibly locals, and I am obviously not. I hear the words "Gringo," and "dinero," and "Hijo de puta." One of them produces a knife, and I am quite clear on the insinuation despite the language barrier.

I pull out my wallet and remove all the cash from it: $500. I hold the money out, and one of the men takes it. He also decides to take my entire wallet. The other man grabs both of my duffel bags, says something in a threatening tone, and runs away. Still holding my wallet, the other man lunges toward me and slices his knife across my left forearm. The cut hurts, but at least it's not deep.

I gasp and take one step back, covering my arm with pressure from my right hand. The man strikes again and, in an instant, plunges his blade deep into my gut, just a few inches left of my belly button. I look down at the damage, and it feels like everything is in slow motion as he slides the blade out of my stomach, which is now painted with my dark red blood like a thick merlot that is spilling onto my shirt. The man darts off into the darkness with my wallet and cash as the rain begins pouring down more heavily.

For a moment, I stand in shock before dropping to my knees. I press my right hand against the wound in my belly and am surprised that my only thought is that this is the first time I have encountered any issues at all during my escape south.

My heart is pounding, and I am sweating from the ordeal and the climate. Luckily, I still have my backpack on, which contains my passport, the debit card for accessing my crypto, and the keys to my car. About $8,000 of the $12,000 I had left was in the duffle bags, which the thieves will be pleased to discover later.

In Mexico, the average annual income had been nearly $17,000, and I had to assume that the number was likely even lower here in Nicaragua. The average laborer in these parts might work long and arduous hours just to bring in somewhere around $20 a day, so I am wondering whether the eight grand those two men just made off with will change their lives for the better, or if it will push them further into crime and violence, as it clearly worked out for them in this case. At least I still have a few thousand dollars in my backpack, and if I don't encounter any more issues, I should be able to stay on course. That is, if I don't bleed to death on this wet sidewalk. There is a dog barking as I struggle to my feet.

Slowly, I stumble into the hotel's entrance and tell the woman at the counter in my stuttered broken Spanish that I am there to check into my room, that I was mugged out front and stabbed, and that I urgently need a doctor.

Then I say, "Gracias," and lie down on the warm tile floor in front of the reception desk and slowly bleed while holding both my hands over my wounds. I begin to fall asleep, and once I manage to open my eyes, someone is picking me up and dragging me outside to their car. This mystery hero drives me to a hospital and makes sure I am treated.

CHAPTER 20

ABOUT FIFTEEN MINUTES northeast of Santa Marta, Colombia, there is a small beach town called Taganga. It was once just a tiny fishing village, but it has become more popular for tourists in recent years. Taganga is small compared to beach cities like Santa Marta or Cartagena, but there is a lively community there, and many of the residents know their neighbors, as they've spent their entire lives in the town.

Maria was born in Taganga and married a lovely man named Esteban, and they had two children, who are now nine and twenty-two. The youngest is a boy, named Esteban after his father, and the other child is a girl named Ana. Esteban Junior is a happy child, usually smiling and always curious. Ana was born with intellectual disabilities that make her unable to live independently. Still, Ana does not require constant care, as she has always been very positive and strong. She has a cell phone and is obsessed with watching makeup tutorials and funny videos from other girls on social media.

The beachfront property was renovated a few years ago by a couple who purchased it when they moved to Colombia from Austria. The Austrian couple live in Medellín and seldom visit the property during the popular tourism months, so they rent out the larger beachfront house in Taganga. Esteban and Maria have their own smaller home closer to the road and act as housekeepers for the larger home.

The first house is a small, modest, traditional Colombian home with bright exterior paint and hammocks on the front porch where the family lives with three dogs and nine cats. Farther down the road, close to the water, is the larger, beachfront house that is usually rented out to tourists and designed more like an oceanfront villa, with five bedrooms and a large outdoor pool, bar, and dining area facing the secluded ocean. The property occupies nearly three acres of land, and it is uncommon to run into many neighbors.

Once a week, Maria and Esteban clean the beach house and change the sheets on the bed, and a few days a week, Esteban cleans the pool and looks after the yard. In addition to this work, he also takes care of three other similar properties nearby for their owners, who also rent their beach homes to tourists. Sometimes Esteban gathers the coconuts on the properties and goes into town to sell them, and some days, he works as a freelance laborer for local construction projects. He is always busy and usually working.

Over the past decade, they had seen all manner of guests in their rental home, but none had seemed as secluded and eccentric as their newest tenant: a fat, drunk, bearded gringo calling himself Walter who always tips them well. Walter rented the house for twelve months and paid with cash up front, which by itself is highly unusual. Most guests visit from nearby countries for only a few weeks at a time. Walter is obviously an American and hardly ever leaves the house, except to buy groceries. Esteban and Maria refer to their new tenant as "the gringo" rather than as Walter when alone with their family, but they have no issues with him and do not mean the term in a derogatory fashion. He paid in advance and tips well. He is quiet and clean and keeps to himself.

In his second month in Taganga, Walter bought two Jet Skis and began to haul them in his truck on his daily trek down to the busier beach areas near Santa Marta to rent them out for an hour at a time to the tourists. He bought the newest model Sea-Doos, which are called *moto agua* by the Spanish-speaking locals. The watercrafts are both large enough to seat three people. Both have black polytech hulls and 150-horsepower engines that can reach up to around sixty miles per hour in sport mode. One of them has a red seat and yellow handles, while the other has a turquoise seat and blue handles. His Spanish has improved some but is still a fumbling gringo version of Spanglish.

Walter eventually hires a local boy named Alejandro to work for him and help run the Jet Ski rentals a few months after moving to town. Alejandro lives nearby and has no parents that Walter is aware of, as the boy had been raised by his grandmother until she died. Walter does not need the assistance so much as he needs the company, and the boy needs some guidance and a father figure to teach him and give him some purpose to stay busy each day.

Like a true American entrepreneur, Walter rents space on the sand near his Jet Skis to set up a small stand to sell smoothies and coconuts. In a short period of time, he is able to get permission to also sell alcoholic cocktails from his stand, and that is when his business takes off. Walter thinks it odd how many women around here like to drink either gin or rum. His Spanish improves a little more, and he becomes friendly with the locals, though none of them know much about him beyond his work with the Jet Skis and the smoothies and that he takes good care of Alejandro. He cares for him almost as if he were Walter's own child. Occasionally, Esteban and Maria take their kids to meet friends on this beach, bring coconuts for Walter's smoothie stand, and talk with him, and this all becomes a matter of routine in a lush, tropical paradise on the sand.

One thing that Maria can't understand is how Walter had enough money from these small businesses to thrive so well. The rental cost for the large house they manage is too expensive for even Esteban and Maria to ever rent, at least at the prices the tourists pay. Maria suspects Walter already had a lot of money but enjoys having some job to do and is only working as a way to pass the time. Walter originally planned to stay in Colombia for only a few months, but the months passed, and he was still renting the same house and paying in advance in cash, and he had begun treating the local neighbors like family.

The Jet Ski business improved. The first year, Walter had two wave runners, and now he had four, with plans to buy new ones before spring break each year and resell the previous years' models after the summer. The business is a simple one and only requires having the newest models each year for tourists.

One day, Walter and Alejandro are closing the smoothie stand early for the day, as they need to take one of the Jet Skis in for repairs. The tourist renting it that day had driven over a kite surfer's line, and the rope was sucked in the propeller of the Jet Ski. The kite surfer had waved over the Jet Ski driver asking for help, as his kite had crashed and deflated far from shore, leaving him drifting out in the open water.

When the Jet Ski came close, the driver failed to turn off the engine, as he was a tourist and unfamiliar with such devices. Within a quick moment, one of the thin ropes from the kite was sucked through the intake grate, and the kite surfer realized the rope was wrapped around his leg. The rope squeezed and popped, tearing itself just as the driver turned off the engine.

The two of them swam to shore, slowly dragging the Jet Ski and deflated kite behind them, until embarrassingly reaching shore an hour later in front of multiple onlookers. They tied the craft to an anchor in front of Walter's smoothie stand. Luckily, no one was hurt. The kite surfer had a bruised calf, but the rope had broken in time to save his leg from a tragic ordeal. Accidents happen, and the Jet Ski's propeller could be easily fixed, so Walter went and grabbed a three-wheeled trailer the size of a Jet Ski and waved for the boy to help him.

"Just another terrible day in paradise," he tells Alejandro in English, and the boy nods as if he understands.

"Solo otra puesta de sol de mierda," the boy replies. Something like, "Just another shitty sunset," and Walter nods.

They both smile, and Alejandro goes into the water, unhooks the craft from its anchor, and pulls it to shore. Walter and the boy begin loading the snafued Jet Ski onto a trailer. It must be through some combined leverage they'd perfected over time that the two of them, a small young boy and a fat drunk using an ancient pulley and a crank, are miraculously able to lift the thousand-pound machine from the wet sand onto the device. They pull the trailer over to an old pickup truck, where it is hooked and taken to Walter's house for repairs.

Maria figures Walter probably hasn't worn shoes or trimmed his beard even once since he arrived. He has gotten much fatter, and his beard has grown wild. On days when there are no tourists around and the weather is good, Walter takes a small boat out early in the mornings, fishes, and sells his fish to the local restaurants.

While out on his small boat, he watches the large fishing boats sailing out and crossing the horizon. Rugged, anonymous men from nearby villages work on these large boats catching fish, going out to sea for twenty-eight days at a time. There are about four months a year when they will do this. They are paid better for one month of work than many natives in town earn in an entire year, but the effort required is grueling and never predictable.

Walter admires these hardworking fishermen and knows he could never sustain that sort of physical labor. Still, he enjoys his work and never complains. He just likes to watch the boats going out and imagine what that sort of existence would be like.

For all his strangeness, Walter is kind to the locals and often smiling. Anytime someone doesn't understand his broken Spanish, he quotes some old man called Hoban and says, "Who even speaks the same language, even when they speak the same language?"

Some days, Walter is overheard talking to himself about some lost family as if he is talking to them, and when he is drunk enough, he will recite the few phrases he actually knows in Spanish. On those nights, you will hear him muttering a phrase he learned while in the Yucatán state of Mexico, "¿Qué más le pido a la vida si esto es lo que tengo que vivir?" The English translation of which would be something like, "What else do I ask of life if this is what I have to live?"

He is happy enough to live without luxury or first-world benefits, as it is far better than any prison. Some days, he considers that by escaping literal incarceration, he has exiled and isolated himself, abandoned everyone he ever cared about, and built himself a metaphorical prison instead. Some days, this tears him apart, and he medicates himself with even heavier amounts of alcohol than usual. Then, once properly sauced, he says, "I can always kill myself later."

He is content with the simple life and assumes he will learn to deal with the mosquitoes and the loneliness. He writes letters each week to his daughter, Alicia. The letters are always quickly sealed in envelopes once he finishes writing them out with pen and ink on a fine, beige parchment paper, and they are carefully placed inside a desk drawer attached to a beautiful desk expertly crafted from tropical walnut wood.

On the desk sits a framed photo of a once-happy family seated on a couch together, with him in the middle holding Ruby and Alicia, and Roscoe and Frankie seated next to them. The emotional and heartfelt letters sit in their fine drawer, never to be stamped or delivered.

THE END.

ACKNOWLEDGMENTS

Thanks first and foremost to J.S., who has always been willing to read the rough drafts of my nonsense and respond with supportive advice.

Thanks especially to my editor, James Osborne, who helped me immensely in shaping this into a better story.

Thanks also, in no particular order, to the following people, who read drafts of this novel and provided me helpful and honest feedback: Alyssa Matesic, Nic De Castro, Michael Bolus, Rich Peters, Erik Johnson, Aaron Pettijohn, Jim Jonesson, Haley Noteboom, Serafima Kobzeva, Shadon Hamedani, and Evan Strome. Your feedback was invaluable, and I am eternally grateful.

AUTHOR BIO

Nathan Pettijohn is an author and entrepreneur. Nathan is a contributing writer for *Forbes* on topics related to what business leaders need to know about innovations in media and technology. Nathan is also the author of a travelogue called *Travels with Hafa*. In 2011, Nathan founded Cordurouy, a digital strategy agency based in Los Angeles, where he serves as CEO. He resides somewhere in Central or South America with his dog, Raphael.

You can contact Nathan on social media at @nrpettijohn